FAR SIDE OF THE OCEAN

HILARY MURRAY

Other books
by
HILARY MURRAY

The Bordello Girl

Past Sin

For Brett and for Beth

1

DILYS COULD NEVER WORK OUT why so many blokes loved their ale when the stink from the brewery over on Queen Street was enough to put anyone off the stuff for life.

"Bloody hell," she grumbled, swabbing the top of the mahogany bar, "when the wind's blowing this way the pong gets right up yer nose."

Couched down on his haunches her husband hooked another four bottles of India Pale Ale from the wooden crate alongside him and thrust them to the back of the empty shelf.

"It's just the malt," he said. "That, and the hops cooking."

"Think I don't know that after all these years?"

Wisely, he remained silent.

"Still don't get why it has to smell so bad," she went on.

Seeing he was more interested in sliding, jostling and chinking more bottles into place she straightened. "We having this conversation or not?"

"Seems that way. Not that I can see why though, 'cause there's nothing to be gained from it."

"Look, it's an observation, that's all," and fixing the back of his head with a withering glare, she added, "like I might mention the weather we're having. Or the amount you've been supping lately."

Grasping the edge of the counter Jim hauled himself to his feet. "Man's entitled to a spot of relaxation after a long day."

"A long day? You wouldn't know one of them if it leapt up and bit yer. Besides, you need to realise it's our hard-earned profits you're throwing down your neck."

She regretted the words immediately they were out of her mouth. Not from any sense of foreboding since in all the years they'd been married - and that was more than she cared to remember - he'd never laid a hand on her, never even come close and he could have done, a bloke of his size. She thanked her lucky stars for that. Some women got hidings so bad they couldn't leave the house for days. Black and blue they'd be. She wouldn't stand for it herself, but then she wouldn't have picked anyone with a temper in the first place. Not if he were the last bugger on earth. So no, she shouldn't have come down hard on him. It was hardly his fault after all.

Swiping a strand of hair from her forehead with the back of her wrist she splashed water into the sink, and dunked and wrung out the cloth.

The writing had been on the wall since the war ended, not that you'd have known back then. But a couple of years on and the economy began sliding downhill. Then the Royal Naval Dockyard started laying men off and being the city's largest employer that affected everyone one way or another. In hindsight they should have got on with the improvements the brewery suggested - not that they'd offered to cough up a penny towards it, God forbid - like replacing the cracked tiles either side of the public bar door and tarting up the sign between the two upstairs windows. Even putting a lick of paint on the window frames might have helped. Problem was, it wouldn't have ended there. What about the peeling wallpaper? Or the damp in the gents lav? Start one thing and the list becomes never-ending, and while it didn't seem worth spending the time at first, it was money they were short of after that.

What they needed was the clientele of the better establishments down on the Hard. The dockyard supervisors and gaffers and Naval senior rates; anyone in fact who could count on having a job next week. Not the officers, of course, she wasn't given to dreaming and from what she'd heard they were no longer spending up big anyway. Trouble was, how could a gloomy back-street boozer entice that trade? No, they were well and truly stuck with what they had; regulars who could barely scrape enough together for a second pint. Nor did it help that the soft lummox she'd married had become a little too free with the tick of late. She'd had to bite her tongue a few times, but she was keeping an eye on things and that was why, at the first sign of a few bob in a man's pocket, she was leaning over the counter quick-sharp and having a quiet word about a certain unpaid account. It usually did the trick.

There were no two ways about it, their chance for better things was long gone. And why? Because these two bars - one a public, the other a snug behind etched glass and timber panelling for the old biddies with their stout and Sergeant O'Brien who, regardless he was still in his police uniform, couldn't make it home without a nip of Bushmills - suited Jim Doherty nicely.

For until recently he hadn't an ambitious bone in his body.

It had to be said that despite the bee he'd got in his bonnet, she and Jim had been a good match. They'd lasted the course, hadn't they? And there was no getting away from the fact he'd been a looker back in the day, despite her mother complaining he was too thin. 'Bony,' she sniped, 'not an ounce of meat on him.' And, 'one puff of wind and it'll be all over.' Dilys had seen only gentle eyes and lustrous dark hair swept back with a dab of grease, then nudged forward into a rakish wave. Other's had noticed too, not that he'd ever taken advantage, he wasn't the sort. Twenty-seven years later he still wasn't bad looking, once you got past the softened jowls and the wildly tufting eyebrows the girls were always threatening to trim. And what about her? Did he ever consider how nature had fashioned her over the years? If so, he never said. The loosened skin under her upper arms had appeared without her noticing. The lines around her eyes and mouth had been a different matter, and she'd a drawer full of creams that had promised so much and delivered so little. Nor could she do a great deal about her graying roots, other than have them regularly bleached. And those were the changes he'd be aware of. There were others, things she couldn't tell him. Things that left her staring at the ceiling some nights. But what was the point in dwelling on stuff she could do nothing about? Better to concentrate on what was important, like finishing what she was doing, then giving the mirrored-backed shelves behind her a quick once over. Or could that hold off until tomorrow? She'd rather have a sit down; she knew that much. Get the weight off her pins for ten minutes before opening up time.

"You realise we've been here eleven years?" she said, tipping the stale contents of a slop tray down the sink. "Gawd help us. Eleven years in this rat-infested hole. *The Saracen's Head*? More like the Saracen's arse if you ask me. We should have moved on years ago. Got out of Portsea and gone up in the world."

"No one was stopping us, doll."

"So why didn't we?" she wanted to know.

"Timing I suppose. It just never seemed right."

Giving the brass tray a flick with the cloth she glanced over. He was frowning at the painted wooden shelf above the till, and the precise rows of Woodbines, Players and Gold Flake cigarettes. Now what? Was he thinking of fetching up a few more packets from the locked cupboard in the cellar that safeguarded their stock of spirits and fortified wines? Forget the expensive stuff, she wanted to tell him, it's loose tobacco and another lot of Rizla papers needed. If he didn't already know customers were trying to eke out the cost of their habit, one look at the mush of soggy yellow-brown butts in the ashtrays and spittoons would soon tell him. Most were no thicker than a matchstick.

"Trouble is, girl," he said all of a sudden, "nothing's cut and dried anymore. Can't count on anything. 'Specially not from the brewery."

Here we go again, she thought.

"Look," she said, "it's not the end of the world. Like I keep saying, we should - argh!" her face contorted, and dropping the tray into place and still clutching the cloth, she screwed a raw-knuckled fist into the small of her back.

Jim winced but said nothing. It was as if he knew better.

"Mary, Mother of God!" she groaned. Then, having counted to twenty continued through gritted teeth, "We'll talk to the bosses again. See if they've found another place for us yet."

"And if they haven't?"

"Then we'll keep on doing the same as now."

Shaking her head, she concentrated on the pain in her back. Willing it to dull, so she could get on with the last of the trays. She'd be done for the morning then.

But he wasn't finished.

"For how long?" he wanted to know.

"For as long as it takes. For God's sake Jim, what choice have we got? Anyway, for all you and I know, it might never happen."

"What, you think they're going to change their mind about knocking this place down?"

"I don't know what they're going to do. And neither do you."

"I know one thing. They won't leave it standing. Not even as a tribute to the working class drinker. No, you mark my words, girl," he said, though in a more resigned tone. "Once these streets are rubble, everyone'll be gone. Including us."

"The dockyard will still be here and blokes'll still want to get a pint on their way home."

"Not if they're living outside the city."

"But they won't all be outside the city," she argued, head lowered and leaning on the counter. "Some'll still be here. Stands to reason."

"Good job one of us has your optimism." Reaching down for the empty crate he hoisted it up. "Funny really. All these changes because of one woman."

"Not again," she groaned.

"You have to admit, no one bothered us before."

"How many times…?" her knuckles were still pummelling her back. "Look, she didn't ask to be murdered, did she?"

"Course not, but had she still been alive the do-gooders wouldn't have been round to poke their noses in our business. And you could argue from that there'd be no talk of clearance either."

"You don't get it, do you? Some nutter killing Brighton Mary didn't bring the council around here. It's these pokey alleys and courtyards, they're slums. In fact, they're worse than that. They're disease ridden just like half the people living in them and the sooner they get pulled down and proper homes built, with running water and electricity, the better."

"But that's just it. How do we know they're going to build houses again? What's to stop them building factories or warehouses, or whatever else takes their fancy once they've shifted everyone out. Either way, there's going to be a lot of changes." Focusing on the window as if half expecting the demolition ball to come crashing through at any moment, he added "and once they're gone, our customers won't be back."

"You don't know that."

"Of course I do. They'll be out in them new council houses in Hilsea."

She'd had enough, for when he got on his high horse there was no stopping him. "I give up. What's the point fretting when we don't know for definite what's going to happen? I'm going for a cuppa. You want one?"

Hitching up his trousers he shook his head. "Nah. I'll finish bottling up first."

"No pulling a swift half behind me back."

He was sizing up a half empty shelf of Brown Ale. "Give it a rest!"

"After all these years I know you better than I know myself, Jim Doherty," she threw over her shoulder.

"Before you go…"

She'd barely reached the curtained doorway.

"…you given any more thought to us emigrating?"

She'd known he'd been leading up to this and when she turned back he'd plonked the crate on the counter. One elbow perched on it, a fingernail was prising dirt from beneath his thumbnail.

"You know my thoughts. I think it's a crack-pot idea," she said. "Why New Zealand? What wrong with here? If we have to, we'll just go further out like everyone else."

"I want something better. For all of us."

"At our age? Are you stark, raving mad?" she wanted to say. But seeing his expression, she checked herself.

"And you reckon this *something* is on the other side of the world?" she said instead.

"Won't know 'til we try."

"But Jim, listen to yourself. You're talking about uprooting us. Your family. Taking us away from everything we've ever known. And for what? A dream? A whim?"

"It's more than that, doll. A new life in the empire could be the answer to our prayers."

He'd stepped forward as if doing so would strengthen his case.

She shook her head. God, he could be so pig-headed when he wanted. "You know Ruby and Lil aren't interested. And what about Alfie? He didn't spend all those years on an apprenticeship for nothing. He's well on his way to being a skilled tradesman. With prospects," she emphasised. "You know that."

"I do. But what's to say the dockyard doesn't lay him off in the meantime? Look," he added quickly, no doubt caught off guard by her ferocious look, "I don't want that any more than you do. But we have to face facts. Life's been getting harder and harder round here. Nothing's written in stone anymore."

"He's got a good job, and a solid future."

She too could be obstinate when it suited.

"In that case," he said, "it'll be just us and the girls."

Her tone was incredulous. "You mean you'd go all that way without our boy? I don't believe you!"

"I had to find my own way in the world when I was his age. No one mollycoddled me." Pulling back his shoulders, he puffed out his chest as if waiting for someone to pin a medal on it. "Besides," he added, with what he no doubt hoped was a reassuring smile, "he might come out later, once he and Alice are wed."

"Oh yes! And pigs might fly! Her parents would never approve. And what if they've got kiddies by then? Which they will have. How can I be expected to live in one place when they're in another? You listen to me, Jim Doherty. I need my family about me. All of them."

"We've got family out there too, don't forget."

She had to give him credit, he was standing his ground. But he was also riling her up good and proper.

"Your brother?" it was her turn to step up. "And when was the last time you saw him?"

"You know when girl. When he left."

"That's right. Nineteen-nineteen. And after that? Nothing! How many letters has he sent? How many Christmas cards? Even your old ma doesn't hear from him anymore."

"It doesn't change the fact he's my brother. And you know the saying, blood's thicker than water."

"I give up. New Zealand, indeed."

"I'm going to write to him," Jim called to her retreating back.

"Know his address, do yer?"

"No, but ma does."

"Good luck to that."

"Does that mean you'll think about it?"

But she'd already disappeared.

2

LIKE THE REST OF *The Saracen's Head*, the dingy kitchen was nothing to write home about. The linoleum was worn through in places, the paintwork a bit rough, and no matter how much she cleaned, a faint smell of mildew hung in the air. The rug beneath Jims battered armchair by the range gave the place a lift though, and then there was the glass fronted cabinet in the corner. The only decent bit of furniture in the room, never mind it was already second-hand when she'd bought it. Jim had asked what on earth she was going to put in it.

"Me best china, of course."

"You got any?"

"I will have. When you put your hand in your pocket."

Setting the kettle on the gas stove, Dilys was worried. This emigrating lark, well, it was alright for some. But not her. Nor Jim if the truth be known. Heaven's above, New Zealand! He might as well suggest they went to live on the moon! And while she didn't know the first thing about the place she knew it would be nothing like Portsmouth. No neat rows of houses, no pub on the corner. And where on earth would she get fresh milk or a loaf of bread when needed, let alone a bit of gossip?

The idea didn't bear thinking about.

Why couldn't he be happy with her suggestion they find another place right here in the very city she'd been born in? The same one he'd been drafted to all those years ago when he was in the Navy? It was where they'd met and married, and made their life. And if not for all those reasons, then for the fact it was the only home the kids had ever known.

But she already knew the answer. Local drinking holes in mean streets of two-up-two-down houses might be thick on the ground in a port that had serviced His Majesties Royal Navy since Noah was a boy, but so were those queueing to tenant them. And that gave the brewery the upper hand. Not that she was expecting special treatment, regardless they'd always paid their rent on time and never put a foot wrong. But still, she doubted they'd any chance at a place like the brewery's latest jewel in the crown. Recently built out at Eastney, it had a smart frontage and a carpeted saloon bar - Axminster, she'd heard, which meant they were spending a bob or two. On the other hand, would she want the worry? Given it was a new venture the bosses would likely be turning up every five minutes, demanding to look over the accounts or tally the stock. Jim wouldn't appreciate that one little bit. And starting from scratch would mean hard work, regardless of all the new-fangled labour saving devices they'd supposedly put in. Kitty over at the New Inn said everything was electric, and there was even a separate office for the landlord to do the books without anyone looking over his shoulder.

'An office, can you image that,' she'd said, one hand under her elbow as she puffed on her ciggie. 'What's wrong with the kitchen table, that's what I'd like to know.'

Dilys sighed. If she wanted to talk Jim out of the notion of leaving England, she'd have to come up with a better idea than applying for that particular tenancy. And sharpish.

With the kettle whistling, and after warming the pot and spooning in Ceylon tea, she filled it with boiling water. Ruby's one and only attempt at knitting, a garish red, green and yellow cosy, was slipped over the spout and handle and snuggled around the belly.

There wasn't just one thing to be taken into account either, she thought, settling back to wait. Alfie for instance. Wherever she and Jim lived, he and Alice should be within walking distance, for if anyone thought their son wouldn't want a pint with his father every now and then they were sadly mistaken. That's what fathers and sons did. Put the world to rights over a mild and bitter. On top of that, she had no intention of missing out to Alice's mother when it came to grandchildren. The woman already had half a dozen, thanks to the way her eldest popped them out on a regular basis, and that meant she certainly wouldn't have time for Alfie's as well.

And then there were the girls.

It was important for Lilith to be close to that school she taught at. Not that there was anything wrong with the corporation's bus service but waiting around at draughty bus-stops in winter brought on any manner of ailments, everyone knew that, so why invite trouble?

Ruby was another matter altogether since she hadn't found a job yet. At least, not one she liked enough to go back the following day. It didn't help she never had her nose out of a fashion magazine either, but times had changed and things were different for girls these days. Even she could see that. At fourteen she'd been handing over a pay-packet to her mother and getting pennies back for her trouble. Ruby would take to her bed for a week if she were forced to do the same! It had to be said though, her daughter had a mind of her own *and* a good idea of what she wanted out of life. Wasn't she already on the lookout for a husband - not that she or Jim were supposed to know - nor could it be denied she'd get one soon enough with her looks. If only she'd wait a little longer. What was the rush? Still only nineteen, once she'd taken that journey down the aisle there'd be no more shopping and fancy clothes. Not with a softened belly and swollen breasts. And if she'd set her sights on a sailor like just about every other girl round these streets - and please God, make it a Petty Officer or someone with a bit of aspiration - she'd be bringing up her babies alone for the most part. It would be a hard life.

She wouldn't be told though.

Lilith, on the other hand, never gave any trouble. At least not in the same way. But all that spouting off about women's rights and labour policies wouldn't get her anywhere in the long run. And time wasn't on her side. Another couple of months and she'd be twenty-three, and that meant if she didn't pull her head in soon it would be too late. Of course, she could spruce herself up a bit. Take a leaf out of her sister's book and work on her appearance. Then she might stand a chance. But with a shortage of good blokes out there she had to get a shift on or she'd lose out altogether.

Fetching her favourite cup and saucer, the only survivor of a pair given her and Jim as newly-weds and used only when the mood took, she poured a dribble of milk from the jug kept on the cold shelf in the larder and added two heaped spoonful's of sugar from a silver plated, ornate handled bowl. That too had been a gift to mark the occasion, this time by her mother's sister who, despite her upbringing, managed to marry above her station. Well-to-do and snooty with it, no doubt the intention had been for her contribution to stand out from all others. It had.

Holding the strainer over the rim and pouring the tea that had stood brewing for the last few minutes, Dilys thought how different their three children were. Lil was Jim all over again, another dreamer, while Alfie and Ruby were the practical ones, like her.

Surely it couldn't be that hard to come up with a solution for everyone? She'd put her mind to it once Christmas was out of the way. It would be her New Year's resolution.

3

FEBRUARY IN PORTSEA WAS ALWAYS grim and standing at the kitchen window, elbow deep in suds, Dilys stared out at the sodden hooped barrels and stacked beer crates. For days now and with no let-up, rain had been splattering into bloated ale-flecked pools and the yard was awash with gritty water. Worse, the hint of a breeze as she'd darted out to the lav at first light hadn't meant a change in the weather at all. Rather it was a cruel joke, and the cloths and towels she'd quickly hung out, draping them over the thin rope that stretched from one brick wall to the other, were sopping.

She wondered why she'd even bothered.

She ought to nip out and get them all in. Put the whole lot through the mangle and chuck them on the clotheshorse in front of the range. Didn't mean they'd be dry in time for opening though.

On top of that, her belly was playing up again. She wasn't sure which was worse; the cramping or the chronic back ache accompanying it. Not that there was much point complaining, not at forty-four. Old age was knocking and even the devil couldn't keep that door closed.

"Still giving you gyp, is it?"

The change to the licencing hours bought in by a war-time coalition government and never repealed, that a landlord could only open his premises from midday to two-thirty, and again from six-thirty until nine-thirty at night, meant Jim was settled in his armchair, his waistcoat unbuttoned, his shirt sleeves rolled back, his legs stretched out to the range, and his feet encased in the plaid slippers Lilith had given him for his birthday.

"It'll get better in New Zealand, you'll see," he said.

Dilys closed her eyes. "Oh, will it? And how's that going to happen then?"

There was the familiar rustling of a page being turned. "Because it's warm there. Do your aches and pains a load of good."

"And how do you know it's warm?"

"Stands to reason, doesn't it? It's on the other side of the world. Like Africa. And you can't say it ain't hot there."

"You don't know the first thing about the place."

The newspaper rustled again.

"I know one thing. It's the cold here that's doing you in. That and the rain."

"So it doesn't rain in New Zealand then?"

"Of course it rains. How else would anything grow? But not like here. All this damp and drizzle. That's what's plaguing you."

"Nothing to do with being worked to death then."

She didn't move. Just stood there, staring out at the gray yard and the washing on the line. Saturated and listless and dripping.

"I can't believe you're still going on about it," she picked up the thread of conversation again.

"Can't see as why I wouldn't be. Nothing has changed here as far as I know."

"So what's it been now?" she spoke as if the question was rhetorical. "A couple of months? And you're still pinning your hopes on a reply from your brother? You even said yourself Ma wasn't sure she had the right address anymore. Suppose he didn't get your letter? Then what? You going to sit around forever going on about it? Anyone else would have seen the light ages ago. But not you."

The newspaper shook. Another page turned. "He'll reply. Mail doesn't get to New Zealand and back over night."

"But why should he? Let's be honest, you might have been brother's once but after all these years? You as good as strangers now."

Another page turned. And another.

"I think you're mad, you are," she went on, gripping the edge of the sink as yet another cramp seared her insides. "And it's not only me who thinks so. Even the kids believe the idea of emigrating is ridiculous. You know that."

"They'll come around."

"Not this time, they won't."

"We'll see."

"What's wrong with you?" Her tone was frayed, her breathing not quite under control, and not only from the pain tormenting her back. "Why won't you see what's under your nose."

"And what's that, doll."

"That when you weren't looking, those three grew up. They're adults now, with lives of their own. You can't tell them what to do any more than I can."

"I'm aware of that."

She wanted to scream. No, worse than that, she wanted to grab him by his shirt-front and shake him until his teeth rattled. "Then listen to them."

"I intend to."

"That's not how it sounds."

Reaching up on top of the cupboard she closed her fingers around the amber glass bottle.

"Look, they're none of them daft," he was saying, "and I accept it might be a bit hard at first, being a new country and all that. But nothing comes easy in life. Any fool knows that."

"So why even think about it?" she said, tugging on the stopper and taking a swig.

"Because it's our one chance to get ahead."

He was reaching for the half-smoked roll-up smouldering on the rim of his ashtray when she finally gave him her full attention.

"You don't believe that any more than I do."

"You're wrong, doll. Take a look around you. We live in a slum, in the worst part of the city. A slum that's going to be razed to the ground any day now and that means everyone we know, our neighbours, our friends, will be gone. The entire community moved out one by one to places some of them have never even visited. Not even as a kid. We'll be strangers, all of us, strangers in our own town." Fingers curled around the home-made fag he put it to his lips. "And even if you think you can live with that," he said, inhaling and exhaling long and hard, "what am I going to do for work? The brewery hasn't exactly been forthcoming, has it? And let's be honest, they've had plenty of time these past months to make us an offer. So let's assume for one minute there won't be another pub. What have you in mind for me to do, should we find ourselves in one of these new-fangled houses the council is building? I've no trade and no experience of anything other than pulling pints and keeping a tidy cellar."

"There'll be something."

Balancing his roll-up on the rim once more he said, "Like what? Come on girl, who's going to employ me at my age? Especially when there's already hundreds out of work. And they're not all old codgers like me either. They're young blokes. Strong blokes. Blokes who can do a full day's graft without taking a breath."

"There's more to a job than brute strength."

"Such as?"

Dilys took a moment to breathe through the ache. Another ten or so minutes and the foul-tasting concoction would have kicked in. Then she'd be fine again.

"Being good with customers for one thing," she managed. "Handling money for another. People want employees they can trust."

"And if I can't find anything, because let's not forget those jobs aren't thick on the ground, that what? You really want to see me joining the ranks of the unemployed and drawing the dole, my signature in exchange for a weekly handout that'll barely feed this family, let alone pay the bills?"

"It won't come to that. Anyway, Ruby'll help. She'll get a job and it'll be another wage coming in."

"Oh, so now I'm to rely on charity if I want the odd pint or packet of fags?"

"You know I didn't mean that. You're giving in too easily."

"No, doll. I'm being realistic. Like you need to be."

Retrieving his newspaper, he shook it and found his page.

"I think you're wrong about the kids," he said eventually.

"Oh?"

"I think once it's all explained to them, they'll see trying our luck in another country might be a good thing all round. And don't forget, we're not the only ones. Hundreds are leaving every month with the same thought in mind. And not only for New Zealand but for Australia and Canada as well."

"Really!" she couldn't keep the scorn from her voice.

"Uh huh. Sam Rudkin's boy went to South Africa. Doing very well by all accounts. Even owns a motorcar, or so his old man says."

"Well, that's one then. Know anyone else from around here living the life of Reilly in the Dominions?"

"The Martins. They went to Canada. And they haven't come back."

"You ever thought they might not be able to afford the fare?"

"Or it could be they're settled and happy."

She eased from one foot to the other, shifting her weight and contorting her spine ever so slightly. "Still think it's a stupid idea."

"I know you do. But I think it's worth the risk."

"And you're going to try and talk everyone round?"

"I am."

"And how on earth are you going to do that?"

"By starting with the voyage, and the magnificent ocean liner we're going to be sailing on."

"What...?" she stared. "What ocean liner?"

"The one getting us to New Zealand of course."

She was gawping at him.

"Calm down woman," he was reaching for his roll-up again.

"Calm down? How do you expect me to calm down?" Pain forgotten, instead she couldn't believe what he was saying. "You haven't really, have yer? Tell me you haven't gone and booked our passages without waiting to hear from your brother? You have, you've gone and done it, haven't yer. I know you. How could you do such a thing? You knew how I feel about it. And to think I swallowed all that rubbish about moving out to Cosham or Hilsea, or wherever. Because that's what it was, wasn't it? Pure and utter baloney to tug at my heart strings. Well, Jim Doherty, you've pulled some fast ones in your time, but this takes the biscuit."

"No one's booked any passages yet. Like you said, we need Joe's reply first. Have to hear what he has to say," and he expelled a stream of smoke in the direction of the ceiling. "On top of that, we both know if he agrees it's the right thing to do, there'll be a whole lot of paperwork to get done first. And no doubt a few hoops to jump through as well."

"Then what did you mean about the ship?"

"I'm just thinking we should all take a trip to Netley. Have a picnic and make a day of it. We could invite Alice too."

Had he taken leave of his senses?

"A trip out? In this weather? It's bleeding freezing outside if you hadn't noticed." It was a good job she didn't have anything to hand with which she might hit him. A rolling pin or a wooden spoon. Either would do. "And then what? You expect us to sit on the grass while one of them big steamers sails past on its way down the Solent, all bunting and brass bands and waving from the decks?" she shook her head. "And that's your big idea?"

Turning back to the sink she plunged her hands into the water and brought out a cup, which, after a cursory glance she placed upside down on the wooden draining board.

"You live in a dream-world, you do," she muttered just loud enough for him to hear.

"I can't show them where we're going, but I can show them how we're getting there. Might put things in a new light," he said.

"Might not, as well."

"It's as good a place to start as any."

"Still don't know why you want to start at all."

The newspaper slapped the arm of his chair. Then a loose spring twanged as he stood. Coming up behind her, he slipped his arms around her waist and leaned close.

"Imagine you and me on a big ship, girl. All dressed up at the Captain's table."

Her back twinged, and holding onto the sink she bit her lip.

"Good looking woman like you," he went on, "you'd be the star attraction. Turn heads, you would."

"Not looking like this I wouldn't."

"I'll buy you a dozen new outfits," his breath was warm on her neck. "Skirts, blouses, dresses, you name it. All as blue as cornflowers. Same as your eyes."

She couldn't help smiling. He'd always been a one for flattery. Knew just how thick to lay it on, too.

"And how are you going to manage that?"

"Got a little set aside for a rainy day."

"You never told me."

"Been saving it up to spend on you, girl."

"Get away with you."

But the magic was working.

"There'd be dancing every night. In a ballroom. You know how you love a bit of a shuffle, girl. Remember? You and me?" and with his lips nuzzling her shoulder, and his groin pressed against her bottom, he swayed and hummed a few bars of some long ago tune. "And walks along the deck in the moonlight. Think of it. All those stars in the sky. More than you've ever seen in your life."

"And how would you know that?"

"You're forgetting, I've been to sea."

"Three years," her eyes were closed and with her head back against his chest she breathed coal tar soap and tobacco. And a whiff of the ale he'd had at lunchtime. "That's how long you lasted in the Navy. Three short years. The way you tell it nowadays you were Admiral of the Fleet."

"Who knows, girl. I might have been if it hadn't been for poor health."

"Poor health be buggered. You pulled a fast one to get out."

As if wanting to make the most of her good humour he'd snuggled even closer. "Only because I wanted to be with you, doll. Not have us spend years apart."

"And who benefitted from that? 'Cos it certainly wasn't me," she managed.

"How can you say such a thing?"

"Easy. From the day you put a ring on my finger I've worked each and every one of them to the bone for you."

"Sounds to me like you're playing hard to get."

She was a little breathless, for his lips were nibbling and sucking just below her ear. "Should've played harder back then if you ask me."

Oh God, it had been ages since they'd last mucked around. Ages since either of them had bothered with the other. They managed the odd quickie when he'd had a little too much to drink of course, but that was just leg over and on with it.

This was what she missed. The closeness. The oneness.

"You always did like me chasing after you," he whispered into her hair. A hand was cupping her once proud breast. "I remember you flirting with other blokes when you knew I was watching. You liked it when I was jealous. You were a shocker, you were."

"I did no such thing," she felt herself blushing.

"Oh yes you did. What about Joey Dawson? You only had to click your fingers and he'd come running."

"That was a long time ago. And it wasn't my fault if someone took a shine to me."

"Of course not. Though it wasn't without a little encouragement."

"Ohh, that's a terrible thing to say!" but there was no outrage to the words.

His hand was sliding down over her belly, pressing gently and she sucked in her breath.

Not this. Not yet. Couldn't he just hold her a little longer?

He was inching up her floral pinafore, ruching it as he went. Next he'd be working on her skirt. Then his hand would run up her leg, the fingers splayed and lingering on the metal clasp and thick elastic of her suspender before savouring the expanse of warm flesh between stocking top and girdle. And when that wasn't enough, he'd move on, blindly but surely.

"For heaven's sake Jim, what are you thinking?" She twisted out of his grasp. "Anyone could walk in. Ruby's in her bedroom. What was to stop her coming down?"

He'd stepped back, but he quickly recovered and holding out his arms again, waggled his eyebrows suggestively. "You're right doll. Let's nip upstairs, out the way."

"You must think I came down in the last shower, Jim Doherty," she said, her hands flat against his chest. "I know what you're after. And a bit of what you've got in mind won't make me any keener to go to New Zealand."

She couldn't look at him. Instead, knees trembling, she turned and leaned on the chipped and stained sink again.

"And don't forget, I'm having my hair done at four," she added. "So you've got plenty of time to get down that cellar and give it a good going over before opening."

4

THE BEDROOM OVERLOOKING THE BACKYARD might have been the largest of all three, but with two brass beds and Aunt Maud's heavily embellished mahogany dressing table and wardrobe taking up so much space it was standing room only. The single window didn't offer much relief either, even at the height of day, for the light penetrating the heavy lace curtaining brought a dismal tinge with it. Of course, it was different in summer when finding its way between neighbouring rooftops the sun lifted the room's decoration from a flat and dreary lilac to a warmer rose-pink. But with the long winter days clinging on it was as much as Ruby could do to lean into the into the oval mirror and tilt her head while shifting a lamp this way and that, all in the hope of highlighting her best features.

"I really don't know why you're bothering. It isn't like mum's going to let you out." Hunched into her pillow, Lilith barely glanced up from the page she was reading. "She'll catch you the moment you try to sneak out the back door, and then you'll be for it, dressed like that."

Transforming each heavily plucked eyebrow into a perfectly shaped arch with a few deft strokes of her pencil Ruby considered any number of acid-like responses in return. But no. She would treat the remark with the contempt it deserved. Though why her sister had to be such a damp squib all the time she'd no idea. Of course, it could be something to do with the lack of a boyfriend, though for heavens' sake whose fault was that? Just look at her, dressing gown tucked around her and hair twisted up in a towel. She couldn't remember the last time she'd seen her in face-powder or caught a trace of perfume on her wrists. It wasn't natural. And she was pretty enough after all, so why didn't she make the most of what God had given her like everyone else did? It wouldn't be difficult, for she'd got a heart-shaped face to die for, not to mention a complexion that had never seen a spot or a blemish, not even at *that* time of the month.

More to the point, why couldn't she be like Elsie's older sister and get her into places she shouldn't go and introduce her to deliciously wicked men? Some might call her obsession with her job and her politics a tad selfish, all things considered.

Instead, she said, "We'll see about that."

But it appeared Lilith had more to say.

"I just don't understand why you always make life hard for yourself. You know what mum says about short skirts and loose women."

Ruby tightened her lips. "This is hardly short. Anyway, everyone's wearing hemlines that finish just below the knee these days."

"She won't like your jumper either," her sister came back. "She'll say it's too tight."

"Well that's just too bad, Miss Snidey. Bert likes it, and that's all that counts."

"Bert? Is that the one on *HMS Repulse*? Or is that Stan? Sometimes I just can't keep up with all the men in your life."

"Then don't. Leave me to my business and you get on with yours."

Uncapping a tube of plum-red lipstick and twisting the base Ruby turned back to the mirror and with three or four strokes transformed her lips into a flawless cupid's bow.

"I can't help it if I'm popular," she said, checking to ensure the colour hadn't bled on her teeth.

"Some might call it something else."

"Is that a note of jealousy I hear from the old maid in the corner?"

"Hardly. But really, you should do things to please yourself, not other people."

"I do."

"But didn't you just say this is all for Bert?"

"I can't see there's any difference."

"Then you do have a problem."

"Not as far as I'm concerned."

Lilith's book closed with a *thwack*. "Oh Ruby, can't you hear what you're saying?"

"Yes I can. Loud and clear, thank you very much. What I want to know is when are you going to realise there's more to life than staying in night after night studying?"

"I would say that depends on the future I want."

"And I'm more concerned with the present."

"I know."

"And what's that supposed to mean?"

"Live for today, for tomorrow we die. Isn't that the catchphrase?"

Her patience was wearing thin. "You think you're so clever sometimes."

"No I don't."

"Well, that's how it sounds."

He sister sat up, hugging her knees. "Your life could be so different. You could so easily make something of yourself if you really wanted to."

"Why would I want to do that?"

"So Bert's the one, then?"

She had to contain her temper. "And suppose he is? What's wrong with that?"

"Nothing. If you're sure."

"I am. And even I wasn't, I'd still marry him. The good ones don't hang around you know. Someone like Bert knows how to treat a girl, and that means she would never have to work, though why she would even want to when he earns good money I wouldn't know. So it may not seem like it from where you're sitting, but my life is just tickety-boo, thanks."

"I see."

"No, you don't. You don't see anything."

"I know you and I live in two different eras. Your dependence on a man is positively Victorian. When are you going to take a good look around you? We're in a new world now."

God, she could be so annoying at times Ruby thought, wondering what it would take to wipe that smug look off her face.

"These days you can so easily have a fulfilling life of your own," her sister was continuing, as she had on so many other occasions. "Women everywhere are forging ahead and embracing their right to independence -"

"Yeah, yeah, and casting off their shackles. Get off your soapbox, Lil! Not everyone wants to be a spinster for the rest of their lives."

Lilith didn't seem at all put out. "Well I'd rather be in charge of my own destiny than tied to a man for all the wrong reasons."

"You're forgetting one small detail. In order to have a husband you have to be asked first, and last time I looked I didn't see a long queue for your hand in holy wedlock. Actually, I didn't see any queue at all."

"And that suits me just fine."

"How would you know when you haven't had much experience in that department. In fact," and leaning her pert little bottom against the dressing table she put a theatrical finger to her cheek and frowned, "I can't remember any bloke asking you to walk out with him recently. Other than Reggie Harper, of course. And he's so desperate he wouldn't care who he was with, just so long as they were breathing."

"Don't be cruel. It's not becoming."

"Wasn't me who started it."

Turning away she reached for her small cardboard pot of Bourjois rouge and dabbed furiously with the soft cotton puff.

She'd overstepped the mark, of course, but it was so easy to do. Not that her sister deserved to be treated that way, but why couldn't she understand that not everyone wanted to be like her? Some just wanted a normal life.

Feeling a tad guilty she said, "Anyway, I do love Bert."

"Then I'm pleased for you."

"And…" she decided to take her into her confidence, "you never know, I think he might propose soon."

"Gracious. I had no idea it was that serious."

"Well it is."

"Does mum know?"

"Don't be silly! Of course not!" she felt her smile fade.

"Dad?"

"No."

"Well, you'll have to tell them."

"I know. And I will, when I've got something to say and the time is right."

"Have you made any plans?"

"Only that it'll be a long engagement."

"Why?"

"He's sailing soon, that's why," and she sighed as if she carried all the world's problems on her shoulders.

"How soon?"

"A few weeks."

"Oh. Will he be away long??"

"Two whole years."

Suddenly it was all too much. "Oh Lil, he's going to the Indian Ocean. That's miles away. And it's not just his ship. There're others going as well. How am I supposed to cope?"

"Time will pass. You'll just have to keep busy."

"But I'm not like you. I'm not interested in books and studying."

"There are plenty of other things you can do."

"Like what?" Accepting her sister's outstretched fingers, she dropped onto the bed.

"Well, you're certainly needed here. Mum's having a lot of trouble with her back these days, and you could take on some of her workload. I'm sure she'd be pleased with the help."

"She's got you for that. When you're not at school, that is."

"But I haven't always got time. I've got lessons to prepare and studying to do. I'll never get a decent position if all I have is my preliminary certificate. I've got to get into college and sit formal qualifications if I'm to have any chance of proving my proficiency in the classroom. You know that."

"You don't think you're being a little selfish?"

It was meant as a joke, but it obviously wasn't taken that way. Her sister's eyes had widened in outrage. Nudging her with an elbow Ruby added quickly, "Dad always said out of all of us, you were the one with the brains. You know we're all proud of you. Oh, Lil," her fragile mood was ebbing fast, "at least you've got your teaching. What have I got? I want to do something exciting with my life while Bert's away."

Lilith must have decided to forgive her, for she answered, "Like what?"

"I dunno. That's the problem."

"You could always find a job. That would help pass the time."

"A job? That's your solution?"

"I can't think of anything else. Though to be honest even that isn't easy anymore. Not many businesses seem to be hiring, though I suppose you could always go into service. It would mean a lot less freedom than you have now, of course. And don't forget Dad's talking about New Zealand, so going through the whole rigmarole of applying for interviews might be pointless anyway."

"Oh lord, let's not even think about that. I couldn't imagine anything worse than starting out all over in some foreign backwater, and that's saying something. No, if I'm to have any happiness over the next year, it'll be because I've made a drastic change to my life."

"Such as what?"

She'd just thought of the most perfectly thrilling idea.

"I'll go and live in London."

"London? Good grief! Why London?"

"It's the place to be. Everything happens there. Don't you keep up with any of the gossip?"

She could already see herself at the Kit Kat club in the city's West End. Champagne would be flowing and she'd be wearing fabulous jewellery and an outrageously expensive costume of gold thread and beads. Or being wined and dined by her latest admirer in a swish restaurant. She'd be the focus of everyone in the room. And the men! Oh, she'd be surrounded by them. All terribly good-looking of course. And royalty too. She pulled herself up short. Well, perhaps not a duke or anything. A viscount maybe. Even so, he'd have a yacht in Monte Carlo and a sumptuous apartment in Italy for when he tired of his aristocratic pile in the Shires.

"You can no more go and live in London than I can go and live in Russia."

"Why not?"

"Well, let me see." Lilith held up her thumb. "First, you have no job, a minor detail I know, but without a good income you can't afford to live anywhere. Second," her forefinger came up, "we don't know anyone in London, and you know what mum's like for worrying. And third," her middle finger uncurled, "you're only nineteen."

"I'm nearly twenty," she retorted.

"Not for another seven months. And even then you wouldn't be allowed to go."

"I would if you put in a good word for me. Mum thinks you're sensible."

Resting her chin on her knees Lilith gave a wry smile. "I know. Not exactly complimentary, is it?"

"Oh Lil, you know what I mean. And you would stick up for me, wouldn't you?"

"No. Not this time."

Her resolve hardened. "In that case, I'll do it without your help."

"And how will you do that?"

"I'll run away."

"Send me a postcard when you get wherever you're going," Lilith snorted, unfolding her legs and retrieving her book.

"I might just do that."

Flouncing, she got to her feet. Why she bothered trying to be friends she'd no idea. It was hardly worth it half the time.

"So where are you and Bert going tonight?" she was asked a moment or two later, and recognising an olive branch when she heard one, she softened a bit.

"Not sure. Probably for a stroll along the Esplanade. But don't tell mum. She thinks I'm popping over Elsie's."

Lilith was rolling her eyes. "I don't believe you sometimes. Well, you'd better wrap up then. And if you intend to get as far as the pier, wear a decent pair of shoes. Last time you had blisters the size of duck eggs thanks to your friend's heels."

It was just as well her sister's nose was back in her book, for she'd no idea how close she'd come to the truth. Had she glanced up the whole game would have given away, for regardless she wasn't allowed anywhere near South Parade Pier at night, the Carlton Dance Band were playing in the Pavilion and that was exactly where she and Bert were going. Blisters or no blisters.

"I know. But it's the style these days. Low heels in the mornings, high at night. Anyway, they make me took taller - and thinner," she gushed, hoping at the same time she wasn't opening herself for another lecture on accepting herself as she was, flaws and all. "I'll be getting my own pair as soon as I've saved up enough, and in the meantime…" she flashed the back of an ankle where newly attached sticking plasters could just be made out beneath her nude stockings. "Look. Should do the trick."

"Only you would come up with such a thing."

"I try, sister dear."

"You know you'd have your own stuff a lot sooner if you didn't spend every penny the moment you get it. It seems to me you're keeping Woolworth's and Boot's cosmetic counters in business all by yourself."

Turning back to the mirror Ruby pulled on her hat.

"I can't help it if I want to look good," she said, tweaking her blonde Marcelled finger waves into place. "After all, one of us has to."

5

"GAWD ALMIGHTY, YOU gave me a scare!"

Having stepped into the alley, Ruby spun around, one hand still on the gate latch, the other clutched to her chest. "What on earth are you doing here? I thought we were meeting round the corner."

The uniformed sailor in the navy cap, ribbon slewed so that rather than sit at the side the tiddly bow was over his left eye, took a long drag on his cigarette before flicking it into the gutter. "We were. Thought I'd save us a bit of time," he grinned, pushing away from the wall and offering his arm.

"Bloody hell," she swore, "what if someone had seen you?"

"But they didn't," he said, a little too carelessly for her liking.

"But they might have," she argued back.

Hustling him to the end of the alley she told him of the brush she'd just had with her mother. Far too close for comfort, she'd been caught at the bottom of the stairs with her mother wanting to know where she was going.

"Over to Elsie's," she'd lied, trying for a haughty *is this really necessary* tone.

"Dressed like that?"

Stuck on the last but one linoleum tread and with her mother forced to look up, she should have had the advantage of height.

It didn't feel that way, though.

"I *am* taking my coat."

"I should hope so. Otherwise you'd catch your death in that outfit. Run out of wool, did they?"

"This is how it's supposed to look," she'd said, tugging at the sweater's dark green ribbing. "It's all the fashion."

"Really? Looks more like you're advertising your wares to me. And what will you be doing round Elsie's?"

"Nothing much. Go for a walk up town probably."

Her mother waited.

"And look in the shops," she finished, the answer sounding lame even to her.

"Just as well they're closed then. And I see you're still wearing her shoes."

Would she ever stop finding fault? What about the skirt? Or her hair, trimmed and lightened only that afternoon? Or her lipstick? Or anything else for that matter.

"Does her mother know how she spends the money she gets from working at the bakery?"

Ruby shrugged. "Probably."

"Somehow I doubt it. I can't see her being let out in anything like what you're wearing."

"Well, she does."

"Don't give me any lip, young lady."

Knowing the threat was real she'd had to look away. Pushing her mother any further could so easily mean she'd be kept in. And that was the last thing she wanted.

"I expect you home by ten-thirty," her mother turned away. "Don't be late."

Hurrying over to the row of hooks behind the back door Ruby first pulled on her scarf.

"Don't wait up," she muttered under her breath.

A mistake in hindsight, for her mother called back, "That's exactly what I will be doing. Ten thirty on the dot, or I'll send Alfie over to fetch you."

The stench from the communal toilets and overflowing dustbins didn't usually bother her, nor did the general decay and slovenliness of the place, but it didn't mean she was comfortable dragging Bert through the depressing labyrinth of alleys and crumbling brick courts with bleak faces peering from cracked windows and doors wedged permanently ajar. Rather she was all too aware of it, and her pace didn't slacken until they'd emerged onto St Georges Square. Then, believing they were far enough from the unwanted attention of anyone who might know her or frequent *The Saracen's Head,* she slowed to a provocative swing and fluttered her eyelashes.

"Have to say you're keen, turning up on my doorstep like that."

"You complaining?"

She shrugged. "Suppose not. Though you'd better not make a habit of it."

"Thought you might appreciate it."

"What if my mum had popped her head out the gate for some reason? Then what?"

"I'd have said a polite good evening and charmed her with my light-hearted conversation."

"Oh, Bert! You are a one!"

"Won't do it again if you don't want me to."

"It's not that…"

"It's alright. Only meant to save us a bit of time."

"Hmmm. You did, did you?" her eyes travelled in any direction but his. "Time for what, that's what I'm wondering."

"Time to be with my girl."

Though it was no more than she expected to hear, she simpered. "So I'm your girl, am I?"

"Don't I keep telling you?"

"You might *tell* me…" she said before shrugging as if perhaps it didn't matter after all. Though it did of course, since her hopes were pinned on him being *the one*.

"Oh," he said, "you want me to *show* you."

"Maybe. A girl likes to be sure of these things."

"Then I'd better try harder."

His expression, as dark and mysterious as any film star's, sent a delicious tingling through her. As if she were at the fairground on one of those rides that took your breath away, even as you clung all for all it was worth.

"You are a devil," she said, giving his elbow a squeeze.

"And you love me for it."

"Maybe."

Right there on the pavement, he stopped and spun her towards him.

"Only maybe?" and lowering his head, he touched his lips to hers.

She thought she'd die with the sheer pleasure of it. But this wasn't the time or place for any malarkey and he should know that. Middle of the street indeed! Coming up for air she gave him a little shove. Not hard enough to push him away, more to emphasis she wasn't *that* kind of girl.

"Bert! Not here!"

"Thought you liked a bit of a cuddle," he said, his arms still about her.

"I do, but not in public. Someone might see us."

"Like who?"

Pressed up against his regulation serge jumper her cheeks were warm. "I don't know. One of our customers perhaps."

"And we wouldn't want that, would we?"

"Not if they went straight round home and told my mum."

"You win," crooking his finger Bert tilted up her chin, "but only for now."

This time his kiss was a little more chaste.

Ruby tried to hide her delight. She and her tall, handsome Naval rating might have only known each other a few weeks, but she loved it when he was all masculine and in charge. That was why she tottered and blushed when loosening his grip, he drew her arm through his once more.

Had she been asked, she would have said that as well as height Bert possessed two other things she found so necessary in a man; broad shoulders and a powerful chest. The attraction had been instant, and why she'd agreed to have tea with him that day in Southsea when she and Elsie had been oohing and ahhing at the latest fashions in Handley's window and he and his shipmates had emerged from *The Osborne* public house on the other side of the road.

Crossing over he'd come up behind them.

"Ladies,' he'd grinned, sweeping off his cap. "May we offer you an escort?"

Having given him the once over, Elsie's eyes had widened appreciatively. Ruby though was made of sterner stuff.

"I doubt you're in any fit state to steer a true course," she said, and having matched his cheek with her own, thought she'd flummoxed him.

But far from it.

"I'd say that would depend on the helmsman," he replied, his eyes dancing in the most wicked way.

The wink that followed had been her undoing.

Now, easy in each other's company and with his long pace shortened to hers, they strolled towards the fortified sea walls at the harbour's entrance. Past rundown townhouses, the once elegant pediments, fanlights and cornices testament to better times. And shiplap cottages three stories high, yet little more than eight feet wide. Past a red-brick reform church and a soberly painted board displaying just three lines of services, and around a drunk spilling out from the dingy public house next door, waving and shouting farewells to those still inside. From somewhere a dog barked, no doubt agitated by the sudden commotion. A woman shouted and the yapping ceased, only to start up again a moment later. And all the while flickering, eerie-green gas light pooled over chilly cobbles and gutters of stagnant water.

"I have to say, you look good in uniform," she complimented him.

"Oh?"

"Yeah. Can't say that for every bloke. It's because you're tall. It sort of sets everything off."

"So it's not the colour then?"

She frowned. "The colour?"

"Navy blue. You reckon I'd look just as good in pink, do you?"

"Perhaps not," she giggled.

"Well, I'm glad I pass muster."

"And what about me?" the question floated on the air.

"You?"

"Yes, me!" and nudging him in the ribs with her elbow, she swung against him.

"Can't see much of you under that thick coat."

"Well, if you take me somewhere warm, I might undo a few buttons."

"Is that so?" lifting an eyebrow he grinned. "Best I take you somewhere hot then."

"Bert! You say the wickedest things."

"Only to my girl."

"So you keep saying, but how do I really know?"

"What? That you're my girl? I'd have thought that was obvious."

"But you know what they say about matelots. A girl in every port. I'm sure a good-looking bloke like you is no different."

"You know me better than that, Rube."

"Do I?"

"I should hope so."

He said no more, and she looked away. Seemed like pushing a man towards a proposal wasn't going to be as easy as she'd thought, though why it should be that way she'd no idea. Wasn't a wife what every man wanted, after all?

She'd have to try a new tack.

"I wish you weren't going away," and she sighed in a way guaranteed to tear at the hardest of male heart-strings.

"I wish I wasn't too."

"You need a regular job, you do."

"Thought you liked me in uniform."

"I do."

"Well then, can't have it both ways."

That hadn't got her very far.

"You told anyone about me?" she asked.

"Like who?"

"Well...you know...family. That sort of thing."

Bert shrugged. "Told my mum."

"Ohhhh, you never said."

"Well, I'm telling you now."

"When did you write to her? What did she say?"

He frowned as if trying to recall. "She said you sounded like a nice girl."

"I am," she said, happy at last. "Maybe she might want to meet me one day."

"She does."

"Did she say that? Really?"

"Why would I make up something like that?"

"I dunno," she lapsed into silence for a moment. "So are you going to take me home before you go?"

"I wanted to. She wanted me to as well. But I haven't got any leave due."

"Oh. Well, maybe I can write to her instead."

"She'd like that."

"You'd better tell me her address then."

"I'll jot it down for you. Give it to you next time," he said easily.

Next time, a little voice said? What was wrong with now? Say it slow and have her repeat it so she'd remember. Or did he have something to hide? Like perhaps he wasn't as free and single as he was making out? He was twenty-six, and old enough to have a wife and kiddie somewhere.

No, she told herself firmly. Not her Bert. He was as honest as they came. Look at how he never broke a date and how well he treated her.

"You won't forget me while you're away, will you?" she persevered.

"You are a silly. How could I possibly forget you?"

"Easily I would have thought, with all those foreign girls chasing after you."

"There's only one girl for me, and I'm looking right at her."

He stopped and pulled her into his arms again. This time, she didn't complain.

6

BOWED AGAINST THE GUSTING WIND, and with one hand clamped on her hat to prevent it being whipped off, Lilith crossed the street and headed towards the three storey school building, but not before noting the cluster of girls sitting on the kerb and singing of the big ship sailing on the *alley alley oh!*

"*And the captain said it would never, never do. Never, never do*," they chorused, wagging reddened fingers at each other.

Hadn't she sung that very same ditty not so many years ago? And if not that, she'd played two ball against brick walls, or hopscotch on narrow pavements, or five stones on doorsteps.

"Shouldn't you be getting ready for school?" she called out in the voice usually kept for the classroom.

The children scattered.

If they were late, she knew who they were. The tall girl's mother took in sewing, a respectable enough occupation, but Lilith had heard she'd set her heart on her daughter achieving good grades and around these parts that was enough to raise eyebrows. Or worse, encourage talk of certain folks getting above themselves. It drove her mad. Why shouldn't girls be encouraged in the same way as boys? There was certainly no room for discrimination in her syllabus.

Pushing open the door marked for staff and visitors only she hurried past Miss Somerville's office and down the green-painted corridor with its scratched and scarred wooden block flooring. The Little School; the long room housing all three classes of younger children, was right at the end. Not yet eight-fifteen it would be another three-quarters of an hour before the desks would fill up, meaning she had enough time to light the stove, go over her schedule, and write up the first lesson on the board.

"Ready for another gruelling day, Miss Doherty?"

"Good morning Mister Haslem."

Crouched over and arranging lumps of coke on the kindling there was no need to look over to the doorway, for her colleague's appearance first thing was a regular occurrence.

"I wonder what delights this overcast and blustery day has in store for us today," he said.

"I would be happy with a few hours of sunshine."

"I was thinking of something a little more extreme. Perhaps an epidemic of snotty nose or itchy scab to keep the little blighters at home."

"You don't mean that," hand on the unlit stove she turned, frowning, for having suffered greatly in the trenches of France Lawrence Haslem was known to behave strangely even after all these years.

"Oh but I do. Have you any idea how difficult it is to enthuse a bunch of guttersnipes with the finer points of English literature?" His eyes were flitting over the room as if uncertain where to land. "Unless of course it is Tennyson's *Charge of the Light Brigade* or something equally as glorifying of the machinations of war."

"They are probably wondering how the subject will benefit them when they are working a shift in the dockyard," she replied, back at her task and holding a match to a twist of paper.

"And yet there are plenty in that very establishment who might be found reading Marx or Engle's."

"There are indeed. So you must persevere and enthuse your charges with a thirst for knowledge."

Haslem gave a rumbling sigh. "You are right of course. And I do have one or two promising students."

"There you are then," she replied, banging the stove door and straightening. "All is not lost."

"Not yet. Though it will be if there is no knuckling down and studying for the eleven plus. You are lucky, Miss Doherty, in that you do not have that trial to contend with."

She understood the reference, for school boards took examination results very seriously indeed. But lucky? She would have liked to dispute his assertion, for while her pupils could hardly be considered difficult, being only five and six years of age, she wanted more. A challenge, even! She yearned to fire up young minds and get them thinking for themselves, not just learning their lessons by rote. And while that would come with a formal qualification, patience had never been her strong point.

The second interruption came as she was completing a line of chalk script on the blackboard.

"Lilith, dearest. You haven't forgotten about the meeting tonight, have you?"

"Of course not, Nora. Why would you think that?"

Her friend had a more distracted look than usual as if she'd something on her mind. That, or she'd gotten up late, which judging by the hastily caught up frizz of curls might just be the case.

"We need to stand together. A sisterhood," Nora said, choosing to ignore the question and coming to the front of the classroom.

"You are preaching to the converted," Lilith pointed out gently.

"I know," hands bunched into the pockets of her long cardigan, Nora's cheeks were a vivid shade of pink. "I just feel so strongly about it. And time is running out. It's all so terribly unfair. Why am I being forced to choose between the work I love and the man I love? Wasn't the war supposed to get rid of all this inequality?"

Lilith tried not to smile, for it was a big leap from defeating the Hun to employment conditions in English classrooms.

"It shouldn't, you're right," she sobered. "But we have to make it a general issue, and not just a concern of female teachers. We have to look outside our profession, to other organisations discriminating against women. Use the might of numbers."

"Gosh, you put it so well. What would we do without you?"

"You would find someone else, I'm sure. It's a just cause and we have a lot of support. Even from the trades unions."

"Hmm. I'm not so sure about that. Not when so many are out of work."

"And how can that be our fault?"

Nora stepped back, blinking. "It isn't, of course. But you know how stubborn men can be."

"And that's why things need to change. It's time we women stood up for ourselves."

"Absolutely! Oh Lilith, you're so inspiring. You're sounding more and more like a politician every day!"

"Rubbish! I just want a world that's fair. That's all."

Making her way to the front of the hall and slipping between the second and third row of chairs, Lilith arrived at the seat Nora had saved for her.

"Hardly a good turn out," she complained, casting her eye over the scattering of union members before shifting the other's girl's belongings to the floor.

"It's still early. Plenty of time for a few more to arrive. Toffee?"

A paper bag was held out.

"No thanks."

She'd barely time to settle before her friend leaned in.

"Have you seen who's behind us?"

Lilith made a show of scanning the entire room.

"I suppose we shouldn't be surprised," she said, turning back. "There's been enough gossip going around."

"Notice she's had her hair done?"

"I feel sorry for her poor husband."

"You think he knows?"

"I doubt it. But that doesn't make it any better."

Nora shifted her toffee to the other cheek. "They say Owen's wife is getting suspicious."

"Well, you can't blame her. It's not the first time she's had cause. For heaven's sake, the man's a serial adulterer and you'd think that knowledge alone would be enough to bring Ada to her senses."

"Nothing's going to do that. She likes the way his lordship struts about as if he owns the place and everyone in it."

"He's only a union official," rummaging in her handbag, Lilith was trying to find her notebook and pen. "And not a very good one at that."

"That's not the way she sees it."

"Then she should."

"Perhaps there's more to it."

Glancing up and catching the shrewd look on Nora's face, she asked, "Like what?"

"A certain little bird has told me she might be using him."

"How?"

"Well, we all know she's desperate to get back to into teaching."

"And you think she's hoping Owen will argue her case?"

"Why not? Four years wed and no babies in sight? It must be worth a try."

Lilith found herself nodding. "She must be going mad shut up in that house all day."

"And with only her mother-in-law for company."

Wasn't that the dreadful part? Two women, both with too much time on their hands, trying to organise the same household? She couldn't think of anything worse, especially for someone like Ada who'd taught at senior level for a good few years before marrying. And as if that wasn't bad enough, the rumour mill had it she was sorely missed and would be welcomed back, if only the rules could be changed.

"Well if it works, I'll be the first to congratulate her."

"Calling the meeting to order…"

Stepping onto the platform the handful of union officials took their seats at the long table. Bill Marsden, as befitting his position as Chairman of the Executive Committee, was already standing behind the centremost chair. Legs planted firmly apart and back ram-rod straight - like so many others he'd also served in France all those years ago, though in his case in a supply depot well behind the front line - he returned his fob watch to the pocket of his waistcoat.

Half a dozen rows of general members, dotted in twos and threes, hushed.

"We will start as usual with a roll call of the officers present, the reading of the minutes of the last meeting, and the financial report," he stated.

The secretary, a rather timid-looking man with both prominent cheekbones and nose, nodded as of to offer a polite *thank you*. However, Bill was not finished.

"But before that," he boomed as if it were necessary to reach every corner of the room. "I'd like to introduce a visitor…"

He turned to the only female at the table.

"Miss Stowell is here from the National Union of Women Teachers. She will be giving a small talk on the common aims of our two organisations."

Picking up on the slight nuance, an arrogance even, as if no one could possibly believe themselves in the same league as the NUT when it came to fighting for rights and conditions, Lilith's eyes narrowed. But Bill had already moved on to what he seemed to consider a more important reminder.

"Furthermore, there is a goodly amount of unfinished and new business on tonight's agenda, and I would ask if you would all keep your questions pertinent and timely. That way we should be able to conclude at a reasonable hour."

He was glaring at his audience as if to identify any challenge to his authority. Or was it merely disappointment at the low turnout? Either way, Lilith couldn't hold back an exasperated sigh, for it was well known he was the worst offender. Liking the sound of his own voice he could ramble on for ages before finally getting back to the point.

Having little interest in the first items on the agenda, she studied their visitor, noting with some surprise that on closer inspection Miss Stowell appeared only a few years older than herself. That led to wondering as to her qualifications, for surely she was a teacher first and foremost? Was she perhaps fully certified? Or possibly even a school mistress? For some reason she doubted the latter, not because of her age but because being a union official required commitment, and there weren't enough hours in the day to do that and manage a class with any level of success.

She was also very pretty, though not in the same way as Ruby. Ruby was fashion personified in that if she read in a magazine that Hollywood actresses were painting their cheeks blue this season she'd not rest until she'd searched out that very same shade. Miss Stowell's features spoke for themselves. Her eyebrows were defined rather than plucked to oblivion, and her complexion pale. If she resorted to powder and rouge it was done sparingly. Her lips, however, were definitely tinted, so perhaps she wasn't averse to a little cosmetic enhancement after all.

Most amazing of all, she appeared to be following the mundane details of the branch's financial report with avid interest. That is until she glanced in Lilith's direction and smiled.

Mortified, she retrieved her pen and bowing her head, started writing furiously.

7

REACHING DOWN FOR HER BAG Nora was more than a little disgruntled.

"Well, that didn't offer us much."

"It didn't, did it," Lilith agreed.

"They barely touched on married women returning to the classroom, and I thought that was the whole point of it being on the agenda. Why else include it?"

"I've no idea."

"It just raises people's hopes unnecessarily. And to gloss over something so important to talk about raising the school-leaving age to fifteen? Why are we even considering it?" she said, scuttling after her to the end of the row. "By then boys should be in apprenticeships and the like. Not stuck in a classroom causing trouble and wasting everyone's time."

"I thought Miss Stowell had some interesting points," Lilith offered over her shoulder.

"Did you? Well yes, I suppose so. But even she didn't mention it. And being a woman I thought she would."

Having made it to the aisle, Lilith stopped. "So did I. Look, do you mind if I stay back? I'd like to catch up with one or two of the delegates and see if I can work up a bit of interest. If nothing else, they need to know we won't be going away any time soon."

"Do a little politicking, you mean?" Nora was buttoning up her coat. "Be my guest. I'm seeing George anyway. He's coming round home to go over some of the wedding details."

"Don't you be too hard on him now!"

"Chance would be a fine thing. He and my dad just nod at everything mum and I suggest. One day I'm going to ask for something totally outrageous just to see if they're even listening. Like a dozen bridesmaids, all in fancy dress."

Giving her friend a quick hug, Lilith headed towards the group who'd been on the platform earlier. Now huddled together, they were clearly involved in discussions of some sort, and taking a deep breath she touched her fingers on the sleeve of a jacket.

"Excuse me, Bill."

The chairman swung round, his brow lowering. She guessed he wasn't at all pleased at the interruption. Or did he have a problem with her in particular? She suspected it could be the latter since their dealings, when she could get hold of him that was, were usually a little strained.

"Oh, Miss Doherty."

"Yes. And I'm wondering when this union will finally get around to giving full and proper consideration to the issue of married women being allowed to continue with their vocations. Tonight, frankly, was a waste of time."

The rheumy eyes hardened. "All in good time, all in good time. These things can't be rushed as I've told you before. We need to tread carefully. And you," the last word was heavily emphasised, "need to remember the number of men who are presently out of work."

"What has that got to do with the number of qualified women currently in teaching positions who have no desire to leave them?"

"Miss Doherty," as if aware the conversation might draw the interest of others he'd fixed a smile in place. "You and I have spoken on this subject time and again. Those women knew the rules when they elected to be educators and if they feel so strongly about their careers…" he glanced to the side as if to muster support, "…they should reconsider, perhaps, their marriage prospects. You girls can't have it both ways, y'know."

There was a shuffling of feet. One official looked at the floor. Another simply turned away.

Lilith was furious.

"And yet a man can," she re-joined sweetly. "You, for example. Not just one career but two if you count your union work. And a wife at home."

Her gaze hardened, for it was a poorly kept secret that despite his blustering demeanour outside the four walls of his home, Bill's wife ruled the inside of the roost with an iron rod. And from the moment he stepped back through the front door.

This time, he didn't bother hiding his displeasure.

"Miss Doherty, I don't have time for this now. Talk to Wilson," he jerked his head in in the direction of the secretary who, having put on his coat was in the process of wrapping a thick woollen scarf around his neck. "Get him to add it to our next agenda."

"When, due to time constraints, it will be passed forward to the next meeting. And the one after."

But Bill had already turned his back.

"Miss Doherty…" Miss Stowell took a step towards her. "I would very much like to talk to you. That is, if you have a moment?"

Her tone was courteous, more so than earlier when speaking to her audience. Then, it might be said, she'd practically hectored at times. As if she were used to giving orders and getting her own way.

"Of course."

"Shall we find somewhere to sit?"

"I hope I haven't inconvenienced you," she began, having commandeered two of the remaining seats in the front row. With the folding and stacking of chairs continuing around them the sound of clattering wood might have seemed accusing.

"Not at all. In fact, you've probably saved me from being barred from all future meetings."

"Is it that bad?"

"I don't know why I bother sometimes," Lilith stopped. "Actually I do. But you can only bang your head against a wall for so long."

"Before what?"

"Before you murder someone."

Miss Stowell's eyes twinkled with amusement. "I see. And your intended victim?"

"I'd probably start with Bill Marsden, and then hack my way through the entire chain of command."

"So, multiple crimes then?"

"As many as I could get away with."

"Hmm. You would need to be judicious. Not everyone is opposed to new ideology and you don't want to alienate those who might prove friendly, given the right opportunity."

"You think I should ask them the colour of their politics first?"

"It might save embarrassment later on."

It was hard not to laugh. Of all the ridiculous conversations...

But Miss Stowell was asking, "Do you really feel that strongly about the rights of married women to teach?"

Heaven's, those eyes were the most amazing colour, Lilith thought. Like a troubled sky, they were more gray than blue and so pale as to be almost translucent. And those sweeping lashes.

She couldn't tear her gaze away.

"Miss Doherty?"

"Yes, I do," she said in a rush.

"Can I ask why?"

She blinked. Surely it was obvious. "It's the unfairness of it all."

"But there are many other areas in which we are discriminated. Pay parity, for example."

"Yes, I know. And that makes me angry too. Is it really too much to ask that men and women carrying out the same task receive equal remuneration?"

"You might have noticed the world isn't perfect."

"I certainly have. But one day…"

"Miss Doherty, are you more of a militant than you're letting on?"

Having opened her mouth to reply Lilith thought better of it. The charge was not that far from the truth.

"Not really," she blushed, conscious of the same amused expression as before, "I'm just getting a little carried away."

"Actually, I admire your spirit, and that was why I wanted to talk to you."

"Oh?"

"You see, the NUWT needs women like you in its ranks. Women who aren't afraid to stand up for what they believe in."

"But I'm not the only one. There are plenty more of us."

"Without wishing to offend you, I think not. At least, not with your fire."

Caught off guard, she was thinking fast. "Please don't think me rude in return," she said evenly, "but my enthusiasm is very grass roots. I'm really not sure I have what you are looking for and I'd hate to disappoint you."

"Oh, I'm sure you wouldn't do that."

"But even if I was interested in joining your organisation - and I'm not saying I am - you of all people know how difficult it is for a group of women to be taken seriously. Trade unions are notoriously misogynist."

"I agree. And that needs to change. It won't happen overnight but that is what we're pushing for. A more even gender balance at every level."

"I see. Would you admit to being a feminist organisation?"

"Without a doubt. And I'm proud of it too."

"With interests in other areas?"

The question was deliberate, for accusations levelled against such groups included anarchy and subversion. Some even went as far as suggesting members wanted to change society out of all recognition. A society, it was argued, that had existed in its present format for centuries.

There was no preamble. "Yes."

"Areas outside of the trades union movement?" she persisted, a little breathlessly. For wasn't this what she had been looking for all this time? To be influential in advancing women's rights and find others who wanted to do likewise?

Miss Stowell was nodding. "Would that type of support bother you?"

"Only if the activity were illegal," she admitted. "I would rather not go to prison if I can help it."

"And that is something I would prefer to avoid too," Miss Stowell agreed. "But you know as well as I do, that level of commitment has been required on occasion. Look, why don't I give you an example of some of the issues I'm involved with. A woman's right to contraception. Now there's something that would solve so many problems, and for society as a whole too. And then there's the on-going battle to relax the absurd rules around women and voting eligibility. Some of the restrictions are far too stringent."

"You see that as a conspiracy to keep the reins of power firmly in male hands?"

"Of course. Don't you?"

"Indeed I do."

"You see," Miss Stowell beamed. "We are already of like mind."

Lilith hadn't finished. "Miss Stowell, you have implied your members share a certain amount of radical thought. And yet your contribution here today was hardly more than tacit support for more innocuous NUT issues."

The other woman did not seem at all put out.

"Of course. You must remember I'm here tonight only as a guest. One who has expressed a desire to promote solidarity with the officials of your branch."

"Just as you are doing with other branches," she guessed.

"Indeed."

"And did you?"

"We shall see," was the cryptic reply. "Lilith... may I call you Lilith?"

"Of course."

She quelled a sudden desire to shift in her seat, for the enigmatic eyes were boring into hers once more.

"The fight for rights and conditions isn't about which union is the more powerful. It's about uniting different factions for the good of the whole. Think of it. As individual organisations we all have our strengths, but by coming together we have numbers. And that's the key when it comes to bargaining with the education ministry or anyone else for that matter. Even at a local level."

"So why have a separate union for women teachers at all? Why not return to the NUT?"

"Because there would be no benefit in doing that. We exist to pursue issues affecting our female membership. That's our focus. And for that reason, while we're ready to lend our support to any cause serving a common need, we do expect that assistance returned. Either in the short term or the long term."

"A case of you scratch my back and I'll scratch yours," Lilith nodded. "And you accuse me of being militant!"

"Touché," Miss Stowell laughed. "And now I should go back and make my farewells, or your Mr Marsden will think his already poor opinion of me quite justified. Please do say you'll give serious thought to joining us. Like I said, we need to keep bringing on board others of like-mind, especially if they have your get-up-and-go."

"I will think about it," she said, knowing she was blushing again.

"Good."

"Miss Stowell," she said quickly, "how should I contact you… if I have reason of course."

"I'll give you the telephone number of my lodgings. And its Grace. Not Miss Stowell."

8

HAVING STARED DOWN INTO THE darkened yard for what seemed an eternity, Ruby let the lace curtain drop back into place.

"What am I going to do, Else?"

"No idea," beneath the rouged cheeks and kohled eyes her best friend was looking a touch bored. "Never had to think of how to get a bloke to propose before."

"Then try."

"I am."

"Then try harder. We need to come up with a plan."

Stretched out and comfy on Lilith's satin eiderdown Elsie studied her newly varnished nails. One of the unpainted half-moon cuticles was looking a touch lopsided and she worried that it might need re-doing. "Trouble is," she said, holding her hand at a distance to get a better look, "we don't really know if he wants to. Marry you that is."

Ruby knew that only too well. "He does. He just hasn't got round to realising it yet."

"And will he? 'Cos you know; you can push a bloke too hard sometimes," Elsie pointed out reasonably.

"Since when have you been an expert?"

"Just saying."

Leaning against Aunt Maud's dressing table and folding her arms Ruby said, "We have to think clever."

"Thought that was what we were doing."

Her glare seemed to have little effect.

"Shame you don't know if you're going to New Zealand or not," Elsie said. "'Cos if he thought you were off; it might spur him into action."

"Oh! That's it, Else. I'll tell him it's all settled and he's bound to get down one knee."

Even Elsie looked animated. "And don't forget, he's not the only one around. There always Frank. Or Wilbur Steadman. He's reasonably good looking. And he does have a good job with the council. You know, either one would slip a ring on your finger if asked. In fact," now her face really lit up, "you could play them all off against the other. See who comes up with the best offer. Though if you pick Will," her face clouded once more, "you'd have to put up with the rest of his family."

"Aren't you listening. I don't want Will. Or that dopey Frank. *I want Bert.*"

Elsie went back to her fingernails. "Just saying. That's all."

"Then don't. Not unless you've something worthwhile to add."

"So when's he going away?" she asked, her tone properly subdued.

"In a few weeks."

"You'd better do something real fast then. Otherwise, you might end up leaving for real. Cor, just think about it, you could be waving to him from a ship of your own."

And quickly lowering her head she put a hand over her mouth.

"It's not funny, Else."

"Not of course it isn't. You still have a problem, though," she said, once she'd recovered from her fit of giggles.

"What?"

"Even if you do get him to pop the question you're not left with much time to get the banns read."

"You think I don't know that? If I can't get him to ask me in the next day or so, we'll have to be married by special licence."

"In a registry office?" Elsie stared. "Your mum won't be very pleased."

"She'll just have to put up with it."

"Will you still have bridesmaids and flowers?"

"Don't be silly."

"A dress then?"

"Of course I'll have a dress."

"Can I come along?"

Never having attended a civil ceremony Ruby had no clue as to what was involved. But she wasn't about to let anyone know that. Dropping onto her own bed she propped herself up on her elbow. "I'll see what Bert says."

"Gosh, it's all so thrilling. You know, if you were really pushed for time you could run off to Gretna Green," her friend sighed long and hard. "So romantic."

Feeling a touch smug, for here they were discussing her wedding when poor Elsie hadn't managed to hold on to a boyfriend any longer than a few weeks, at least not anyone decent, Ruby basked in her superiority.

"It won't be easy of course, having a husband at sea for the two years of our married life," she said, flipping over onto her stomach. "But I'm sure I'll cope."

"Of course you will. He'll be a lucky man to have you."

"Hardly luck, Else. This is true love."

"If you say so. But will you still come round our house once you're Mrs Bert Wilson?"

Ruby's eyes opened wide. "Oh, my giddy aunt!" and rolling onto her back she gazed up at the ceiling. "Mrs Bert Wilson," she savoured the title. "Mrs Ruby Wilson. Mrs Ruby Maud Wilson."

"I didn't know Maud was your middle name! You kept that quiet."

"Yes, well, it's after an aunt. And I hate it."

"It'll have to go on the licence."

"I know. And then that will be the end of it. From then on I'll be known as Mrs Ruby Wilson."

"And what about his family?" Elsie fingered the indented lines of stitching on the eiderdown. Up, across and down again.

"Well, his mother knows all about me of course. She can't wait to meet me."

"That's a good start."

"Yes. She thinks I sound like a nice girl." Ruby was still looking up at the ceiling.

"Which you are."

"Absolutely."

"So when's he taking you home?"

"Why? You want to come along, or something?"

"Don't be daft. Just curious, that's all."

"Not until he gets back. He hasn't got any more leave."

"That's a shame."

"But I'm sure his mum will come down for the wedding. Maybe with more of his family too."

"What about his dad."

"He's dead."

"Oh. So when are you seeing him next?"

"When I visit the cemetery I suppose," Ruby giggled, for she was feeling on top of the world now. "Be a bit hard otherwise, wouldn't it?"

"I meant Bert, silly."

"I know. Tomorrow. We're off to the pictures again."

"Make sure you see something romantic then. That is if you want him to declare his undying love."

Ruby sighed. "Thought that might work the other day. Trouble is, he's not like us. He thinks love stories are boring."

"Well, he's hardly going to be in the mood to propose after a Western, is he?"

"I know. Why must men be so difficult?"

"Dunno. That's just the way they are I suppose."

9

A CHILLING SEA FOG WAS rolling in off the Solent, and emerging from the bright lights and glamour of the Palace Cinema and pulling up her collar, Ruby snuggled close.

"Cold?" Bert wanted to know, slipping an arm around her shoulders.

"Freezing."

"Best I get you home then."

"Suppose so. Oh, that was such a lovely picture."

"It was alright if you like that sort of thing."

"You just can't beat a love story. Especially one like that. Does things to a girl, it does," she said, as they stepped off the kerb and crossed the road.

"Really? Like what?"

"Oh I don't know. Makes her think a little bit more about the man she's with I s'pose."

"So it's a good thing then?"

"Don't films like that make you think about the way things are and how they could be? If that's what you wanted, of course."

"Can't say they do. But then I prefer something with a little more action."

"Good job we're not all the same then. Ohh, Ivor Novello gives me goosebumps, he does," she said, glowing happily. "He's so handsome!"

"As handsome as me?"

"No-one's as handsome as you, Bert Wilson," she assured him.

Having turned into Nelson Square his gaze had been flitting from one side of the road to the other, until halting a few doors short of *The Oddfellows Arms*, he stared pointedly at the hanging sign.

"You good for a quick one? No more than ten minutes?"

"Shouldn't really," but feeling the almost imperceptible stiffening of his body she relented. "Alright, go on then. But just the one. You know what my dad's like. If he finds out I've been in a boozer he'll kill me."

"That's rich coming from a landlord. Though I suppose he wants to keep you safe from the riff-raff in this town. Which I can't argue with."

Ruby was delighted. "So that's what you want to do too?"

"Course," he grinned down at her. "I want to keep you all to myself."

"Oh Bert!"

Giving him a playful tap she lowering her head and looked up through her darkened lashes. "You know, if that was really what you want, you only have to say."

But all he did was kiss the tip of her nose.

"Come on," he said, his arm still around her shoulder, "let's get inside before you turn into a block of ice."

Managing to get seats close enough to the fire, Ruby settled back, undoing the buttons of her coat. Bert went to the bar to order their drinks. A pint of bitter for him, a port and lemon for her. Not that she was a drinker, but having served it enough times to the made-up tarts making free with their old man's weekly pay-packet, she'd poured one for herself when no one was looking and decided it was infinitely better than London gin, the only other thing she'd tried.

Careful not to make it too obvious she checked out the blokes huddled around a cribbage board and those hunched over and leaning on the bar. In every case, the flat caps and ill-fitting jackets were practically indistinguishable from any she'd seen in *The Saracen's Head*. Still, it wouldn't do to run into someone who might recognise her.

"Warm enough?" Bert set her glass down in front of her.

"Lovely."

"Like what you're wearing, Rube. The colour really looks good on you."

Ruby simpered. The dress was far too flash for the pictures but the moment she'd seen it on the rail in that new shop in Commercial Road, she'd wanted it. She wasn't going to let him know she'd had to go to her dad for a small loan, which of course he gave her, just like he always did. The only proviso was the usual one, that she didn't tell her mum. 'Keep it between us,' he'd said, planting a kiss on her forehead. 'It's better that way.' It was so annoying. She should get a regular wage for all the work she did around home; cleaning, helping with the cooking and even deputising behind the bar when necessary. Instead, she had to rely on charity and the odd bob or two.

Dropping his cap onto the table and with his pint in one hand and arm over the back of another chair, Bert launched into an incident that day when having given an all-too-trusting boy seaman a bucket, he'd ordered him ashore to get it filled with salt water.

"You didn't!"

"We all went through it, Rube. It's a rite of passage."

"And did he realise it was a joke?" she wanted to know.

"Nah. He went to the stores, daft 'appoth. They sent him away with a flea in his ear for wasting their time."

"Oh, the poor thing."

"You wait. He'll be doing the very same thing to another sprog in a year or two."

"A year or two," she toyed with the stem of her glass. "You'll be a leading hand by then."

"Keep my nose clean and get a few good reports under my belt and there's no reason why not."

"Do you think you'll ever make Petty Officer?"

"You're thinking ahead there, Rube."

"Doesn't hurt to have dreams."

Leaning in and putting his glass down, he ran a finger over the back of her hand. "And what are yours?"

"Oh," she flushed. "I just want to be happy."

"Then I reckon that's what we both want."

Her breath caught. Did he mean…? Was this it? *The* moment?"

But he'd picked up his pint again.

"My dad has a dream," she tried to keep her tone level.

"Oh yes? What's that then?"

"He wants to go to New Zealand."

"That's a big dream."

"In fact, he wants us all to go. His brother's already there."

"And is it what you want too?"

She played with her glass again.

"Maybe. He says it will be a good life."

"There's plenty that think the same."

"Oh?"

"Life in the colonies? Why not? Not much left here her in Blighty anymore. Not with all this unemployment and jobs going right, left and centre. It'll get worse before it gets better, mark my words."

She felt encouraged.

"My dad says exactly the same. Do you ever think of settling down?" her gaze travelled over other tables.

"Leave the sea, you mean?"

She nodded.

"Most matelots do at some stage," he shrugged.

"I suppose it depends if a man's married or not," and when he raised a quizzical eyebrow she added quickly, "Whether his wife is happy with the situation. Not everyone would like their husbands being away so long. Especially if they have children."

"Is that how you'd feel?" Bert was looking thoughtful.

She swallowed. Which way to jump? *'Yes'* would show him how much he meant to her. On the other hand, *'no'* might seem as a little less demanding since they were still only stepping out - at least as far as he was concerned.

She racked her brain.

"I suppose it would depend on who I was married to."

Her heart was beating so loudly surely he could hear it. She wanted to reach out and lay her hand on his arm. Assure him that while nineteen might seem young in his eyes, she was mature enough to have thought long and hard about the step they were taking and so there was no need to worry she might say no. Heavens, he didn't even have to go down on one knee. At least, not in the public bar of *The Oddfellows Arms*.

But instinct told her this was something he had to do for himself.

He was looking at her, his eyes intent, a gentle smile on his lips.

"Time for another? Or should we be on our way?"

And reaching for both glasses, he shoved his back his chair and stood.

10

AS THE INFANTS TRACED LINES and shapes in trays of sand under the watchful eye Lizzie Passmore, her fifteen-year-old assistant, Lilith was further down the classroom, ruler in hand.

"Five threes?" she pointed to a child with freckles and unruly red hair.

"Fifteen, miss."

"Four twos?" The ruler swung in another direction.

"Eight, miss."

"Good. Three fours?"

The ruler hovered before settling on a freshly nicked scalp. The owner's features immediately contorted into an expression of absolute horror.

"Come on. We did this yesterday. Three fours?"

The boy fidgeted and Lilith sighed.

The ruler moved on.

"Three fours?"

"Twelve, Miss."

"Excellent."

Glancing at her wristwatch, a treasured twenty-first birthday present from her father, she saw it was almost midday. Time for a senior to step into the corridor and, when the large hand on the clock over Miss Somerford's door clicked into the upright position, ring the hand bell. Then, all hell would break loose with the banging of desk lids and pupils pushing their way into the aisle and out of classroom doors, heading for home and the bite to eat that would - in most cases - be waiting for them.

She'd barely reached the front row when the first peal rang out.

"Quietly, please. No talking."

She didn't need eyes in the back of her head to pick out the usual suspects.

Five minutes later she was dropping her packet of sandwiches onto the table in the teacher's common room and falling into the nearest armchair.

"Gosh, I'm in need of a cup of tea."

Nora was already putting the kettle on the gas ring. "Hard morning?"

"No harder than any other day. You?"

"I took Lawrence Haslem's class for country dancing this morning. Do I have to say anymore?"

Lilith grinned. She'd heard the tinkling of the piano, and the same bars being repeated over and over again.

"Did you see the latest copy of the Chronical?" Nora asked while spooning tea into a large brown pot.

"No?"

"Your Miss Stowell is in it."

"Really? And she's hardly my Miss Stowell, silly."

Sitting up she reached for her lunch and unwrapped the greaseproof paper. "Did she write an article or something?"

"No, she just rated a mention."

"Oh."

Looking at the thin smear of fish paste between two slices of bread Lilith wondered how on earth it could have possibly looked so inviting earlier that morning.

"Are you still thinking of going over to the NUWT?" Nora asked, leaning back against the cupboard and, as was her habit, pushing her fists firmly into her pockets.

"Yes, I am."

"Me too."

Lilith's eyebrows shot up. "You?"

"Why not? You aren't the only one wanting to improve our lot."

"No, of course not. Sorry. It just came out a little wrong, that's all."

"I want to do my bit too. You're just more vocal than the rest of us," Nora said pointedly.

"I know. Too vocal for my own good sometimes."

"Apology accepted."

"Thank heavens for that. I don't think I could have coped with eating in silence."

"Who has to eat in silence?" Having just arrived Miss Somerford regarded first one then the other, both times lowering her head and peering over the top of her spectacles.

"No one, headmistress," Lilith laughed. "We were having a little joke."

"Oh good… good. Thought you might have been talking about one of the children."

"Not at all. Though I have no doubt most of them are required to keep quiet at the table."

"As it should be. Is there a cup for me?" She was glancing at the teapot with a hopeful expression.

"Of course."

But then Miss Somerford frowned and turned on her heel. "Ah. Back in a moment."

"So when will you make the switch?" Nora asked once they were alone again. "Bill Marsden won't be too happy at losing members."

"Oh, I don't know. He'll probably be glad to see the back of me at least."

"Have you thought about trying to rope in others?"

"Like who?"

"Like our female colleagues from other schools around here?"

"And how would I do that?"

"Call a meeting. Single out those not already in the women's union and let them know how you feel about things. The pay, the marriage bar, that sort of thing. Tell them there might be an alternative to the NUT's bargaining for us."

"I don't think I could."

"Why not?"

"What? Stand up and speak in front of an audience? I wouldn't dare!"

"There might not be an audience. Other than me of course."

"If that was the case then yes, I could do it," Lilith laughed. "Provided you didn't heckle me."

Nora grinned impishly. "That's right. Take away all my fun."

"I suppose I could ask Grace... Miss Stowell, I mean," despite her best efforts, the heat had risen in her cheeks, "to be the main speaker."

"Good idea," Nora set her tea down in front of her. "Just as long as she's more inspiring than last time."

"Oh, I'm sure she will be."

The installation of a telephone between the doorway to the public bar and the one to the kitchen had been carried out by the brewery a year or so earlier. All part of the modern world Jim boasted when showing off the instrument to his family. Intended for placing orders or for calling the local constabulary or the Royal Naval crushers in the case of trouble, rarely was it used for any social purpose for even had they been able to afford it, no one of their acquaintance saw the need for such a device.

Having given the number to the operator to connect, Lilith was a bundle of nerves. The dial tone was ringing on and on, so perhaps Grace wasn't at home. She could be sick. Or away. On holiday even, although that was unlikely given it was the middle of term. Nevertheless, she imagined her at the seaside. Somewhere sophisticated like Torquay. Or Eastbourne.

Strolling along the promenade, her face framed by a large white hat, her companion, a handsome man, would lean in and say something and she'd laugh delightedly.

Or perhaps she wasn't enjoying a day out at all. Perhaps she and her gentleman friend were with friends at a house party. They might have spent the afternoon playing croquet on the lawn, he in flannels, she in a pleated dress. Or tennis, to enthusiastic applause and choruses of *Good shot* and *Jolly well done* as she returned serve after serve with surprisingly little effort. And as the ball whizzed back and forth, those long legs would have flashed across the court...

"Portsmouth 7913."

"Oh..."

"Hello. Grace Stowell. Can I help you?"

"Yes. Sorry. Miss Stowell... um... Grace... it's Lilith Doherty. We met at..."

She got no further.

"Lilith? Of course! Lilith. Our little militant. I'd almost given up hope."

She blinked. Given up hope? It had only been a week!

"I'm sorry," she said. "I didn't realise..."

"I'm teasing. Rotten of me, I know."

She'd no idea what to say. Receiver in one hand, her fingers worried at the flex, twisting it around and around. "Are you sure I'm not calling at a bad time. I'd hate for it to be an intrusion."

"Not at all. Is this a social call?"

"No, sorry. Not exactly."

"Please don't apologise. Though I'm always up for a chat. But how can I be of help?"

"It's about the NUWT."

"Yes?"

"Well, I've been giving it a great deal of thought."

"Always a plus in my book."

"And I would like to join."

"That's wonderful. Like I said, we need women like you."

"There are others too. Well, one at least. For now. But I'm sure there are more." She was rambling. "Anyway, I was wondering if it would be at all possible for you to come and talk to some of my colleagues. Explain the union's goals and aims, and suchlike. You would do it so much better than I could, and at the moment everything we know is second-hand, or what people like Bill Marsden tell us and he's not exactly complimentary."

"I can imagine. Look, it's a great idea and I'd love to. Why don't we meet for coffee and discuss it?"

"Oh, um…yes…yes. That would be lovely."

"Shall we say Saturday morning? Eleven o'clock? Do you know Betty's? It's a dear little place in Palmerston Road where they have the most sumptuous selection of cakes."

"I do."

"In that case, I'll see you there."

Lilith was giddy with it all. She could hardly breathe. And the hundreds of butterflies trapped and whirling around in her stomach didn't help.

11

NEITHER THE LACK OF STREET-lighting nor the carpet of dense mist deterred the rat from scuttling across the alley and slipping beneath the broken timbers of a gate. In a neighbouring yard, a cat yowled. A window was forced up and something hard and metallic ricocheted off a wall. The noise stopped.

"You're quiet," Bert said, ensuring his stride matched hers as they made their way home over the slippery cobbles.

"Am I?"

"Normally you'd be chatting ten to the dozen."

Ruby managed a tinkling laugh, though what she had to be happy about was anyone's guess for hadn't they just wasted hours of their precious time together watching grown men in fedora hats and black shirts running around on the screen and shooting at each other with machine guns? The only saving grace had been the fabulous outfits worn by the actresses. Bought with the proceeds of crime, she supposed.

Stopping three doors up and pulling her into his arms, her chosen fiancé leant against the backyard wall.

"It's one of the things I like about you," he said, lifting her chin.

"Is it?"

It was hard to raise any enthusiasm when inside she was wondering if these last weeks all been for nothing. He certainly hadn't given her any hope he was ready to give up being single, so what was she supposed to do? Cut her loses and run? But she liked him, that was the problem. Surely everyone wanted to get settle down at some stage in their lives? Some did it sooner that was all, she told herself, finally slipping her arms around his waist. If his ship wasn't leaving she'd play it differently. A gentle tease here, a light nudge there, then nothing as if she didn't care after all. According to mum, all men like to do a bit of a chasing and a girl that was too easy to catch was not the kind to marry. At least that's what was said whenever she was caught trying to sneak out in the evenings. But Bert's lips were already on hers, and craning on tiptoe she lost herself in the urgency of his mouth, and the taste of ale and the peppermints they'd shared in the pictures.

"Mmmm," she sighed, coming up for air.

"And what does that mean," his arms stayed tight around her as if he wanted more. More kissing and more of her.

"It just means *mmmm*."

"So you like being kissed?"

"Depends on who's doing it."

He leaned back, the better to see her. "Ruby Doherty! Are you flirting with me?"

"Me?" she opened her eyes wide. "Heavens, what on earth makes you think that?"

And then his mouth was back, and even more demanding.

"Ruby… Ruby… Let me show you how much I love you."

His tongue clashed with hers and with her head forced back at an un-natural angle, her neck hurt. But it didn't matter. Nor did the fact she could hardly breathe. He loved her. He'd said so. Lifting her arms, she clung to him and while her heart was still beating wildly, it was nothing to the delicious churning in her stomach. She couldn't think straight. Her lips were being crushed. She was being crushed. He was so big, so strong, it was as if she was being swept up by something she had no power over.

"Oh, Ruby…"

She pushed away, needing to catch her breath. But just as quickly he drew her back.

"Let me, Ruby…"

Fumbling at her coat and with his mouth back on hers, he worked open the buttons and felt his way inside. Then, with one hand pressed against her back, he cupped her breast with the other. Only the presence of his arm prevented her falling and shocked and a little afraid, suddenly it was all too much.

"Ruby, it's all right," he said, as with her hands flailing against his chest she fought her way back to arm's length. "It's all right. I thought you loved me. I wouldn't have done it otherwise."

"I do love you," she protested.

"But not enough."

His crestfallen expression tore at her heart.

"Oh, Bert. Of course I do. I was just surprised, that's all."

"I thought we had an understanding."

Her breath snagged, and staring up into those oh-so-disappointed eyes she allowed him to take her hand.

"We do," she said, stepping back and laying her head on his chest.

"You're so beautiful," he was saying. "And wonderful. And sweet. Any man would get carried away if he had you in his arms."

Their lips met again, though this time, the kiss was gentle.

"But I won't do it again if you don't like it," and he laid his cheek against hers.

"I did like it," she said quickly, "it's just that no-one's ever touched me there before. You're the first."

She heard his breath quicken.

"Oh." And then, "You're such an amazing girl."

Nestled against him, she basked in the praise.

"Do you really love me, Ruby?"

She nodded.

"Then let me love you back," he begged.

She nodded a second time.

Eyes closed, she fought the fluttering in her stomach when his hand settled on her breast once more.

"See? There's nothing to be scared of," he murmured. "People who care for each other do this all the time."

Holding her breath, and with every fibre of her being unwittingly concentrated in just that one place, she realised not only was he was right but now she knew he loved her it really did feel rather nice.

"Oh Ruby," he murmured.

But even as she gave herself up to his mouth she was thinking hard. She would let him touch her a little longer, and then he'd have to stop. For everyone knew what happened to girls who let men have their way with them. No, if he wanted to love her like this in the future, he'd have to put a ring on her finger first.

Coming up for air she took a full step away.

"Bert, I have to go," she said, re-buttoning her coat at the same time.

"Sweetheart…"

"Sorry. I can't be late, otherwise I'll never be allowed out again. But you can walk me down to the gate. Just don't make any noise."

For a moment she thought he might argue with her, even try to grab her again. But if that was his intention he obviously thought better of it. Instead, looking down and dipping his knees he adjusted the crotch of his bell-bottomed trousers.

"Jeez Rube. You sure know how to give it to a bloke."

She wasn't sure what is was she'd given him, but if it went anyway to convincing him they should get married, then as far as she was concerned it wasn't a bad thing.

12

"WHAT'S WRONG WITH YOU?" Ruby grumbled, poking her head over the blankets.

"Nothing's wrong with me," Lilith threw back. Still in her dressing-gown, she was crouched over an open drawer. "Why don't you just go back to sleep? It isn't even ten o'clock and everyone knows that's far too soon for you to think of waking up. Especially on a Saturday."

"Heavens, we did get out of bed the wrong side this morning," Ruby yawned and stretched. A little more awake, she frowned. "What are you doing?"

"Trying to find something. What does it look like?"

"Why?"

"Why do you think? Because it's morning, and some of us get up and get dressed regardless we don't have to go to work."

"You don't normally make this much fuss."

"Maybe that's because I can't find what I'm looking for."

"And what's that?"

"My new blouse."

"Which one?" Ruby yawned again.

Slamming the middle drawer closed, Lilith yanked open the bottom one. "The only new one I have. The cream one with pearl buttons and embroidered collar."

"Oh, that one."

"Yes. That one."

She looked up, alert to some nuance in her sister tone. "You don't know where it is by some remote chance, do you?"

"It could be in the laundry."

"In the laundry? How could it possibly be there when I haven't worn it yet."

"No, but I did."

"What! You wore my new blouse?"

"That's what I said."

"How dare you! How dare you touch my things!"

"Don't get in a strop. It's only a blouse. Wear another."

"I'm going to kill you."

Getting to her feet, Lilith saw Ruby's eyes widen. Though more in surprise than fear, she realised. No doubt because she rarely lost her temper. She was normally the placid one. The peacemaker.

Not this time.

"What's the matter with you?" her sister squawked, grabbing the covers and dragging them higher.

"I'm going out, and now I'm going to be late."

"Because of a blouse? Find something else to wear."

"I wanted that one," Lilith stood over Ruby's bed, hands balled into fists.

"Borrow something of mine instead."

That brought her up short. Something of hers? Why not? She did have some nice clothes, though God knows how she afforded them. And they were a similar size, at least from the waist down. Her sister had more up top, anyone in Portsea could attest to that. Even in the school-yard, she'd flaunted her budding figure. But that aside...

"Where are you going anyway?' pushing back the bedcovers, Ruby sat up. "I've never known you so grouchy before."

"Union business."

"Is that all. Heavens! Anyone would think you were meeting the king the way you're carrying on."

"It's important to me. You know that."

Head inside the wardrobe she was sending coat-hangers flying. Some things might be a touch over-the-top, she thought, dismissing one garment after another, but not all.

"What about this?" she asked, fingering a soft, drop-waisted tunic.

"Be my guest. You need something to go underneath, though."

"My lemon blouse would do."

"Lemon and navy?" Ruby had screwed up her nose. "Not sure that's you. What about your sage green one? It'll be a little less *here I am*. Oh, and wear shoes with a heel. You can never be too tall. Especially when dealing with men."

Opening her mouth to say she was meeting with someone from the National Union of Women Teachers she quickly thought better of it.

"Actually, I think I'd like to be a little adventurous for once," she said, holding the dress against herself.

Ruby shrugged. "Then go with the lemon," and throwing back the covers she swung her feet to the floor and shuffled for her slippers. "I'm going for a wash. God, it's cold," she shivered.

Lilith desperately wanted to make a good impression. Grace had to know she was serious in her desire to help improve conditions, and in that regard could be called upon to serve the union in every capacity, even politically.

She stopped. Perhaps it was time for a change, especially if she was going to be mixing in new circles. And if she was going be a little more confrontational, though in an intelligent way and not run at things like a bull in a china shop as she usually did, would it hurt to take a leaf out of Ruby's book and pay more attention to her appearance? Wasn't that what their mother was always telling her?

Dragging a brush though sleep-tangled hair brought another consideration, and turning sideways to the mirror she scraped back the mousy, shoulder-length mess. Grace had a perfectly sleek, ash blonde cap. Would a style like that suit her? Or was her nose a little too long for such a daring cut, or her chin too pronounced? Grace's features were elfin and she had the most perfectly shaped ears. Small and delicate with the sweetest lobes. But not everyone could be so lucky, she told herself, turning the other way. Dare she? She felt a surge of excitement. Wasn't she already thinking about making one major change? Why not two, and call into Maisie's on the way back? Even if they were too busy to see her right then and there, she could make an appointment for early in the week to have her hair cut short, like a boy's - though with perhaps a feminine curl on each cheek.

If nothing else, such a rebellious act would give the old biddies in the snug chance to talk about her, instead of whatever Ruby had been up to lately!

The bell above the door jangled loudly. Too loudly. Grace had said eleven o'clock. Not five past, not even three minutes past and standing just inside the delightfully warm tea shop and glancing over the nearest tables Lilith was only too aware her silver-grey cloche hat, her fur-collared coat, her flesh-coloured stockings and her two-inch heels were all being weighed up without the lowering of a tea-cup. Having been forced to dash for the bus, she hoped she didn't resemble something the cat had dragged in. That would be mortifying.

"You made it," Grace smiled broadly, once Lilith had eased between cramped tables, and around busy waitresses and carrier bags of shopping left out for the unwary.

"Yes, and I'm sorry if I'm late."

"You're not. I've only just arrived myself. How was your journey."

Draping her coat over a neighbouring chair and feeling altogether frumpy beside Grace's smart black and white jacket and matching hat, she wanted to say something profound, something clever. Or at least offer a witticism to make her laugh.

"Good," was all that came to mind.

"I haven't ordered yet. I thought I'd wait until you got here. They do a good range of teas, though I must confess my preference is coffee. And at this time of day, the stronger the better. Are you a fan too?"

Smoothing her dress under her bottom and sitting down, Lilith reached behind the vase of tiny orange narcissi trumpets for a menu.

"Not so much."

"Then I must convert you. It's just the thing to give you a boost."

She had no idea how to answer, for while they might have the odd bottle of Camp or tin of Bantam powdered in the larder at home, she'd never met anyone who drank it in any quantity.

"So, what are your vices?"

Grace had leant in, and caught out by the unexpectedness of the question Lilith could only offer, "Gosh! I have no idea."

"Does that mean there you have too many? Or not a single one?"

To her annoyance, she felt herself blushing. "I suppose it means I haven't any. At least none I can think of."

"Then your education has been sorely lacking. But don't worry, once you've found your feet we'll soon put that right."

Dazzled by the fact they were separated only by the width of the table, and bewitched by an expression that was both challenging and mischievous she dared to ask, "Do I take the purpose of this meeting is to lead me astray?"

Grey eyes sparkled, pinning her as surely as any butterfly in a display case.

"Would you like that?"

Lilith's mouth dried. Worse, she felt her cheeks burning again.

"I think that would depend," she managed, dropping her hands into her lap.

Determined to hold her own in the conversation, for this was certainly some kind of test, she waited to see what might be said next.

Suddenly Grace laughed. "We must be careful you don't end up like me, with far too many sins to count."

"Surely not."

"You wouldn't say that if you really knew me."

"So it's not just coffee then?"

"Not at all. I'm afraid I have a quite a few weaknesses. I hope you're not disappointed."

Lilith had never felt so reckless. "Name one."

"I'll name two; jazz and Turkish cigarettes," and with her elbows on the table and her chin resting on intertwined fingers, Grace said, "And here's another, the urge to make a difference. Do you smoke?"

"No."

Glimpsing a new world, one that was unconventional and therefore by definition exciting, dangerous even, Lilith felt her heart race. This was what she wanted. This was what she had been searching for. It was heady stuff, for as much as some wanted to comply with society in finding a husband and having children, she wanted to kick out against it. Reshape it into a fairer and more egalitarian model.

Until that moment she hadn't known how.

"Well, now you know you know all about me," Grace said, "tell me about you."

She looked away, for whatever she might offer would be tame in comparison.

"There's very little to say."

"I can't believe that."

"I'm afraid it's true."

Returning to the menu she hoped Grace would do the same.

"So, what shall we order?" Needing a moment to compose herself she was reading through every item. Slowly. "Are you having coffee?"

"Most definitely. You?"

"I think I'd rather have tea. Earl Grey would be lovely. And a buttered teacake."

"So why don't we get down to business," Grace said, once the waitress had taken their order. Watching the girl scribble and bob, Lilith had wondered if such a position might suit her sister while Bert was away. But given the uniform of frilly cap and apron, the thought was quickly dismissed. Not only that, she would never be so amenable.

"I have to say I was rather pleased to get your telephone call," Grace continued.

"Oh?"

"Don't pretend you didn't know how much I wanted to recruit you to our cause."

"I didn't actually."

"Then consider yourself flattered. Now, you said you would like me to address a small meeting?"

"Yes."

"Of your fellow teachers?"

At last she was on firm ground. "Yes. At least one from the school at which I teach, and as many as I can interest from those nearby. I thought I'd post a flyer in every staff room if they would allow me to."

"I'm sure they will. Have you given any thought as to when you would like to hold the meeting?"

She shook her head. In fact, she hadn't thought much further than the idea itself. "I would say sooner rather than later. Perhaps in three weeks' time? That is, if it suits you, and of course if I can book a hall."

"I'll have to check my diary, but at this stage I can't see it being a problem. And what would you like me to talk about? Specific issues and grievances? Or the broader picture? Women in the workplace. That sort of thing."

"Perhaps touch on both. It might help to generate a sense of camaraderie to start with. Then discuss the fundamentals of the NUWT. And after that, you could mention other areas of interest and organisations you are affiliated with."

She stopped, horrified. "That is," she cringed, knowing she'd completely overstepped the mark, "if you think that would be the right approach."

Grace was nodding. "I can do that. And although I can't promise to keep it light, I will try to keep the rhetoric to a minimum.'

"I'm sure whatever you say will be well received."

Moving her cutlery aside as if in need of a distraction, Lilith cursed. How could she have rattled on like that? Now she was being regarded with the strangest expression.

Perhaps it was just as well she had no idea how wonderfully her face lit up and how animated she became when speaking of issues that roused her. Nor had she had the faintest notion that her tendency to lower her eyes when she blushed left Grace wanting to sweep her up and protect her. Perhaps that was why she looked at her for a long moment before saying, "You know; you really will be an asset for our organisation. I'm so glad you decided to ring me."

13

RUBY WAS GOING TO LAY it on the line since it had never been her intention to allow things to go on this long. If Bert wanted to carry on doing what he was doing at the end of the evening, murmuring sweet nothings while his hand roamed over her - and just last night his fingers had glided down over her bottom to linger where no man's should - then he would have to make an honest woman of her first. She was sure it was in his mind to suggest it anyway. He was just waiting for the right time to ask her. That's all. Shame there wouldn't be any chance of getting married before he sailed though. Time had seen to that. But it could just as easily be planned for when he came back.

And that would solve the another little problem, for once the engagement between Miss Ruby Maud Doherty and Mr Albert Wilson was announced there would be no more talk of emigrating - though to be fair to her father, he'd been rather quiet on that front lately. But just in case the subject came up again she'd be quick to remind everyone they'd a wedding to plan and naturally, as the father of the bride he would be expected to give her away. Which he could hardly do from the other side of the world.

So, a forthcoming proposal of marriage would neatly kill two birds with one stone.

Emerging at the far end of the alley and seeing her sailor waiting on the other side of the road, her heart skipped.

"'Lo Bert," she said, crossing over and taking his arm.

"What do you want to do tonight?" he asked, setting back her on her feet after a quick kiss. "Pictures or dancing?"

"What's on?"

"Laurel and Hardy at the Victoria. Haven't seen the billboards for the pier, so it would be pot-luck there."

She screwed up her nose. "Can't we just go for a walk somewhere."

"Fine by me, if that's what you want."

As usual she hastened him away from the vicinity of *The Saracen's Head.*

"Here, ease up Rube," he said, pulling her back once they'd emerged from the narrow lanes, "it's not route march. We've got all night."

"You wish."

Slowing to a more amenable pace it seemed like he had something on his mind.

"All right, we've got a few hours then," he said. "But you could change all that if you wanted to."

"Oh yeah? And how am I supposed to do that?"

"You ever thought about telling your mum about us?"

She had to catch her breath.

"You reckon there's something to tell then?"

"What do you think?"

"You looking to make us official or something?" she tried again, desperate to conceal her excitement.

"Could be."

"Like how official?"

"Suppose that depends on you."

"Oh?"

"Don't forget, I'm off soon. Won't be back for a long time."

Ruby didn't need telling.

"So all we've got left is this week and next," he continued. "That is if they don't bring the trip forward."

"They wouldn't!"

She'd stopped in a circle of gas light just as something trickled from the side of a building and along a crack in the pavement. The odour was decidedly unpleasant.

"There's rumours going around," he planted his hands on her shoulders. "Talk we might be sailing earlier than planned."

"But why?"

"Search me."

"But you must have some idea?"

"The Admiralty doesn't exactly take the lower deck into its confidence when making decisions like that."

"But that's not fair!"

"I'll tell their lordships, shall I? Next time I'm talking to them I'll say my Ruby's not best pleased with the way they do things."

Despite the nasty shock he might be leaving sooner than either of them had thought, she squirmed with pleasure at hearing herself referred to as *his* Ruby. It sort of established things even more.

"You do that," she said, as they stepped forward once more. "And if they want to come and talk to me, you can tell them where I live."

"That would be something, wouldn't it," Bert chuckled. "The Lords in their number one dress uniforms gathered in your dad's public bar."

"It would be a first," she giggled. "He'd have a fit!"

They strolled on.

"Do you really think you might go early?" she asked, all merriment gone.

"Have to be prepared for any eventuality. And there's a lot of activity going on around the ship."

"Like what?"

"Coaling, victualling. That sort of thing. And lots of stuff at the bottom of the gangway for a bloke to fall over when he wants to get ashore and meet his girl."

"Oh."

He gave her arm a little squeeze. "Don't think about it now. Let's just enjoy ourselves."

"But I can't unthink it, now you've told me."

"Does this mean you're going to miss me?"

"Oh, Bert," her voice was plaintive.

Pulling her into a doorway he gently placed his hands either side of her face.

"Rube, you will wait for me, won't you?" he said, looking into her eyes.

"Of course I'll wait."

"You're my girl. You know that don't you?"

"'Course I do Bert."

"Let's go somewhere, Rube. Just you and me."

"Where?"

"Anywhere. But let's be alone for once. Really alone. Just the two of us."

His lips found hers and with the world spinning and sensing something momentous, for surely he was building up to the big question, she almost panicked.

"We could go for a drink somewhere if you like?"

His expression was unreadable. But then he broke into a wide grin.

"That's my girl."

By the time she'd finished her third port and lemon Ruby was finding everything Bert said to be either amazingly clever or side-splittingly funny.

"No, you didn't!" she spluttered as he came to the end of yet another tale.

"I did. You should have been there to see it."

"Oh Bert. You are a one."

"So you keep telling me. Top up?" he gestured to her glass.

"Shouldn't," she said, wondering why the word seemed so fill her mouth. Like cotton wool. Or candyfloss, but without the sugary strands. She frowned. "Shhh…".

He was smiling. She loved it when he smiled. He had lovely teeth, he did. All straight and white. Not like some. She'd gone out with a bloke once who had one front tooth that crossed over the other. She couldn't recall the name of his ship, but he was from Scotland, she remembered that much.

Chair legs scraped the floor, then Bert was holding out his hand.

"Oh! Are we going?" she pouted.

"Think we should."

"But I'm enjoying myself."

There was a strange look on his face. As if he was considering something. Maybe he was trying to think of somewhere else to take her before he saw her home.

"Oh Rube," he said, softly.

"Yes, Bert?"

"You really don't want to go back yet?"

"Not really," she smiled happily. For a dreadful minute she thought he was cross with her.

No sooner had the pub door swung shut behind them than he'd slipped his arm beneath her coat and around her waist.

"All right Rube? Not cold?"

She shook her head. How could she be, when they were snuggled up together?

"You still want to go somewhere else?"

"'Course."

"Somewhere we can be alone?"

"Uh huh."

Stepping awkwardly on a cobble she lurched against him. When had it become so hard to put one foot in front of the other? But it didn't really matter, 'cos his arm was around her nice and tight. He was smashing, he was. Really smashing. And he'd make a good dad too. She could see it all now. A proper little house for him to come home to. One with a garden. And apple trees...

"It's just a little walk," he was saying.

The so-called guest house was scarcely a cut above a doss house, but Ruby didn't know that. All she knew was that they were out of the wind and it was warm in the hallway. Even nicer, when Bert bent down to sign his name in a book the proprietor gave her a really friendly smile. That is, once he'd folded the money he'd been given and slipped it into his pocket. Then they were climbing the stairs, first one flight then a second until, after making their way down a short hallway, Bert inserted a door key into a lock.

"Here we are. Number six. You sure you're all right, Rube?" he asked, pushing open the door and switching on the light.

At the rear of the house and next to a reeking lavatory, the room contained a brass bed, a wardrobe and a chest of drawers. The curtains, drawn to hide the back of the house in the next street, were thin and worn in places. Another length of the same fabric attempted to hide a wash-stand. Devoid of ornaments or trinkets, the only attempt at homeliness was a print on the wall above the empty fireplace.

Ruby didn't notice any of it.

"Oh Rube," having thrown down the key, Bert had taken her into his arms again. "You are amazing... the best ever. If only you knew how much I've wanted this… all those times outside your gate…,"

He was trailing kisses down her neck and she wanted to giggle. No more than that, she wanted to fling herself back onto the bed and stretch out her arms and legs like a starfish.

"What, Bert?" she questioned in a singsong voice. "Oh, you are silly. Here, let me," and removing his hands from where he'd been fumbling with her coat, she slipped the three buttons and shrugged it from her shoulders.

"Where shall I put it?" she wanted to know, looking around for the first time.

"Give it to me. I'll hang it behind the door."

"That's a good idea."

He was so practical, her Bert. But then most sailors were, in her experience. It had something to do with the way they lived. Sharing a small space, and all that.

His arms were back again. "Oh, Ruby… Oh, Ruby."

The mantra went around in her head. Then he was kissing her, and while at first it was fine, after a moment she felt a little dizzy. As if the floor had tilted. She had to have air, so she tried to push him away.

"Bert… wait."

"What is it, Rube?"

His voice seemed to come from a long way off.

"I thought we were going to go somewhere to talk," she said.

"We have. We're here. Look, do you want to sit down?"

Ruby couldn't see anywhere to do so. Other than the bed, of course.

"All right."

There was something she had to ask him. Or was it the other way round. Should he be asking her something? She couldn't remember.

Taking her place at the foot of the bed, she clasped her hands in her lap and crossed her ankles. Bert sat next to her, his arm draped around her shoulders.

"It would be like this all the time if we were husband and wife," he said, drawing her closer so she could lay her head on his shoulder.

And then she remembered. Of course! He was going to ask her to marry him. But was that the proposal? If it was, it was awfully short. She'd expected a bit more. Like how lovely she was, and how he couldn't live without her. And wasn't she supposed to say something back? Like *I do*?

He was popping the buttons on her cardigan. The one at the top. The next one down. The one below that. All the while kissing her. But softly, gently this time, and reaching up she slipped a hand around his neck. This was so much better. He must have guessed she was a little giddy. How clever of him to suggest they sat down. And when his fingers trailed over her brassiere-clad breast she thought how nice that was too.

"I won't hurt you, Rube. You do know that, don't you?"

What was he talking about? How could he possibly hurt her?

"I know that Bert."

110

"Oh Rube," he was pressing and squeezing her flesh just as lately when he took her home. But then he snuck inside her underwear and found her nipple, and suddenly it was hard to breathe. And not just because his mouth was clamped on hers either. A feverish ache like nothing she'd never known was coursing through her, and she arched, thrusting against the palm of his hand, wanting the torment so badly.

Until even that wasn't enough.

When he eased her back onto the pillow she threw her arms around his neck and clung to him once more, shutting her eyes and retreating to a place she'd never known existed. The truth was she'd stopped minding his attentions in the alley, but this... oh, it was so much better and if he wanted to, he could keep on doing it all night. She wouldn't stop him.

His mouth was still on hers when rolling onto her he propped himself up on one hand and used the other to fiddle with his trousers. That same hand then slipped up and under her skirt and travelled along the inside of her thigh, leaving her bucking and jerking when his fingers brushed over the gusset of her knickers. She needed more but had no idea what it was she wanted. Nor did she recognise her own voice, pleading over and over.

"Yes... yes..." he was assuring her, his knee between hers. He was pushing her skirt up, trying to bunch it up onto her stomach, and somewhat pinned by his weight the only help she could give was to wriggle from side to side. Suddenly her legs were free and as she pulled them up, he was shoving down his trousers. He was panting, and his movements were careless, frantic even. Then, with a sound that was somewhere between a groan and a grunt, he fingered aside her knicker leg.

Clarity returned, but only for an instant. Something smooth and unyielding was pushing against her private parts. She had a vague notion what it was of course, though she'd little idea of exactly what it - his *thing* - actually looked like, but even as she tried to squirm away he was soothing her, telling her it would be all right and that he loved her.

He was kissing her again, his mouth wet, his tongue probing, his breath ragged. The ache in her belly returned, this time worse. She was on fire, burning up even as the invader kept trying to force its way inside her.

Only now it was hurting.

She tried to tell him, tried to make him understand it wouldn't fit, but his eyes were screwed shut and his face contorted in what she could only think was a similar agony to her own. Then, just when she thought she could take no more, something gave way and a strange warmth flooded her opening and coated the top of her thighs. The release seemed to have an effect on him too, for he now seemed even more determined. Every thrust into her slickness brought forth louder and louder grunts, which would have been funny at any other time, and while thankful the passage was now easier, even so lying beneath him she wondered when the ceaseless pistoning would end.

Then to her relief, he suddenly gave a hoarse shout and crumpled down on top of her, heaving and sweating.

Holding him in her arms, she stared up at the dark and shadowy ceiling. She could feel a headache coming on, but at least her mind wasn't fuzzy anymore. Funny how things happen. All the hinting she'd done, all those evenings with Else trying to come up with a scheme. In the end, none of it mattered. He'd have to marry her now. All that remained was to set the date. Her mother would be thrilled - not that she would ever learn what had just taken place. She'd be even happier to plan the wedding, since Alfie's nuptials to that wishy-washy Alice hardly counted, regardless of what anyone said. It was the bride's family that ran the show not the grooms and even though Bert wouldn't be back for a long while, there was still plenty to do. The church would have to be booked, the dress chosen, and the cake made. And that was the least of it.

Dropping a kiss onto the top of his head she wondered if he had any sisters. It would be a nice gesture to ask them if they would like to be bridesmaids. Along with Lilith and Elsie of course.

That was when she realised she was more than a little uncomfortable *down there*. Sore and stinging, and decidedly sticky, she needed the lav.

"Oh Ruby," he muttered, his eyes closing and his breathing levelling regardless she was trying to ease him off her. "Oh, Ruby."

14

THERE WAS LITTLE WARMTH IN the kitchen at such an early hour, despite the fact the fire in the range had been banked up overnight and brought back to life with a little riddling and a fresh layer of coal.

Jim was waving the envelope he'd retrieved from the public bar doormat and opened just five minutes earlier.

"At least give it a thought," he urged.

"There's no point."

Dilys's stance brooked no argument. She might only come up to his shoulder, but what she lacked in height she made up for in sheer determination, and when she set her mind to something it took an awful lot to budge her. He knew that.

"You not thinking straight, doll. It's the perfect opportunity, and one that won't ever come around again."

Dropping another rasher of bacon into the spitting lard she spun around, fork in hand. "You don't get it, do you. I told you last year none of us wanted to go. But oh no! You had to send that letter, didn't you? Put out feelers, you said. Well, you've gone and done it now, haven't you?"

"I'm going to talk to the kids again. Let them know I've had a reply and exactly what Joe is suggesting."

"You do that."

"I intend to."

"They won't listen."

"I think they will."

"They didn't want a bar of it last time."

"Well they might see things differently now we've got something to get excited about."

Dilys took a deep breath. "Look, we have to see our family happy and settled. We agree on that. But here," she emphasised, turning over one rasher after another. "Not in some God forsaken place on the other side of the world."

"Everything's changed, doll," Jim shook his head. "We've got an opportunity to make money. Good money. We'll be comfortable in a couple of years. Imagine that."

"And that letter told you all that, did it? In detail?"

"Read it yourself." Pulling out his chair and taking his place at the head of the table Jim thrust the two pages towards her. "And that's not all. Joe says there's a government emigration scheme in place just for the likes of us."

Sliding the bacon from the heavy pan onto one thick slice of bread and slapping another on top, Dilys pushed his breakfast towards him. Then, after wiping her hands down her pinny took the sheets of close-formed script.

"Hmm," she muttered, turning over the first.

Jim set about his food, though not without keeping one eye on her.

"Well?" he asked when she'd come to the end of the second page.

"A hotel," she was staring at him.

"That's it, girl."

"You really think your brother is going to put up the money for a hotel?"

"That's what he says. If we want it, that is."

"More fool him. And he expects you to run it."

"That's the idea."

Closing her eyes, she shook her head.

"What?" he wanted to know.

"You couldn't run a tombola."

Jim's pent up breath escaped with a rush. "No, but you could," he grinned, swiping away the fat running down his chin. "Think about it. No more pub landlady. Instead, you'd be a hotel owner. A lady of means."

"Oh yeah? And how do you work that out when it'll be Joe Doherty's name over the door."

"Just until we pay him back. Then it'll be our name up there, fair and square."

It was as if he was letting her have a moment to think things over.

"Com'mon girl. It's the answer we've been looking for. A quality place in a booming town. What more could you ask?"

"Somewhere local," she said tonelessly, folding and handing him back the pages.

"Do I have to tell you again that England's gone to the dogs? There's no work and no prospects here nowadays. Bloody hell girl, some blokes can't even afford the price of a pint anymore, and you know that better than anyone."

"Listen to yourself. All doom and gloom. And I've told you before, it'll improve. It has to. And all the time we got the Navy on our doorstep we'll manage."

"But it won't be on our doorstep when the council moves us out."

"Then we'll have other customers."

"Only if the brewery sees fit to giving us another pub," Jim reminded her, before sinking his teeth into his sandwich again.

"Haven't we been over this time and time again?" she said, though without her usual fire.

"And we'll continue to do so. At least until you agree to take it seriously," mouth full, he waved the letter at her.

Crossing to the window she dropped the greasy frying pan into the half-filled sink. "Your brother must be doing alright then."

"Looks that way."

"Got kiddies of his own now. Or so he says. Wedded to a local girl I suppose,"

"You could be right. Or maybe it's someone he met on the boat going over."

"Wonder how he made his money?" she reflected, lighting the gas and putting the kettle on to boil.

"The same way all of us do. Hard work."

"He could have married into it."

Licking bacon grease from his fingers, Jim shrugged. "Could of. But even as a nipper he was always willing to roll up his sleeves. That's the one thing I do remember about him."

"How much younger than you is he?"

"Eight years. He came after Maggie and Bridie. Would have been another one between us, except she died."

Dilys nodded. Wasn't that the way of things? She'd had had a stillborn after Lilith. Seven months into the pregnancy, the baby just stopped growing. It had been another little girl. She'd called her Minnie, not that she'd ever told anyone that. Still thought about her though. Wondered what she'd look like had she lived, and what she'd be doing with her life.

"And what about Alfie?"

"Alfie?" He was staring at her as if he'd somehow missing a turning in the conversation.

"Yes. Haven't really thought how he'll fit into the picture, have you?"

He took a moment, though not to savour the last bite of his sandwich. More like he wanted to choose his words carefully.

"I'd like him to come, of course. And there'd be plenty of work for him in Auckland. It's a big place with a decent sized port."

"And how do you know that?"

"Went to the library, didn't I? Looked it up."

"The library? You? When?"

"Ages ago."

"You never said."

"Maybe I don't tell you everything."

"So it seems. And did the books tell you if the port is run by the unions, like here? They don't like outsiders, you know that."

"Then he could find work elsewhere if he had to. He's a grafter that boy."

"And Alice?"

Jim was nodding. "That's a problem, I agree. But our boy has to think for both of them. Think of their future. And where that might be."

She was considering the very same thing.

For months she'd clung to the notion of the dockyard as being a place their son would have a job for life. But supposing she was wrong? Plenty of others must have thought that way, and now they were on the dole. Of course, things could get better. And they would, she was sure of it. But when? She'd thought too of the remembrance parade one year, and the ANZAC battalion marching through the city. Boys they might have been, but those Kiwis and Aussies were strapping, healthy looking blokes, full of gi'days and calling each other *cobber* and other banter.

"And if it didn't work out, well, we could always come back," Jim was saying. "No one's stopping us."

She could hear it in his voice. Trying to come over as wanting to be fair. Give her options, because despite everything, she was his life. She knew that just as she knew she could squash his dream right now if she'd a mind to.

Gazing out into the backyard she thought about Alfie and Alice. And Lilith and Ruby. And the hotel.

"You'd better talk to him then. And the girls. Let them know exactly what Joe's suggesting and what it means for all of us."

She almost heard his jaw drop.

"I will."

"We need to get something straight though," she said, folding her arms.

Having swung around to rest his elbow on the back of his chair, his face was lit up with a grin that went from ear to ear.

"What's that doll?"

"Hotels big or small don't run themselves, do they? What about all that accommodation? Who takes care of that? All that bedding to be changed. All them carpets to be swept. No doubt that'll all fall on my shoulders as usual."

"You've got Ruby and you've got Lilith, and you'll have other girls too. Cleaners, chambermaids, as many as you want."

"And who'd look after the rest of it, then? According to that letter, that place has two bars as well. And an off-licence. What exactly did he say? That it was the right time to snaffle a going concern? That means busy in my book."

"Like I said, we'll have staff, doll. You and me, all we have to do is sit back and let everyone else run around."

"What rain shower did you come down in, Jim Doherty? Employees need a firm hand."

"And that's what I'll give them."

"That'll be the day."

Dear God, she thought, I can't believe I'm thinking about it. But it was too late, he was on his feet.

"You won't regret it, girl. It'll be the making of this family, you'll see. Come and give us a cuddle."

"Now wait up. I never said…"

She got no further.

Lifting her a dozen inches off the floor he'd planted his lips on hers.

15

WITH ONE EYE ON THE two old biddies in the snug - God forbid they should ever have to wait to be served - Dilys kept the other on the sailor at the end of the bar. She'd not seen him on the premises before, at least not that she could remember. Of course, that didn't mean he hadn't been in with a load of pals at some time. They often did, matelots on a run ashore, since it wasn't unusual for them to start their drinking outside the dockyard gates before moving up into town. It was like they couldn't wait to get a pint down their throats sometimes.

There was something about this one, though. Something about the time he was taking to sup his ale. As if he had a lot on his mind.

"Yes, Fred? Same again?"

Hand on the pump she was already holding his empty glass under the nozzle.

The man in the flat cap nodded. A regular known for drinking two pints at lunch-time, one after the other in quick succession, in all the time he stood at the bar he wouldn't exchange a word with a soul. Not one.

Four full draws on the pump, strong and smooth, and beer rushed into the glass, foaming into a head. A pause, then a further quarter pull topped it up.

"Right you are," she said, putting it down in front of him and receiving the coins in the palm of her hand.

Chucking them into the till she glanced over to the sailor again. He seemed in a world of his own, a bit like Tommy Riley who always sat by the shove ha'penny board, eyes glazed over and breathing noisily. It was the gas in the war that had done for him. Most folks left him alone, even his brothers who could be a rowdy bunch when they'd a drink or two inside them.

But the sailor's eyes weren't glazed over, nor was his breathing remarkable in any way.

Looking up he caught her staring.

"Don't suppose Ruby's in, is she?" he asked, still hunched over.

"No. She's not."

"Oh."

"Why do you want to know?"

"No reason."

Stepping closer, she straightened up. "Sure about that?"

He didn't flinch. Rather he locked eyes with hers. Then, lifting his glass took a large swallow, as if to buy time. Or, she thought, as if he'd more to say, but didn't know how. Unsettling thoughts ran through her mind. Like who her daughter might really be with when she was supposed to be round that Elsie's. She'd had her suspicions all along. Getting dressed up the way she did. All that make-up, and wearing someone else's shoes when she had two perfectly good pairs of her own. Thank God Jim was at the post office sending off his reply to his brother. This sort of stuff needed handling without any interference. It was always better that way.

"Ruby's a good girl," she said firmly. "She doesn't mix with men unless they've been properly introduced to her father and me first."

The sailor nodded.

"It's that we're off first thing in the morning," he said. "Won't be back for a while."

"And what that got to do with her?"

He took another mouthful of ale. "I wanted to say goodbye."

"Do you now. Well, since she doesn't know you from Adam, she can hardly care if you're gone. Can she?"

If she thought that might rark him into saying something unguarded, she was wrong.

"Would you give her a message?"

His gaze was unwavering, and she didn't like it. Not one little bit.

"Depends what it is."

"Tell her they did bring the sailing forward; she'll know what I mean. Tell her they stopped all shore leave and I got lumbered with duties these last couple of nights. Not even supposed to be here now. Tell her…"

"Tell her what?"

"Tell her everything's going to be alright. Tell her…"

He was studying the flecks of foam in the bottom of his glass.

Dilys narrowed her eyes. So, Ruby had been sneaking out behind her back. Well, she'd see about that. Going round Elsie's indeed! Hadn't her chickens come home to roost. She should have guessed something was up because the little madam had been acting very strangely these past two or three days. Sulking and snapping at everyone. Even now she was upstairs, lying on her bed as if the world had come to an end. Well, this little romance was about to be nipped it in the bud. An Able Seaman? She could do so much better. And would, once they were away from *The Saracen's Head*. In a few months she'd be an hotelier's daughter no less, and that meant she'd have the pick of the bunch. And they wouldn't be like this sorry specimen. They'd be young men who having made their fortune were looking for a wife to lavish it on. Funny how life turned out, Joe's letter arriving just that morning and all. Almost like fate was giving things a nudge.

"Like I said, Ruby isn't interested in blokes. So you're wasting your time."

The sailor carefully placed his glass on the counter between them.

"Just tell her. Please."

Drawing himself up to his full height he tugged and straightened his jumper, put his cap firmly on his head and walked out of the bar.

16

THE FLY BUZZED CLOSE TO the ceiling, but Ruby knew its interest lay in the rose-pink fringing on the hanging lampshade. That or the flex, since it had investigated both already. She had no idea what it expected from life or if it would ever find it, and really who cared? She had much more important things to worry about. Like how everything between her and Bert had gone so disastrously wrong. One thing was clear, having had his way with her he'd immediately lost interest. He hadn't even the decency to show up the next night. Nor the one after that, and that was one of their regular dates.

Was it something she'd said? Or did? He'd seemed alright, hurrying her home, and checking her over before taking her in his arms and giving her the most loving of kisses. And he'd waited as she carefully eased up the gate-latch and slipped into the yard.

She couldn't understand it.

She went over again how she'd crept in through the back door and hearing the muted conversation coming from the public bar as glasses were washed up and floors swept - the last of the idlers having been encouraged out the door after the usual ten minutes drinking-up time - had shot up the stairs, and torn off her clothes in the darkened bedroom before jumping quickly into bed. Even Lilith hadn't woken to question the time, or what she'd been doing at such a late hour. The bloodstained knickers were balled up and hidden under the bed, ready to be prodded and poked into the glowing range the next morning when no one was around.

And now she was being summoned from below.

"I'll be down in a minute," she groaned, only to hear the sound of trudging on the stairs.

"Do you intend staying up here all evening?" her mother snapped, striding across the room and flinging open the bedroom curtains. Any evidence the day had once been bright enough to promise spring had indeed arrived, was gone. Instead, the sky was low with cloud and the sun setting fast.

Touching a hand to her brow Ruby rolled over and faced the wall.

"I don't feel well."

"Oh? And what's it this time?"

"My head aches."

"Again? I'll get you an aspirin."

"I don't want an aspirin. I just want to stay here a little longer with my eyes closed."

"There's no time for that. Alfie and Lilith are home from work, and your father wants to talk to you all"

"Do I have to? Look at me!"

"It's nothing a wet flannel won't sort. And tidy your hair as well. Come on, it'll be time to open up soon, so get on with it."

Slouching into the kitchen she stopped short on seeing her father, for he looked taller, more energetic somehow. As if he'd shed years in what, twenty-four hours? Even the very air about him seemed charged.

"Come and sit down beside your brother."

"Blimey Rube. You're looking a bit worse for wear."

Sitting hard back, and still in his working shirt and braces, Alfie's legs stretched under the table.

"As charming as ever, brother dearest," she replied before taking her place. For while she'd made an effort with a comb she couldn't see the point in hiding the fact she was suffering. Not that she could tell anyone exactly what might be wrong of course, but that hardly mattered. A little sympathy, a little understanding, would be nice.

Before he could make any response, or before she could complete the cutting retort on the tip of her tongue, their father had cut in.

"That's enough."

She stared. First at him, and then at her mother. She was the one who usually laid down the law. But not this time, it seemed.

"You all know I've been talking about us going to New Zealand…" fists on the table and sleeves rolled up, her father was looking at each of them in turn, "well, I've had a letter from my brother Joe."

Ruby's stomach flipped.

"And he's come up with an opportunity we need to grab. It will take work. Hard work. But that's to be expected. Nothing in life is given freely. Nothing."

No one spoke.

"I intend to apply for the forms we have to fill out. Empire Settlement Act forms. That's how we're doing it. Assisted by your uncle and the business funds he's putting our way."

It was as if each sentence was being hammered home.

"Once we've sent everything off and get the final approval, we'll be moving to Auckland. No reason to stay around here any longer."

Focusing on her father's strong, square hands and the wiry hairs between the knuckles Ruby caught a movement from the corner of her eye. Head lowered, her brother was busy rubbing one thumb over the other.

"Alfie," her father acknowledged quietly, "won't be coming with us."

Open mouthed, her eyes flew to Lilith opposite. She too was looking dazed.

Their mother, though, was not. "Let your father finish."

She felt strangely light-headed. As if nothing was real.

"There's a ship leaving Southampton in July and I intend us to be on it."

Only now did Alfie look up and after glancing at their father, turn to her and Lilith.

"I've spoken to Alice," he said. "Explained everything. We're going to be married before you go."

"And so I should hope," it sounded as if her mother was having difficulty getting the words out. "A family celebration! It'll be a good way to say goodbye to everyone."

"Don't make it sound as if we'll never see folk again," her father muttered.

"But we won't. Will we?" Ruby found her voice. "If we go to New Zealand I'll never see Elsie again and Lilith won't get her qualifications. How can that be for the best?"

"Lilith will be able to get her qualifications when we get there. There's bound to be a perfectly good teacher training college in Auckland."

"But how do you know," her voice rose higher. "You don't. You're just guessing."

"Ruby! Enough!" her mother stepped forward. "Your father will go over everything in detail, once he gets the forms. Now I suggest we all take a little time to calm down."

She couldn't believe it. As if what she was going through wasn't enough, now she had this to contend with too...

Twelve weeks. That was all the time she had left? It wasn't fair. How could her father do this to them? Hadn't the whole idea been shelved? It hadn't been mentioned in a long while, not since Christmas anyhow, though it had raised its head once or twice after that, she realised. But not in any definite way. It had just been talk. Now, somehow, it was all settled and she and

Lilith were supposed to go along with it. But just twelve short weeks with Elsie and everyone else she'd ever known? Bert too, on the off-chance he hadn't run out on her after all? No, this was home, this was where she'd grown up and this was where she intended to stay. How could anyone in their right mind want to start all over again, and so far away? And as for Alfie remaining behind? It simply wasn't right. Favouritism, that's what it boiled down to. Well, she would see about that too.

Her sister was rising from the table.

"Why don't we go for a walk," Lilith suggested to her.

"I'm not in the mood."

"Then let's go and sit in the snug."

"So why are we here?" Ruby asked, settling at the nearest of the three marble topped tables and folding her arms.

"I think we need to talk."

"Why? Unless you know more about Dad's plans than I do?"

"No. It was as much a shock to me as it was to you."

"Then what do you want to discuss?"

"You."

"Can't see why?" she huffed.

You've been very quiet lately."

"Have I?"

"Far more than usual."

"And?"

"I just want to know if everything's all right?"

"Of course, it is. At least it was, until just now."

Lilith didn't look any happier. "It was a bit of a turn up, wasn't it? But we can hardly say it was sprung on us. We've known for ages it's what dad wanted. Though I will say I'm as much against the idea as you are."

"Because of your studies, I suppose? Well, I can't blame you. Who's to say you can take your exams in New Zealand anyway? I doubt they've even got a college there. And what does Dad know? If you ask me, I think he's making it up half the time just to make it sound better than it is."

"It's not only my studies," Lilith said quietly, "although of course I'm desperate for my qualification. No, it's more to do with the movement."

"Women's rights and all that?"

"Exactly. Meeting Grace Stowell has opened up a new world for me. One that excites me, and I want to be a part of it."

Ruby nodded, though personally, she couldn't see the attraction. What was the big deal with equality if it meant being stuck in a job for years on end like a bloke? She'd settle for a wealthy husband who treated her like a movie star any day. What sensible person wouldn't?

"So what about your boyfriend," Lilith asked. "Bert, wasn't it? Are you still seeing him?"

"Not anymore."

"Oh? What happened?"

Ruby squirmed. "Nothing really."

"Don't tell me," her sister laughed. "You got bored again."

"Something like that."

Why did they have to talk about her? Why couldn't Lil just say what was on her mind so she could get back upstairs and lie down again.

"I thought this one was husband material?"

She didn't reply.

"So what are you going to do?" Lilith asked.

"About what?"

"New Zealand."

"Dunno. Sign the forms, I suppose. Like a good little girl."

"I'm going to speak to mum. See if I can stay here."

Ruby couldn't believe what she was hearing. "But you can't! Not if I have to go."

"I'm twenty-two and an adult in the eyes of the law. No one can make me do anything I don't want to. Not anymore."

"Oh Lil," reaching over, she grabbed at her sister's arm. "You can't mean that."

"I'm afraid I do."

"Then I'll stay here with you."

"That's not possible. I'm going to have to find lodgings and it will be hard enough on my own without having you to look after as well."

"You won't have to look after me! I promise. I can take care of myself. I just need somewhere to live, at least for now. Then I'll get out from under your feet."

"And how will you pay your share of the rent? And the bills? You haven't even got a job."

"I'll get one, I will. I'll start looking tomorrow. Please Lil, talk to mum about me staying too."

17

First, the applause broke out, then the audience stood to give Grace Stowell what could only be described as a standing ovation.

Lilith was thrilled.

She'd been on tenterhooks for the past week or so, worried that having booked the Wesleyan hall and sent out dozens of flyers, no one would turn up. That would have been a disaster given her enthusiasm when discussing the opportunity with Grace. In fact, she'd never have been able to face her again. Or anyone else for that matter. Instead, all things considered - and that being mainly the drizzling rain that had begun that morning and continued steadily throughout the day - it had been a pretty good turnout. And while she hadn't counted heads, she guessed some forty or so women had been curious enough to come and find out what was on offer.

The applause was allowed to continue a little longer, and still clapping wildly, Nora leant in. "That was marvellous."

"It was, wasn't it," Lilith agreed. "And even better, everyone else seems to think so too."

Above them on the podium Grace was holding up her hands for silence.

"Ladies."

Gradually the noise died away.

"Thank you once again for braving the weather and being with us tonight. I could have spoken longer, and for that reason I hope to see you all again in the not too distant future. Meanwhile, I will be here a while yet, so if you have any further questions, or if you found anything I have said to be of interest… please feel free to come over and chat."

Gathering her notes, she left the rostrum.

"I think congratulations are in order," she said, appearing at Lilith's side.

"Oh, absolutely. Well done! It was a wonderful talk. And look around you, everyone thought so."

"Not me, silly. You. It was your idea after all."

Despite her elation, Lilith knew she didn't deserve all the praise.

"Actually, it was Nora's," she said, dragging her friend forward.

"I only made the suggestion. You did all the work," Nora said. "Putting up the posters, sending out the invitations. Even laying on the tea and biscuits."

"Speaking of which, I'm dying for a cup. Shall we?" Grace indicated the long table where at least two dozen women were queueing up.

They were soon waylaid, though.

"Absolutely. We must continually re-examine our goals," she agreed with a woman with a fox stole artfully draped over one shoulder. Thankfully the only one in the room Lilith thought, edging away uncomfortably. She'd never liked glass eyes and snarling lips, regardless how fashionable they might be.

"You're right," Grace was agreeing with another, "our interests are wide ranging. That is why we remain closely linked to most other women's organisations."

And to a third, "Yes, equal pay for women teachers is of course at the forefront of our demands, but then so is the issue of maternity rights, unfortunately a subject our male colleagues seem to have little appetite for."

Skirting the queue and pushing her way to the front Lilith filled three cups from the large enamel tea-pot, and added a splash of milk. Then, tucking a sugar coated biscuit onto each saucer, waved Nora over and nodding to where Grace had been button-holed by yet another group.

"Can you find us somewhere to sit, while I take this over."

"So tell me more about this business venture of your fathers," Nora said, nibbling at her biscuit.

Balancing her cup and saucer on her knees Lilith replied, "There's not a lot to tell. I know it's a hotel. But that's about it."

"And you're definitely not going?"

"No. I've already spoken to everyone and explained my decision."

"That must have been hard."

"Yes, it was."

"How did they take it?"

"Not well," she admitted. "In fact, it left me feeling quite rotten."

"And Ruby?"

"Very supportive, but she would be. She was hoping to bolster her own case. Not that it worked. Dad's adamant she has to go with them."

"She won't be happy about that."

"She wasn't. You should have heard the fuss she made."

Nora nodded. "So what are your plans now?"

"Well, I need to looking for lodgings."

"That shouldn't be too difficult. There's plenty of widows in this town who'd be only too glad to rent out a room for a little extra money, especially to a teacher. Even my mum would have thought about it what with George and I moving in with his family. That is if Jessie hadn't already staked her claim."

Lilith laughed, "That's what you get with younger sisters. And I should know."

"You don't have to tell me. She's going on and on about the colour of her bridesmaid's dress. Blue, I said to her. How hard can that be?"

"She doesn't like blue?"

"Says it makes her look peaky. Sometimes I wonder why I even bother."

"You won't say that when you're a married woman."

"No I won't, will I. So when do you have to move out?"

"Not for a while yet. But I'll have to start checking the classifieds soon if I'm to be organised in time."

"You should ask around at school as well. You never know, someone might know of rooms coming up."

Lowering her cup, Lilith pulled a face. "Knowing my luck, the one person with available accommodation will be Lawrence Haslem."

"That could be awkward," Nora laughed.

"I'd say it would be downright embarrassing."

"May I join you both?"

"Of course," Lilith said, pulling forward the seat next to her, "though I expect your tea must be cold by now."

Grace smiled. "Don't worry. I'm used to it. Goes with the territory, I'm afraid."

"Can I get you a fresh one?" Nora asked, seeing her looking around for somewhere to set her unwanted cup and saucer.

"That would be lovely."

"Well, I have to say this has been a rousing success," Grace said, even as she continued to scan the room. "Just speaking to some of these women, it's patently obvious we need to get out and about a great deal more if we're to spread the word."

"So you think you might have some new members after tonight?"

"I'm sure of it. But it's more than that. There's also a lot of support for issues outside the union too."

"That's good," Lilith agreed, and placing her own cup squarely back on its saucer ventured, "Perhaps we should do this again."

"I don't think there's any *perhaps* about it. And in time you might even consider a larger venue."

"But we didn't fill this one. Nowhere near!"

"Just wait for word to spread. You'll see."

"It would be exciting."

"Not to mention a feather in your cap. And speaking of caps, I meant to tell you how much how much I like your new hairstyle."

God, would the day ever come when she could accept a compliment without turning beetroot red?

"Thank you. I wasn't sure…" and not knowing how to continue, simply shrugged.

"It's very flattering," Grace assured her. "When did you get it done?"

"The week after we met in Betty's."

"The shorter look really suits you. Shows off your elegant neck to perfection."

Lilith blushed again. "Unfortunately, not everyone feels that way."

"Oh?"

"One or two of the teaching staff seem to think it's a little too radical for the classroom. As if cutting off my hair is merely the start of a slippery slope. Next, I'll be filling little minds with all sorts of disagreeable notions."

"Ah. And that bothers you?"

"No. It would be different if the comments were being made by people I respect. But that's not the case."

"Good for you!"

There was an awkward pause. At least for Lilith, who felt once again as if she was being drawn headlong into those intriguing grey eyes.

And then Nora was back.

"Hope it's hot enough," she said, holding out a cup and saucer. "No biscuits, though. All snaffled, I'm afraid."

"That's fine. Now," Grace said, after taking a few sips, "what time did you say we had to be out of here?"

Lilith checked her wristwatch. "Gosh, another fifteen minutes and Mr McGrath will be over to lock up."

"Then let me finish this and we can make a start on the chairs."

"You don't need to do that," Lilith was horrified at the thought.

"Why not? Don't you think I'm capable?"

"Not at all. That is…"

"Yes?"

Nora grinned. "I'll go and collect up the crockery and take it into the kitchen."

Watching her make her way back at the long table, and the small group of women still happily chatting over their second cup, Grace turned to Lilith.

"You know; I've really enjoyed tonight."

"Yes. It was good fun, wasn't it?"

"I was wondering if you would like to come for tea on Sunday. My landlady's visits her daughter that day, so we'd have the entire place to ourselves."

"Oh…um…" Lilith stammered.

"If it's not convenient, or if you don't want to, you only have to say. I won't be offended."

"Oh no, I do. I do. Really."

"Wonderful. Say four o'clock?"

"Perfect," she managed. "But I don't know where you live."

"Southsea. Do you have a piece of paper? I'll write down the address."

18

Ruby discovered Bert's whereabouts a few days later, after walking down to the main gate and checking the dockyard movements board. It had been hard to take in, especially with the quartermaster watching from his office. She'd wanted to go over and slap the smirk off his face. Instead, she'd stuck her nose in the air and turned on her heel.

"Yes, he sailed last week," she'd told Elsie when it became obvious that even she knew his ship was no longer in port. "And before you ask, no he didn't propose. And no, I didn't want him to either."

Elsie's expression veered from shock to disbelief.

"Oh, don't get me wrong," Ruby continued airily. "I liked him enough. But when it came down to it, just not enough to actually *marry* him, if you know what I mean. I think I need someone with a bit more intelligence, you know. Someone with a future."

"A future?" Elsie was clearly perplexed.

"Yes. Someone who will give me the life I want."

"Someone with a couple of bob in their pocket then."

"Exactly."

Perched on the arm of a chair in Elsie's front room, her mother having popped out for five minutes and her father still on his shift in the dockyard, Ruby smoothed a hand down her skirt. No one would have the satisfaction of seeing her heart was broken. No one. Not even her best friend.

"So, no more sailor boys?" Elsie said.

"Not unless they're officers."

"Aiming high then."

"Should have done that in the first place really."

Her friend nodded, though she still didn't look convinced. "Just as well you found out now."

She frowned. "Why?"

"'Cos you wouldn't have wanted to waste a year only to find out your real feelings when he returned."

"Exactly my thoughts."

"So what did he say when you told him?"

"He was upset, wasn't he. Begged and pleaded for me to wait for him. But like I said to him, some things are just not meant to be. Told him we should both put it behind us and find other people."

"So now what are you going to do?"

"About what?"

"Everything?"

"I'll just have to see what turns up."

"Well, there's always New Zealand. Not that you want to go of course," Elsie added, a touch maliciously.

"Maybe I don't feel that way anymore."

"What!" her friend was incredulous.

"Maybe I've changed my mind," she lied. "Everyone seems to think it's a marvellous opportunity.

Who knows, I might find a rich man on the voyage over. Which is more than I'm going to do staying in this town."

19

THUMPING THE RAW PASTRY ONTO the floured surface, Ruby set about it with the rolling pin.

"I don't care if Uncle Joe is buying us a hotel. I wouldn't even care if he was buying us a palace. I'm not going."

Standing over the stove, ladle in hand, her mother barely looked up from the bubbling contents of a large enamel pot.

"You won't have any choice if it comes to it. And go easy with that. The more you handle it the tougher it gets."

"As if I care."

"You will if we never sell another mutton pie."

"I don't see why you're bothered when we're not going be here much longer."

"It's not a hundred percent yet. We've still got a bit of sorting out to do."

Ruby stopped. "So there's a chance it'll all fall through?"

"Unlikely."

"But it might?"

"I wouldn't waste time raising my hopes if I were you."

"Why not? You know how I feel. And it's so unfair. First Alfie gets let off going, then Lilith."

Dipping the ladle and lifting it to her mouth her mother sipped and smacked her lips.

"For Heaven's sake, why won't you listen to me?" Ruby exclaimed.

"I am listening." And reaching into the crock she sprinkled another pinch of salt over the stewing meat.

"I'm old enough to make my own decisions."

"Not in my book."

"Another month or so and I'll be twenty."

"Your birthday's in September, and that's a while away yet. And anyway, by my count it'll be another year before you can do anything without our permission."

"It's so ridiculous."

"Is it?"

Watching the ladle being dipped again and the gravy tasted a second time, Ruby huffed. Why must her mother be so bloody irritating? After all, it wasn't that long ago she was as much against the idea as everyone else.

But then she frowned. When had her mother begun looking so tired? Worn out, even, as if all the life was being drained from her. It didn't help she was slouched over the pot as if everything was too much of an effort. She tried to think. When was the last time she'd seen her dolled up? Or wearing something new? She couldn't even recall hearing her laugh these past weeks. Really laugh, that is.

147

A chill went through her, as if someone had walked over her grave.

"You alright?" she asked.

"Why wouldn't I be?"

She shrugged. Nothing wrong with her attitude then, and getting back to the pastry she curled it over the rolling pin and after coating the board with more flour, laid it back down and smoothed out the edges.

"Mum," she said in a friendlier tone, "is there no possibility of us being given another pub around here?"

"Not with the clearance coming up. Anyway, your father wants a change. He wants to try somewhere new."

"Has he thought about Fratton?" she asked, pressing down on the cutter for a perfectly round pie base. "Or Cosham? It's nice there. Lots of people are moving out that way. People we know."

"It's not what your father wants."

"Well then, what about a little further out? Like Emsworth? That would be a real change."

Turning off the gas her mother moved the pot to the back of the stove. "I've already told you. It's not what your father wants."

"But what about what *you* want. Doesn't that count for anything?"

Her mother said nothing.

"Perhaps we could persuade him. I don't know…" she pressed out another perfect round. "If we all got together and sat him down maybe we could make him see the advantages in staying here."

Joining her at the table, her mother started greasing the waiting tins.

"We can't just give up," Ruby said.

"Look," her mother sounded exasperated. "Who's to say this won't be right for us all."

"You don't believe that."

"You don't know what I think."

"Then tell me."

"I want what will most benefit our family and your father has decided this is it. So let's not waste any more time worrying about whether we should live in Cosham or Emsworth, or anywhere else for that matter."

Ruby had never known her to be so stubborn.

"But it's not our family that's going," she argued, stamping out the remaining crusts with a little more force and a little less care. "It's just you and dad and me. If it's that wonderful, why aren't you forcing the others too?"

"I see. Well Alfie's situation is fairly obvious and your father agreed, reluctantly I might add, that Lilith could stay behind and get her qualification. But that's all."

"But that won't be for years!"

"Doesn't matter. She'll still be filling out the forms so she can join us when she does."

"Then let me come out with her."

"I don't want to argue with you."

"Then don't. Just agree it's a silly idea."

"I'll do no such thing."

"Please mum, won't you talk to dad? Tell him how I feel? That I really don't want to go."

"I'm sure he knows that already. Ever since that letter arrived there hasn't been one moment when you haven't been bleating."

"Oh mum…"

"Enough!" her mother cut in. "If we go, and it's still not certain we'll be accepted for the scheme, then you will be going too. Like it or not."

20

THE THREE-STOREY VILLA, a mere stone's throw from South Parade Pier and the pebble-strewn beach of Southsea, was one of only a handful of properties in the quiet leafy road offering that type of accommodation, or so she'd been told. Lilith was checking off names fashioned in stained glass over front doors. That *Oban, Rothesay,* and *Bute* blazed in jewel-like, Art Nouveau splendour left her wondering what was it that caused middle-class families on the south coast of England, with husbands and fathers no doubt employed as accountants or civil servants, or in business - though should that be the case always behind the scenes and well away from the public eye - to name their homes after remote, windswept Scottish Islands?

Or a lake in Westmorland, she thought, pulling up outside *Windermere.*

Rapping her knuckles on the door she stepped back onto the tiled path. The house was little different to its neighbours and that meant well maintained with fresh paintwork and clean windows. Capped brick pillars and a smartly trimmed privet hedge enclosed the small front garden, though the only thing she recognised in the terracotta edged flower bed was the thorny stems of a pruned back rose bush.

"You should see it in summer. It's a veritable riot of colour. Pansies, geraniums, fuchsias. The lot."

Grace was a vision of sheer elegance and loveliness. The wide legged trousers might be considered outrageous in some quarters but they were also the height of fashion, even she knew that, while the soft blouse and light coloured cardigan slung casually over her shoulders spoke of garden parties and cream teas.

"Sounds absolutely lovely," she managed. Her heart sank. Why on earth had she worn such sensible shoes? And her hat, for heaven's sake, she'd had it years.

"Come in, come in," Grace held back the door. "Give me your coat. I thought we'd take tea in the front room. It's the official resident's lounge, but with no one else here we'll have it all to ourselves."

Her first impression was of a high-ceilinged, elegant and well-proportioned room. Then she was struck by how bright and welcoming it was, with the afternoon sun streaming in through the large bay window. It certainly showcased the modern floral wallpaper and the mix of comfortable-looking sofas and cosy armchairs.

"I thought we'd sit by the fire," having folded Lilith's coat, Grace was placing it on a chair behind the door. "I know it's not cold at the moment, but in an hour or so it might be a different story."

A low table had been set with bone china plates of tiny sandwiches and savouries, and as if reading her mind Grace offered, "All care of Mrs G., my wonderful landlady."

"Golly, it looks delicious."

"I know. She does tend to spoil me."

"I hope you're not complaining?"

"Not at all. Though it can be a bit much at times. Especially when she's trying to nudge me in the direction of a suitable young man." It was clear from her expression that was a situation she tried very much to avoid. "Tea?"

"This is all terribly nice. How many rooms are rented out," she asked, before adding quickly, "if it's not too impertinent a question?"

"Not at all. Three usually, although one member of our little clique is taking herself off to Paris any day now."

"Gracious!"

"It's quite romantic really. Her intention is to become an artist's muse. And of course, where else would you go to do that?"

"Certainly not around here," she laughed.

"And if that fails," Grace said, passing over a brimming cup and saucer, "she intends to try out as a showgirl."

"A showgirl? What, at a place like the Moulin Rouge or the Follies Bergère?"

"The same."

"Gosh, how daring."

"I have to say, she does have the figure for it."

Lilith thought privately that Grace also had the necessary attributes, for her legs were long and willowy whereas her own could never be described that way. Nor would she pass muster as a dancer of any note. Not under any circumstances.

"So, it'll be just me and Gregory Bateman after that," Grace was saying. "Oh and Mrs G., of course."

"And this Gregory Bateman, is he a suitable young man?"

Grace's laugh was quick. "Not in a million years. For a start, he's wedded to his work."

"As are you," Lilith teased, strangely relieved.

"It's nowhere near the same. He truly is joined at the hip to his hospital laboratory bench."

"Oh. What does he do exactly?"

"Exactly? No idea. Vaguely? Something to do with analysing bodily fluids."

"Ugh."

"Quite. He's also the wrong side of forty."

"Totally out of the question then."

"Totally," Grace agreed, sitting back and lifting one knee over the other. "But what about you. No eligible bachelor in your life?"

Having made her selection from the plate of sandwiches, Lilith had just bitten into a crustless egg and cress triangle.

"Me?" she croaked.

"Yes, you!"

"None."

"And why is that?"

It was a question she'd asked herself often enough.

"I have no idea," she answered honestly. "I just don't seem to meet anyone who might fall into the right category."

"But you must have known one or two possibles in your life?"

"No. I suppose contrary to being in the right place at the right time, I must always be in the wrong place at the right time."

"Or the right place at the wrong time," Grace finished. "And yet here we are in a town bursting at the seams with single naval officers."

"I know."

"We should do something about our plight. Form a lonely hearts society or something."

"I'd rather not," Lilith said quietly. "I rather think I like it the way I am."

"And you know what? I rather think I like it that way too."

Moving the last morsel of her sandwich around her plate Lilith knew she didn't dare put it in her mouth for it would stick like glue to the roof. So instead she looked pointedly at the teapot.

"Would you?" she asked, nudging her cup and saucer forward.

"Of course. You have to excuse me. I might be good at rousing support for our fellow employees, but I can be a shocking hostess at times."

"I'm sure that's not true."

"Believe me, it is. This is me putting on a show."

"Then don't."

"Gosh, that's a relief. I much prefer to be waited on than the other way round. But having said that you must try some of Mrs G's Victoria sponge. If we haven't eaten at least a quarter of it, she'll never make it for us again. And that would be a disaster."

Lilith heard only one word. *Us.*

A tour of the house later revealed Grace's accommodation was of similar size to the resident's lounge, no doubt because it was directly above. A palette of salmon pinks and eau de nil, it even had the same bay window, though without the perfect symmetry of the floor below for with two bedrooms facing the front of the house, this one, though still the larger, had been forced to yield a foot or two of width to its neighbour.

"I'm lucky," Grace said, crossing over and drawing the curtains against the fading light. "This is the best room in the whole place. Not that I've had it from the beginning, but I snatched it the moment it became available and now I'm not leaving for anyone."

"It's lovely," Lilith breathed. To say she envied her would be a massive understatement. Look at the desk tucked into the window recess. And the sweet little armchair. And how clever to fit a cupboard and bookcase to one side of the chimney breast. Oh, and she even had a wash-stand with both hot and cold taps and a curtain to hide her bits and bobs. And an electric fire, though smaller than the one downstairs and with a green enamel surround rather than burnished tin.

This certainly was heaven on earth.

"I'm guessing you're impressed?" Grace laughed.

"Is it so obvious? And what's more delightful, you don't have to share with a sister like I do."

"Never having had one, I would know if that was a good thing or not."

"Believe me, it's not."

"Take a look around. I don't mind."

Lilith was in her element. After admiring the motif of twining plants on the tiles either side of the fireplace she stopped in front of the bookcase and studied the rows of spines. Then it was the desk that had her attention.

"This is rather fabulous," she said, touching a finger to the leaded glass shade of a lamp.

"Wonderful isn't it. I bought it when I was up at union HQ. Dual purpose. I can work by it or read by it if I'm curled up in the chair. Coffee?"

Lilith blinked. For having opened the narrow cupboard and taken out an electric hotplate and coffee pot, Grace was waving a brown packet similar to the one she'd bought in Betty's tea shop that day.

"Indulge me," she was saying. "I promise you won't regret it."

"All right."

"Good. I'll just set this going, then I'll pop downstairs for some milk. Why don't you make yourself comfortable?"

But Lilith remained where she was, picturing herself in such a splendid situation. She too would have a desk in her lodgings, and a lamp—though not one from Liberty's, of course. Furthermore, and like Grace, she would entertain guests. Nora for one. Maybe even other women with an interest in the movement. Women she was yet to meet. And as she took in every detail of her surroundings, she noticed a number of garments hanging on the back of the door, and something red and embroidered peeking out from beneath. Was it a kimono? How delicious. And how very like Grace to own such a thing.

The house was quiet. Deathly so. Just three paces and her fingertips were fondling the silk. When there was still no sound from below, nor on the stairs, she closed her eyes and breathing deeply, pressed it to her cheek. This was what Grace wore when relaxing in the armchair, book in hand. Or in the evenings when preparing for bed. She could imagine her now, turning from the wash-stand. Even with the belt knotted, the front would slip apart with each step...

Dropping the fabric as if it had scalded her she hurried to the safety of the bookcase. What on earth was she thinking? It was wrong, so very wrong and on many levels, the least of which being that it went against everything nature intended. She'd never been one to seek out a member of her own sex, though she'd read about such women of course and it was common knowledge that certain all-female colleges were notorious for that kind of affection. Mannish, was how newspapers described them. Well, no one could accuse her of that. And why should they? If she wanted a boyfriend, she could have one at the drop of a hat. Everyone said so. It was just that she yet hadn't met a man fully at ease with a woman who thought for herself. But she would, one day.

She was busy reading the fly-leaf of a novel when Grace stepped back into the room carrying not only the milk but a plate with the remains of their tea.

"I've no idea if you're hungry again, but I thought I'd bring it up anyway. Don't worry if you're not. Buster will get it all tomorrow. Well, maybe not the cake, but the meat sandwiches, at least."

"Buster?" she asked, glad of the distraction.

"Mrs G.'s Yorkshire terrier."

"Sounds ferocious."

"His yap is worse than his bite," Grace said, switching off the hotplate and removing the bubbling pot. Pouring dark, pungent coffee into two tiny cups and adding a dribble of milk she passed one over.

"Here, try this and tell me you don't like it. Not that I'd believe you anyway."

Looking anywhere but at her friend, Lilith sipped obediently. "Oh! This is lovely. And so different from anything we've had at home."

"Told you so. Now, you take the chair, but throw me the cushions first. I'm going to sprawl in front of the fire. Very unladylike, I know, but to hell with that. Oh, and take off your shoes if you wish. Make yourself at home."

Lilith wanted nothing more than to do exactly that. In fact, she'd have given anything to remain there all night, curled up in the chair, legs tucked under her while they discussed books they'd read or politics they supported. But she just couldn't risk it. Heaven's, she was already shaking like a leaf and if Grace noticed, and asked what was wrong, then what on earth could she say?

Hugely disappointed in herself, she blurted out, "Thank you. But I daren't stay much longer. I've already promised to help out at home, and I can't let them down. I'm so sorry," she added, on seeing Grace's disappointment.

"That's alright. I completely understand. Family first and all that. But I'm not letting you off that easily. You have to promise we'll do this again next week."

"Yes," she smiled weakly. "We should."

21

HAVING BROUGHT THE SECOND POST through to the kitchen, Dilys propped up the cream envelope with its official-looking stamp on the shelf above the range.

"Is that what I think it is?" Spreading a thick layer of butter onto a slice of toast Ruby looked up. "If so, there's little point in my filling out any form."

Dilys didn't bat an eyelid. She was studying the other envelope in her hand. Made of far cheaper paper, this was neither typed nor addressed to Mr J. Doherty, Esq. Instead, it was her name on the front and reaching into the kitchen drawer she pulled out a knife and slipped it under the flap.

"I'm your mother, and I say what goes," she said, extracting the single sheet and glancing over it before continuing in the same monotone, "At least until you've older. Or you've got a ring on your finger. Then as far as I'm concerned you become your husband's responsibility. But all the time you're under my roof..."

"But I won't be under it for much longer," Ruby broke in.

"Oh?" she glanced up.

"Not if you're in New Zealand, anyway. Because I'm staying here."

"Here? I thought we'd gone over this. And more than once."

"That was ages ago," Ruby offered between mouthfuls of toast. "But now Lil's looking for a place to live, things are different."

"In what way?"

"I've asked her if she can find a place for two."

"Oh yes? And exactly how do you think you're going to be able to afford your share?"

"Easy. I'll have a job."

"And you've started looking, have you?"

"Uh huh."

"I'm guessing you haven't found one, though."

"Not the right one, no."

"And have you had many interviews?" She already knew the answer, for her daughter was not the sort to keep anything to herself. And certainly nothing that important.

"What would be the point in agreeing to meet an employer if the right job hasn't turned up yet?"

Returning to her letter, Dilys re-read the last few lines. "How else would you know if a position's suitable?" she said without looking up.

"I'll know."

Re-folding the page she slipped it and the envelope into her pocket. "You're coming to New Zealand with your father and me, and that's an end to it."

"I'd rather not argue with you."

"Well, that'll be a first."

Ruby was fingering the crumbs on her plate. "I'm hoping we can all show a little more maturity than of late."

"Oh do you?"

"I think as a family we should look at what's fair. To everyone, not just one or two of us."

"And what do you have in mind?"

"The way I see it, we should all go, or none of us go."

"Your father has already made his decision. Now, if you want to make yourself useful, start folding those tea towels."

Even before she'd even had time to nod in the direction of the pile of laundry Ruby had whirled around and flounced out of the kitchen.

She understood how her daughter felt. The thought of leaving Portsea was terrifying, and nothing anyone could say would make it any better, especially now two of her precious children wouldn't be coming with them. But Joe's generosity meant they were being handed a golden opportunity, and one she agreed they would never have if they stayed at home.

If only Ruby could see how limited the options really were. Oh, she went on about staying and finding a job, but everyone knew her heart was set on marrying, and marrying well. But how could she? She'd end up like every other girl, with a dockyard worker like Alfie for a husband or a sailor like the one who'd come into the bar that afternoon. And that was something else. A letter had arrived some weeks later, marked Her Majesty's Ship. She'd been watching out for it and checking the post each day, so that when it turned up just as some instinct had told her it would, she'd done her daughter a favour and dropped it into the range to blacken and curl into wafer-thin layers of ash. Ruby was meant for better. And if, as had been hinted at in Joe Doherty's letter, there were a shortage of single women in New Zealand, then she would be fighting off suitors. After all, plenty of young men had chosen the emigration route to fame and fortune. And if it was true that having made their wealth they were in the market for a wife... well then. Like she kept on trying to tell her, with her looks she'd have the pick of the bunch.

Her imagination wandered into the realms of large stately homes, with ornamental gardens, spreading lawns and ancient oak trees. Like the one at Leigh Park they'd visited all those years ago on a trip organised by the local Sunday School - not that the Doherty children showed the slightest interest in going to church or anything. Nor had they cared much for the big house that day. No, they were only interested in the lake and what might be lurking under the surface. Well, Alfie anyhow. Ruby had been a toddler, and Lilith, the quiet one, stayed close by and within reach.

And now she wouldn't be. Close by and within reach, that was.

Reaching into her pocket she spread the letter flat on the table.

She was in two minds whether to ignore the instruction contained halfway down the page. But then what? Would they send another, this time couched in stronger language?

The word *specialist* kept jumping out at her. Not that they had any way of paying for one. Not if they were going to make their home in New Zealand that is, for it would take all their savings, what little they had, to get started. And if Jim found out she wasn't a hundred percent then all hell would break loose, and he'd demand she got herself up to the hospital and checked out.

Only she didn't need anyone telling her what was wrong. She already knew. Not in big words of course. But what was going on inside her. The traces of blood in the lav, the pain in her stomach and the aching in her back. Not to mention seeing how some of her clothes were beginning to hang off her. So why spend money on confirming the inevitable when it could be put to much better use on a new life for everyone.

Having made herself a nice pot of tea she was sitting with her elbows on the table, cup at chin height, when Jim walked in.

"There's a letter for you up there," she said, nodding in the direction of the shelf.

"Oh?"

About to join her at the table he made a beeline for the range instead and after getting down the envelope and studying his name and address, asked with a surprising level of calmness all things considered, "'Nother one in the pot is there?"

"I'll get you a cup and saucer."

"Know what this is, don't you?" he said, as she passed from cupboard to table.

"The Empire Settlement forms?"

"Can't be anything else," and thrusting a nicotine-stained finger under one end of the flap he sawed it to the other.

"Yup," he said, parting the now-ragged edges and withdrawing the thick wad, "it's the forms all right."

"Does that mean we've been accepted?".

Glancing over first one typewritten sheet then another, he replied, "It means we're a lot closer, girl. They wouldn't have sent all this otherwise."

"So what do they need to know?"

"Not too much, by the looks of this. The usual stuff. Name, address,' he turned a sheet over, "name of sponsor... that'll be Joe...details of any assets...and a declaration at the bottom. Seems pretty straightforward." The page was turned back. "Looks like we have to get medical certificates. Can't blame them. Don't want a load of old crocks on their hands, do they? Let's have that tea and I'll start filling these in."

That the emigration board would require proof an applicant was physically fit before it would approve travel and assist with fares and the like had played on her mind for weeks. And for the very same reason Jim had mentioned. The Empire needed the young and the strong, not folk like her, who might soon be a burden. So now what? She had to admit life had a queer way of acting sometimes. Like, her getting her letter the very same day he got his. It was as if someone up there was playing a joke on them. Trouble was, he'd been a different man lately. Look at the poor bugger, reading through the forms again, this time with a little more care. He'd a purpose now. This was the old Jim. The Jim she'd fallen in love with twenty-five years ago. Why, he was even back to charming the old biddies in the snug, and that was something he hadn't done in a while. Cackling hens, he called them now, a far cry from some of the descriptions he'd used behind their backs these last few years.

He was better with the kids too. Even showing a bit of interest in what they'd been up to. He'd always been close to Alfie, but the girls could be a mystery to him, more so now they were grown up. Ruby could twist him around her little finger if she'd a mind, but he puzzled over Lilith, no doubt wondering how he could ever have produced such an impassioned and intelligent creature. Yet he was proud of her, anyone could see that. Who'd ever thought she and Jim would end up with a teacher, of all things, in the family?

"When do you reckon we could get this medical stuff then?"

He didn't even look up, which was just as well as she'd very nearly dropped her tea-cup.

"I'll go round the doctors next week and get us all appointments."

"What's Ruby up to? Couldn't she go this afternoon? Might as well do it sooner rather than later. They might fit us in on Monday or Tuesday."

"Monday might be pushing it. You have to be dying if you want to be seen that quick. But I'll give her a shout," Dilys agreed, trying to sound enthusiastic.

22

"YOU CAN GO IN now, Mrs Doherty."

Gathering her bag, Dilys left the austere waiting room without acknowledging the receptionist; a woman whose high-necked blouse spoke of another era, and whose sole purpose in life appeared to be the zealous guarding of the doctor's time and expertise rather than in showing any sympathy to those who might require it. Passing a man on his way out, his head bowed and eyes averted, she made her way along the corridor and after rapping on a door, opened it decisively.

"Ah, Mrs Doherty."

The acknowledgement came after little more than a flickering glance.

Taking one of the two high backed chairs in front of the desk she sat bolt upright, waiting for the doctor to finish the more important task of writing up notes. Or whatever it was he was busy doing.

"A medical certificate is it?" he spoke at last, rolling the blotter over the page.

"Yes, Doctor."

"Indeed. For purposes of emigration, I understand," he said, mouth tight and eyes unblinking.

"That is correct."

"Yes. I had your daughter in here earlier. Not too keen on the idea of crossing the globe, is she," he continued, removing his glasses and polishing them with a handkerchief he'd pulled from his pocket. "In fact, she made a point of complaining of all manner of aches and pains."

Oh did she? Dilys thought. Well, she'd be talking to that young lady when she got home.

"And I believe your husband and your other daughter have appointments tomorrow?"

She tipped her head in acknowledgement. Just the once.

"Well," the word was drawn out as, with glasses back on the bridge of his nose and elbows on the desk, he formed a pyramid with his fingers. "Unfortunately issuing a certificate in your case isn't quite as simple a matter, as I'm sure you appreciate."

"I can't see any problem at all, actually."

For a moment he looked startled. "Mrs Doherty, are you forgetting something? It's my understanding…"

"I'm not forgetting anything at all."

"Then let me refresh your memory" and he opened a manila file.

"There's no need."

It was as if he hadn't heard her. "You had symptoms and you came to see me," he said, lifting first one sheet then another.

"That was four months ago."

"Are you saying there's been a change since then?'

"I am."

"So why wasn't I advised?"

"Do all of your patient's fork out for another appointment just to tell you the treatment worked?"

"No. But in your case, there has been no treatment. At least, none that had been formally agreed on. In fact, I wrote a letter… now where is it…"

"Doctor, I would have thought you'd be pleased with the improvement in my health. It's all a bit embarrassing really, and truth be known I might have been guilty of exaggerating when I first brought the problem to your notice. But the good news is, I'm not having the same…" she stopped, searching for a suitable word, "…inconveniences."

"Are you sure?"

Clearly he was perplexed.

"I'm certain, doctor."

"Are you saying you no longer want an appointment with the specialist at the Royal Portsmouth Hospital?"

"I am. I really can't see the point of wasting either his time or my money."

The expression on his sallow face was one of mistrust. "If this is a case of financial difficulty…"

"It is not. You can be assured about that."

"But symptoms of this type don't just vanish overnight."

"Hardly overnight. As I said, it was a while ago I saw you. And since then, as you suggested, I have made a point of taking things a little easier and enjoying a little herbal tea every now and then."

"But the abdominal pain? The cramping? The pain in your lower back?"

"Rarely felt anymore."

"You astound me."

"Surely not. I've no doubt over the years you've seen many cases where nature has been carried out her own cure."

"Yes, of course, but…"

"Well, here you have another. It's as simple as that," she pasted a smiled in place. "So Doctor, shall we get on with whatever it is you need to do for the certificate? Oh, and as a token of my appreciation for the care you have given me and my family over the years…" Reaching into her bag she brought out the bottle of French cognac she'd purchased from the vintners on the Hard that morning.

The doctor's glance slid to the label.

"Hennessey," he murmured.

This time her smile was genuine, for seeing the offering as somewhat of an investment she'd spared no expense.

"And you're sure?" he said, his eyes on the bottle. "The…er…symptoms…?"

She knew his workload was heavy. Conditions round these parts meant coughs and colds and other diseases spread like wildfire. Kids were prone to everything from scarlet fever to TB. Would he see it her way? She was offering him the chance to help a family get out and achieve a decent standard of living. At the very least it would be one less to bother about. Or so she hoped.

"I'd have been back a lot sooner if there was anything to worry about, doctor. Right as rain now, that's me. So, will it be pulse or temperature first?" she asked, shoving up her sleeve.

23

"NEVER KNEW IT WOULD be this hard," Ruby complained, waiting only for Elsie to farewell the three other girls emerging from the rear door of the bakery before taking her arm.

"Didn't get the job then?"

"No. And I could have done it with my eyes closed."

"So what happened?"

Feigning an innocent look, she replied. "I've no idea"

That wasn't exactly true. Having arrived a little over ten minutes late for her interview, one look at the manageress's face told her she had no chance of working at any haberdashers *she* was in charge of. So rather than hope for a change of heart, and she wasn't going to crawl for anyone, she'd chosen to advise she'd only kept the appointment out of good manners. For she'd already accepted a position elsewhere.

"You should have seen her, Else."

"Who?"

"Mrs Hobbs. Face like she'd swallowed a wasp. How she keeps her customers I've no idea."

"Just as well you didn't get it then. You two would have been at loggerheads within days."

"Not even that if you ask me. Some people just don't realise how important a smile can be. And I'd know. Don't I have to keep one plastered on my face all the time I'm collecting up empty glasses?"

Elsie uttered her agreement. "Any more interviews this week?"

"No."

"Don't worry. Something'll turn up. You'll see."

"That's all well and good, but I'm getting desperate."

"Shame we're not taking on any more staff. I bet I could get you in with me otherwise."

Ruby would be happy to work at the bakery if it wasn't for the fact the shifts started so early. Elsie and the others had to be there at four-thirty for goodness sake, when normal people were still asleep. Worse, she couldn't keep up in the evenings, and who in their right mind wanted to be exhausted and dropping when everyone else was livening up? It was a close thing, though.

"Thanks Else. I'll keep on looking," and she took on an expression of stoic disappointment.

"So how did it go at the doctors then?" Elsie asked.

Now she tutted and shook her head. For this was another cross she'd had to bear. "You would *not* believe it."

"What happened."

"Clean bill of health. You can't say I didn't try. I complained about everything under the sun. Headaches, back aches, flushes, dizzy spells. I even said I got spots before my eyes."

Elsie laughed. "But he didn't fall for it?"

"Not one bit. And I only went to keep the peace at home. Now I'm stuck with my name on those stupid forms Dad's sending off in the morning"

"Might come in useful, seeing as how things are going on the job front."

"Except I don't want to go," Ruby stated.

"Changed your mind then, have you?"

"Never wanted to go in the first place."

"That's not what you said. Thought you was hoping to find a rich toff on the way over?"

"Yes, well…"

"Here, I've just had a thought," Elsie broke in as they stepped off the kerb and crossed the road. "Isn't the butchers on Kent Street looking for someone on the till?"

"Are you joking? Could you see me amongst all that blood and sawdust? And the flies? Ugh!" and she shuddered.

"S'pose so. What about Lil?"

"What about her?"

"Well, she's allowed to stay, isn't she? Has she found somewhere to live yet?"

"I asked her again last night when she got in from school. She was a bit cagey, but I got it out of her there might be a room coming up in Southsea."

"Big enough for two?"

"I asked her that, and she says no. But like I said to her, we share a pokey bedroom now without any problems, so what would be the difference?"

"And what did she say?"

"It's not the same," Ruby mimicked her sister's tone.

"Then tell her to find somewhere bigger."

"I did."

"Do you think she will?"

"She says it's all to do with affordability."

"You'd think she'd be glad to have you around. You could keep the place tidy while she's at work."

"That's exactly what I said."

"So then what did she say?"

Pulling Elsie into the gutter to avoid the oncoming pram and the two kiddies hanging off the handle, Ruby replied, "She said I should go to New Zealand, didn't she?"

"She didn't!"

"She did."

"Hmm."

"So I'm back at square one. I need that job, Else."

"You'll get one. Don't worry."

Glancing up every now and then from her preparations for the next day's lessons Lilith was also thinking of her future living arrangements, and giving serious consideration to the idea Grace had put forward the second time she'd gone around for tea. It was sheer madness under the circumstances, but on a practical level, Mrs Gainsborough's lodging house would be absolutely perfect if indeed the tenant in room three did decide to go to Paris.

Grace seemed to think it was a foregone conclusion.

"It's just a question of time," she'd said. "And I really don't think she wants to be here any longer than necessary, since she's dropping hints like mad about an apartment on the Left Bank, and a certain painter she's been in correspondence with all this time."

"It sounds terribly bohemian."

"It is, considering the man already has a wife."

"So she's not to be just his muse then?"

"I would say not."

"How very wicked."

"Isn't it? Anyway, the moment I hear the sound of bags being packed I'll corner Mrs G. straight away and say I have just the right person for the room," sprawled on enough cushions to keep a sultan happy, she'd waved her cigarette around. "Another orphan like me, and a teacher to boot. She'll be ecstatic!"

Lilith looked sideways. "Are you truly an orphan? Or just after my sympathy?"

"Well, if you're planning on dishing it out, then yes, send it my way. But in truth, both parents are very much alive and kicking. They live further along the coast in a delightful village by the sea."

"Then clearly you have no need of anyone's commiserations," Lilith admonished, though not without a smile. "Do you see them often?"

"Not as much as I should. Not with everything else going on in my life."

"Ah yes, now you mention it I've been meaning to ask where you taught."

"At an academy for young ladies." Grace screwed up her nose. "Only three days a week, though, taking classes in hygiene and physical education."

"You mean you don't have the responsibility of general classes too?" she was amazed.

"No. That's the lot of the form mistresses. And as far as I'm concerned, they're welcome to it. Besides which, I'm a little too caught up in my other activities."

"The union?"

"Uh huh. That, and various women's groups. You know, there's a local meeting of the Open Door Council on Wednesday. You should come along. I'm sure you'd find it interesting."

Already aware of the organisation from *Time and Tide*, a feminist journal to which she subscribed, much to the disgust of Ruby, she was only too thrilled to accept.

"Wonderful. We can meet here around six thirty if you like? And there should be time for a bite to eat afterwards."

Settled in the armchair beside the desk, the Tiffany lamp glowing and her senses intoxicated, Lilith had told herself that having at last found a purpose in life, nothing should come in the way of it, not even a silly infatuation if indeed that's what it was.

In the cold, grey light of day though she knew it wouldn't be such an easy thing to achieve. Even if she could dismiss the whole thing as little more than childish idolisation it would mean watching every word that came out of her mouth for one thing, and every gesture for another. It would also mean standing back and allowing others to come into Grace's sphere.

Closing the textbook she placed it to one side.

She would have to throw herself into her work and her causes, that was all.

24

DILYS'S BIRTHDAY IN THE FIRST week of May was to be a double celebration, though as far as she was concerned being another year older was no cause for rejoicing. It was just one step closer to the grave, she grumbled when Jim suggested they all went out for supper that night.

"Come on, girl. Forty-five is hardly old these days," and he'd given her *that* look. The one that said he was about to whip her into his arms and steal a cuddle.

"Just you stay there and carry on with whatever you're doing."

But it was too late and holding her tight, he beamed down at her. "Especially when you don't look a day over thirty."

Needing the reassurance of his strength and support, she leant her head against his chest.

"Exciting times, doll," he mussed her hair with his lips. "And now we've got the go-ahead, we can make solid plans. Like telling the brewery for a start. And..."

"Yes?"

"...we have a wedding to help plan. Or had you forgotten?"

"You trying to cheer me up or something?"

Gazing down, his expression was so full of love. And something else, she thought. Excitement. That was it. He was like a kid who'd been told Christmas was just days away.

"I dunno," she said. "There's a lot to do if we're to be ready for that ship in July."

"You can't fool me, doll. You're looking forward to a new start as much as I am."

"That right?"

"That's right," he said, leaning his forehead on hers.

"I just wish the other two were coming with us."

The words caught in her throat.

"I know."

"Even if it were just Lil…"

He was stroking her back. "But she's got somewhere nice to go, and she'll be with that friend of hers. You can't begrudge her that."

But I do, she wanted to say. Even believing that of her two daughters Ruby would get most benefit from emigrating, it was Lil she wanted by her side. Quiet, determined Lilith. And loyal. Yes, loyal, she thought, recalling the numerous times she'd stepped up and taken over when the aches and pains were at their worst. And not a single word said.

Ruby's help, on the other hand, was conditional, and then often upon wages. Which was fine now she had set hours in the kitchen, but ask her for anything else and the chances were she'd have something better to do. Like meet up with Elsie for a spot of window-shopping. So how were they going to get by in New Zealand with just the three of them? And more importantly, how long would it be before her symptoms got so bad she could no longer hold the reins? Then what? It didn't bear thinking about. Of course Ruby could take over, that was the plan after all. But who knew what might be going on in her head when the time came? One thing was certain though, if Lilith didn't come out - and please God she did - eventually it would be just Ruby and her dad miles away from home.

With a light kiss on the top of her head, Jim went over to his chair and his paper, and after rolling a cigarette and putting it to his lips, asked, "Wonder which church the kids'll be getting married in?"

"Which church? Her local one I suppose. Why?"

"Need to get thinking about it." he said, striking a match.

"I'm sure Alice and her mother have all that in hand."

"Reckon it'll be a big do?"

"Not on our side, that's for sure."

"Could have the reception here though, couldn't we. Plenty of room in the public bar."

"Over my dead body," she retorted. "We're not having our son's reception here. So don't you even suggest it."

"Just thinking about saving everyone a bit of money."

"But it's not our place to do that, is it? Alice's parents are paying for things. And as far as I'm concerned, it's down to them to put on a show. Not us."

"Keep yer hair on, doll. I was only saying."

"And I want our boy done proud. Who knows, they might really push the boat out, and have the do in one of those posh hotels in Southsea."

Having lifted his newspaper, the corner now lowered.

"You reckon?" he said.

She shrugged, "Might."

"That family haven't two ha'pennies to rub together so unless they're looking at the tallyman to advance them a few bob, it'll be out of the church and into their front room for a slice of sponge cake and a glass of sherry."

"So why am I bothering with a new hat, then?"

"Mother of the groom, doll. It's expected. And you wouldn't want to be outshone by Alice's mother. Would you?"

25

LILITH HAD KNOWN SOMETHING WAS wrong for a while now. She just didn't know exactly what. Helping fill their allotment of plywood crates with all manner of things, from bedding to kitchen knives - you just don't know what we're going to need, her mother had complained, don't know what we can buy there and what we'll curse not having brought with us - she tried to coax out of her what it might be.

"It's all becoming very real now, isn't it?" she said, wrapping a small china shepherdess in a sheet of newspaper.

Her mother didn't answer.

"Are you still having doubts?"

"Always have had. Always will have. Put your finger on here," her mother indicated to where she'd tucked one length of string under another.

"You never know," she said, reaching over, "you might get there and be pleasantly surprised."

"Let's hope so."

About to select another ornament, this one a clumsily painted dog, she instead seized upon the ornately framed photograph taken on the day of her parent's marriage. Sylph-like in her dress and veil, her mother had been clearly unable to hide her joy. Her father was upright and proud.

"You haven't changed much," she smiled, holding it up.

"Rubbish! Life changes all of us."

"Not always for the worse, though."

"Depends."

"Does it? You can't say life hasn't treated our family well. Alfie's getting married next week. I'm stepping out on my own. And you and dad and Ruby are off on this big adventure. Don't you think all that's something to be proud of?"

"Hardly feels like an adventure at the moment. Just feels more like hard work. Not to mention the worry of making sure nothing's left behind."

Lilith laughed. "Well if you did forget something, I could always send it on."

"I'd rather you didn't have the bother. You'll be in a place of your own by then."

Her mother got to her feet and rubbing the small of her back, bent first one way then the other.

"It will be strange," Lilith said. "I hope I can manage by myself."

"I'm sure you will. You're a good girl Lil. I'm going to miss you."

"I'm going to miss you too. All of you."

"You have to get your father to help you shift all your things over. When is it? Week after next?"

Lilith nodded. "I won't need much, though. Just my clothes and a few personal bits and pieces. The room already comes with most of the furniture I could ever need."

"You'll still have to make it homely, so take your own bed-clothes. You mark my words; you'll need that eiderdown come autumn. I know what these places are like. Perishing, half of them. And you can help yourself to what I'm leaving behind. Should tide you over until you can afford new. This Grace person? You can rely on her to be a good friend once we're gone?"

"Oh yes. She's wonderful. It's amazing, we've so much in common."

Still contorting, her mother raised an eyebrow. "You will write and let me know if things don't work out, won't you."

"Of course, I will. And I'll be straight out on the next boat."

Lilith knew that was never going to happen. Arranging to take the room at Mrs Gainsborough's might not be sensible but the alternative, to move into in lodgings with lingering odours of boiled cabbage and damp, and the continual banging of cold water pipes was unthinkable. Or so she told herself. And now she and Grace had so much planned. Political rallies to attend, speeches to hear, causes to fight. All that on top of teaching, of course. From now on her life was going to be so terribly full and exciting she wouldn't have a moment to call her own.

"You do that," her mother replied, closing her eyes and gritting her teeth.

Lilith stopped what she was doing.

"Are you all right?"

"Just need a moment. Look you carry on. I'm just popping out to the lav." One hand on her lower belly she made it to the door only to stop and place her hand on the frame.

"Mum?"

"I said I'm fine."

Hauling herself upright her mother stepped out into the hallway and a moment later the back door banged shut.

Lilith got on with the cutlery. Each spoon had to be individually wrapped and then, once bundled together, the whole lot tied with twine. After that, it was the turn of the knives and then the forks, all three packages going in the crate along with the best cruet set, two lace tablecloths, the doilies, antimacassars and other treasures.

Having finished one pile, she got to her feet. Her mother had been a while. Surely too long? Peering first from the kitchen window, she went out into the hall and opened the back door. The privy, a brick outhouse with a wooden door and iron latch, was in the corner of the yard, next to the coal shed.

Despite her concerns, she felt a little uneasy at invading someone's privacy.

"Mum?"

The answer was little more than a faint groan, and skirting the empty barrels and crates she tapped lightly on the door.

"Mum?"

"Go away, Lilith."

"Not until you tell me you're alright."

"Of course I'm alright. Now go back inside."

Clearly something was wrong. But the yard was not the place for a fuss. Not with neighbours only feet away. Her mother would die of embarrassment.

"I'll go in then."

There was no response.

"Mum?"

"Just…go…indoors."

Her mother was pale when she re-entered the kitchen.

"Are you going to tell me what's wrong?" Lilith said.

"Nothing's wrong. Just something I ate."

"That's not true, is it? You've been like this for weeks now."

There'd been plenty of clues, she'd just been too busy with her own life to pay much attention. Things like her mother's recent habit of picking at the food on her plate before discarding it altogether. She'd put that down to simple loss of appetite, emigrating was, after all, an enormously stressful undertaking and at her age it couldn't be easy. And how many times had she walked in and found her cradling her stomach, or rubbing her back? And the shadows under her eyes and hollow cheeks? Why hadn't she noticed these things before?

"Do you need anything?" she asked.

Her mother was at the sink, filling a glass with water.

"No. Like I keep telling you, it's something I ate. It'll pass."

She shook her head. "I'm not so sure. I think you should see a doctor."

"Lilith," slamming down the glass her mother spun around, "if you don't want to help me with all this packing, then don't. But stop going on about things you know nothing about. All right?"

26

THE RATTLING OF TEA CUPS in the cafe overlooking the esplanade was frankly, beginning to get on Lilith's nerves.

"I have no idea what is wrong with her," she said, pushing aside the remaining mouthful of apple pie.

Grace lowered her own fork. "You have a right to be worried, you're her daughter."

"But why won't she say anything?"

"Perhaps she doesn't want to worry you."

Lilith shook her head. "I should have noticed sooner. She's complained of aches and pains for ages. I just didn't think."

"Don't blame yourself. She could have taken you into her confidence, but for her own reasons she chose not to. Has she seen a doctor?"

She nodded. "That's the funny thing. She had to, for the medical certificate."

"And he passed her as being fit?"

"He did."

"Then perhaps it's not as serious as you think."

Once again she shook her head, and picking up a knife, set it back down again, squaring it with her plate. "I wish I could be sure."

"It could be an age thing, you know."

"No," she let the word hang for a moment before adding, "I think she's hiding something,"

"But if that was the case, wouldn't the doctor have discovered it when he examined her?"

"You'd have thought so, wouldn't you?"

Grace was clearly sceptical. "So you think she somehow managed to fool him into giving her a clean bill of health?"

Even she had to agree it sounded unlikely.

"I don't know what to think. But I know she wants to see dad happy, and that includes making sure nothing would stand in the way of his dream."

"The way it should be between those who love each other. Has anyone else spoken to her about it?"

Grace's hand had come to rest lightly on hers, and suddenly it was hard to concentrate.

"I've no idea. I doubt Ruby would. And dad? Well, he's so wrapped up in New Zealand she'd have to drop dead before he'd notice."

"You should try talking to her again."

"And have her jump down my throat like last time? No thanks! But I am going to keep an eye on things."

"And if it should turn out to be serious?"

She fought the impulse to turn her hand and let her fingers entwine with Grace's.

"I'd rather not think about that."

"Why?"

"Because if she really is ill and still insists on going, she'll need me with her."

"Surely you don't mean that?" Grace looked horrified.

She swallowed. "What else can I do?"

"There must be something."

"Let's not think about it. I can't bear the thought of losing the room. And then there's everything we've planned. I'll be letting you down as well, not to mention the union."

"You won't be letting anyone down because you're not going anywhere. I won't let you."

Lilith wondered if Grace had any idea her fingers had tightened. Or if she could possibly know how much the gesture meant. For one crazy moment she wished they were somewhere else. Just the two of them. Alone…

"You make it sound so simple," she said.

"It is. At least as far as I'm concerned," and still holding her hand, Grace leaned forward. "I think you need cheering up."

"You could be right."

"Let's go out tonight. You and me."

"Go out? Where?"

"I know a nice little club. It's quiet, discreet. We can have a few cocktails and chat. You can even stay over if you like. Mrs G. won't mind a bit and that way you won't have the worry of the last bus home. How does that sound?"

"A cocktail bar?" she laughed. "I knew it!"

"Knew what?"

"It's what you warned me about in Bettys that day."

Grace looked puzzled, so she carried on, "Mmm. Have you forgotten? You threatened to lead me astray."

"Oh, that's right. It's a yes then?"

"I'll need to change."

"Me too. Shall we fix a time to meet again later?"

"Lets."

Though as she said it, her heart sank.

27

RUBY KNEW EXACTLY WHAT LILITH should wear of course.

"Oh Lil," she gushed. "A cocktail bar. How totally spiffing."

"You might think so, but I haven't got the right clothes for a place like that. I'll be completely out of place. Good grief, I'm not a flapper. Never have been, and never wanted to be."

"Leave everything to me."

"Wait… stop…" thrown by her sister's enthusiasm, she held up her hands. "I don't want you to dress me. Just give me your opinion."

Wardrobe door wide open, she was easing out hanger after hanger.

"No, not that," Ruby said, hovering at her shoulder and pulling a face. "Oh God no! You couldn't wear that either."

"Why not?"

"Because it's drab and it's dowdy. Come on Lil," she pleaded. "Give me a chance. I'll have you looking so snazzy men will fall over themselves to buy you a drink."

"That's not what I want. Grace and I are going somewhere to talk. Just the two of us. No men, and certainly none that would trip over their own feet."

"Yes well, we'll see about that," was the murmured come-back. "Try this," and she pulled out the dress Bert had so admired.

"I'm not quite sure…" Lilith began.

"What's wrong with it?"

"Nothing. It's just a little shorter than I would usually wear."

And a little brighter. And a little more daring.

"Exactly. You're going to a bar, Lil. Not a gathering of underpaid teachers."

"But what goes with it?"

"What do you mean?" Ruby was looking puzzled.

"Well, the neckline is awfully low."

"Not once it's on."

"I'm really not sure…"

The dress was held against her.

"How can you say that? It's perfect. Well, maybe not perfect," her sister stepped back, head on one side, nose wrinkled up, "It could be a little glitzier and it's not exactly as glam as it should be. If you want to get noticed, that is."

"I don't."

"Then it'll pass."

"Ruby… look, I don't think it's me."

"Well I do. And besides, what else have you got?"

That was the problem she thought, wondering yet again why she'd agreed to go out that evening. Grace was bound to turn up in something terrifically stylish and the very latest thing. No doubt bought in London at one of those swanky stores. She, on the other hand, was wearing a borrowed dress. Oh God, she'd think her such a frump. Worse, she'd never ask her out again.

"Oh, all right," she reached for the coat-hanger.

"Shoes?" Ruby asked.

"What?"

"Shoes. What are you wearing on your feet?"

"Oh Lord!"

"Elsie's then. I've still got them."

"Oh, this is going to be a disaster."

"'Course it's not," Ruby insisted, reaching into the bottom of the wardrobe.

"But what if they don't fit."

"Try them."

Balancing on one foot Lilith slipped the other into the strappy shoe.

"Do they pinch?"

"No. If anything they're a little big," she said, looking down and lifting her ankle.

"Easily remedied. I'll just tighten the buckle," and Ruby crouched down. "Now the other one."

The flared heels certainly made her feel different, she thought, straightening and pulling her shoulders back. Provided she could cope with the strain on her calf muscles.

She was reaching for the dress again when Ruby grabbed her arm.

"Not so fast. We've still got a bit of work to do first."

Her sister could be so very irritating at times. "Like what?"

"If madam would kindly sit on the bed, Miss Ruby Doherty, make-up artiste to the stars, will transform her into a goddess of the silver-screen."

"Heavens no!"

"Heavens yes. You don't want to be the only half-dressed female in the place, do you?"

"I suppose not."

"Well then."

Handing their coats over to the cloakroom attendant Lilith thanked her lucky stars they'd agreed to meet at the bus-stop, for she'd have died if she'd had to walk into the club alone. A little dimmer and far more intimate than she'd expected, and with more ebony and gold paint than she'd ever seen in her lifetime, an aromatic fug of cigarettes and perfume enveloped her the moment they stepped through the curtains.

"Where shall we sit?"

One hand on the balustrade, Grace was searching the edge of the tiny checkerboard dancefloor, and seeing those tables were already filling up and must therefore be popular, Lilith suggested one midway between the stage and the bar.

"There," Grace pointed, and having tucked a proprietorial arm through hers and led her down the short flight of stairs, they made their way between clusters of bright young things, all seemingly engaged in amusing small talk.

Grace leaned in to make herself heard over the pounding rhythm of a jungle beat and a rough and tumble trumpet solo.

"Amazing, isn't it? It's the very essence of Harlem."

More than a little overwhelmed, she nodded. "I had no idea such places existed around here."

They didn't bother with the glossy drinks menus littering the table. Instead, and trying not to gape at the waiter's tight matador-style trousers and the revelation of dark, springy curls peeking out from the unbuttoned neck of his white shirt, Lilith nodded her approval to the order of two Sidecars as if drinking cocktails was something she did on a regular basis. Only when he'd hoist his tray and melted into the crowd did she sit forward to ask exactly what she'd agreed to.

"Cognac, orange liqueur and lemon juice."

"Sounds very potent."

"It is rather."

"Well, I suppose there's always a first time."

"And a second, if you like it. And if you don't, we'll order something different."

Grace appeared faintly amused, and Lilith wondered if she'd somehow committed a social faux pas? What it something she'd said? Or did? Or was it what she was wearing? She'd known the dress wasn't right the moment she'd put it on. And as for the ridiculous headband Ruby had insisted she wear... Or was it the make-up. That was it. She should never have let her loose with her brushes and powders, regardless the Cleopatra look - complete with sweeping wings of heavy black kohl - was supposed to be so very *in*.

"I can't get over how different you look," Grace said. "It's as if I'm seeing a completely new you."

Lilith cringed. "Believe me, it was not my idea."

"But I like it."

"As you said, though, it's not me."

"Actually, that's not what I said. I said it's like seeing a new you. And it's quite intriguing."

"Is it?"

"Yes. And I'm wondering what else I might discover about you tonight."

"Oh, I hardly think…"

Blushing and flustered she turned to watch those on the dancefloor. But her mortification didn't end there, for when their drinks arrived she reached for the stemmed glass and took far too large a sip of the concoction. She wasn't sure what was worse, the overpowering waft going up her nose, the intense taste itself, or the unladylike coughing fit she had to contend with afterwards.

"Good?" Grace lifted her own glass.

"Am I required to be diplomatic?" she squeaked, still trying to catch her breath.

"Not at all."

"I think it's a little strong for me."

Grace didn't seem at all put out. "Then let's order something else."

"No, please. I'm perfectly alright for the moment."

Intending to make the drink last all night if necessary, she toyed with the swivel stick while wondering what on earth she was thinking, agreeing to come to such a place. Everyone else, Grace included, was dressed in the very latest style, while she must look like the poor relation, for not only did her dress lack beading or metallic thread, she wasn't wearing dozens of bracelets on her wrists, or ropes of pearls around her neck.

And Ruby was right, hemlines were rising alarmingly.

"Grace, darling! I thought it was you."

He'd arrived out of nowhere, arms wide and smiling broadly, and leaning down greeted her in the continental fashion; with pursed lips brushing each cheek. Lilith dismissed him immediately. The long silk scarf and the flamboyantly patterned waistcoat were so terribly contrived. Didn't he know they were in Portsmouth and not on the French Riviera? Nor did her opinion waver when raising his eyes in her direction he studied her lazily before offering, "I don't think I've had the pleasure?"

"Roland, do behave!" laughing, Grace scolded him. "Lilith, this is Roland Cavendish-Shaw. An absolute scoundrel and a very good friend. Roland, Lilith Doherty."

Bowing low, he lifted her hand to his lips.

"Enchantèe mademoiselle."

Her cool response, merely a half-hearted 'Mmmm', triggered a questioning eyebrow. But nothing more. Rather, he turned his attention back to Grace.

"We missed you at Ginny's last week."

"I know. I just couldn't get up into town, you know what it's like."

"Actually darling, I don't, since I haven't to deal with a headmistress bearing down on me every five minutes. Anyway, she was very cross with you."

"Tell her I'll make it up to her. Soon."

"You'd better. And bring your little friend with you," he fixed Lilith with an unflattering look. "The more the merrier, I say."

"Who was that?" she asked once he'd left, and she'd finished rolling her eyes at the handful of kisses blown in her direction.

"He's Minnie's brother. And before you ask, Minnie is one of the leading lights of the NUWT. That's how I know him. They've not a lot in common regardless they have the same parents, and perhaps that's just as well. He's a shocking ladies' man as you might have guessed."

"He's making that quite clear," Lilith said, nodding to where the subject of their conversation was carelessly topping up the wide-bowled champagne glasses of four giggling young women, each seemingly hanging on his every word.

"Another?" Grace was indicating Lilith's own glass, which still held at least half the original contents.

"Oh no. I'm still enjoying this one."

An incredulous eyebrow was raised. "Really?"

Knowing she'd been caught out, she blushed. "Perhaps something different this time."

But Grace was looking past her and turning she saw a majestic woman in a jewelled turban and long satin coat bearing down on them.

"Grace, how divine. I see the usual crowd are here. Hard to believe this place just gets more and more popular, and it's not as if they don't already charge enough to get in. It's the band of course. Can we share, darling? Or do you want to be alone?"

Before anyone could respond she'd turned to Lilith. "I don't think we've met, at least not that I recall. I'm Rose and this," she announced, "is Constance. Connie for short."

"Or to my friends," the girl stepped forward. Lilith thought her dress the most delightful she'd ever seen.

"We're just having a quiet drink," Grace demurred.

"In that case, we'll stay only long enough to catch up on all the latest gossip, and then leave you to it," and with a meaningful glance, Rose pulled out a chair.

28

"I MUST SAY, you do seem to know an awful lot of people."

Opening the door to her room and ushering Lilith inside, Grace laughed, "don't I! And they all seemed to come out of the woodwork tonight of all nights."

"It was fun."

"It was. But not what I'd intended when I suggested we went out. We've hardly had a moment to ourselves."

"But I had a great time. And I like your friends, especially Connie. She had me in fits over some of the things she was saying."

Dropping into what was fast becoming her favourite spot, Lilith kicked off Elsie's shoes and curled up. She felt so blissfully content. Of course, it could be the lovely evening they'd had and the cocktails she tried, but she didn't think so. It was more the company and the fact she and Grace were uncannily alike, even thinking along the same lines. It just made everything that much easier. The connection had been there tonight too, regardless how many people stopped by their table to say hello, though she'd been a little uncomfortable at first, thinking they might try to monopolise Grace or draw her away. But she needn't have worried.

"Yes, she's a hoot, isn't she? And so different from Rose. If ever there was an example of chalk and cheese, they are it."

"How do they know each other?"

"Through work. Rose is in accounting."

Lilith was massaging her feet. "And Connie?"

"In the typing department. From what I understand they met in the works canteen. Of course, they've been together a while now."

"Together?"

"As lovers, I mean."

"Oh."

She felt incredibly stupid, for while she'd picked up on the shared intimacies and the occasional private joke she'd put such things down to a long-standing friendship. Even when Connie took to the dancefloor. Watching her kicking and wiggling her way through the Charleston, how could she have mistaken Rose's adoring expression for anything other than it was?

Rummaging in a cupboard, Grace looked up. "You're not shocked, are you?"

Was she? Perhaps a little. But not in the way Grace might be thinking.

"No, not at all."

"Good. You'd be surprised how many bigots and narrow-minded people I've met in my time, and I can tell you it's not a pleasant experience. These days I just try to avoid them. Life's too short, as they say."

Mouth a little dry, she ventured, "Do you have many such friends?"

Having found what she was searching for, Grace straightened.

"A few. Mainly in London though, and that's probably due to the size of the place. Being a different race, colour, creed or sexuality seems a little more acceptable up there. Not that it's ever easy at the best of times."

"Why not?"

"You really don't know?"

"No."

"Generally speaking, people tend to be uncomfortable around those who don't conform to society's expectations. So those who are different in any way usually try to fit in. Sometimes it works, sometimes it doesn't," she said, dropping the spare nightdress onto the bed.

"And your friends," Lilith said carefully. "Do they manage to fit in?"

"Not all of them. Some are quite frankly outrageous," and she laughed. "But being creative types like artists and writers the public tend to be more lenient with them. In fact, in some quarters, it's almost expected."

"I see."

"But that doesn't mean it's the same for a teacher."

Lilith gaped.

"If you take this path," her friend continued gently, "you'll be rejecting everything society offers. A husband, children, stability. And respectability. Then there's your career. At best you may be held over for promotion, at worst you could even lose your position altogether."

She was finding it hard to breathe. She knew! Oh God, she knew. But how? She'd been so careful, even finding excuses not to meet up on the odd occasion. She could deny everything of course. Laugh it off as a misunderstanding. Her? Attracted to someone of her own sex? Heavens no! It would be a little embarrassing for a while, but they'd get over it.

Clearing her throat, she asked instead, "How would they know?"

"A chance meeting when you're with your lover. An observation on the lack of men in your life. A comment on your living arrangements. There are all sorts of ways."

"I see."

"You would have to become adept at keeping secrets, even from those you love. Your sister, for example. You'd wear two faces, have two lives, one open and the other hidden. And you'd learn to conceal your emotions and never show affection, such as touching or hold hands in public like any other couple might do. You can't even look too long into her eyes, for fear someone might notice. And then there's the rejection from those whose friendship you thought was invincible. Can you imagine what it's like to confide in someone you've known for years, only to have them turn from you in disgust?"

"No. I can't."

"And it doesn't stop there. There are those who believe that falling in love with a person of the same sex is a medical abnormality that can be treated and cured. But even in our scientifically advanced world, the treatment for anyone willing to undergo it is not pleasant; I can assure you."

Lilith felt herself pale. "Go on."

"Electric shock therapy, chemicals, all very nasty. And let's add being condemned from the pulpit to the list. You will be singled out and castigated as immoral and having turned from God and His teachings, those same scriptures that tell us to love one another despite their weaknesses."

Grace fell silent.

"And is that how you feel too?" Lilith asked quietly.

She hoped for understanding. At worst, she'd take compassion. But searching those pale eyes she saw something else. Something that gave her hope their friendship could survive even this.

"How could you ever think that of me."

Drawn her to her feet she crumpled into Grace's arms. "I love you," she heard the words leave her mouth as if uttered by someone else. "I'm sorry, but I do. It's not something I planned, and the truth is I have no idea what else I can say to put things right. If you want me to go, I will. If you never want to see me again, I'll accept that too."

"Why would I want you to go?"

It was wonderful and it was terrifying. As if a tornado had rushed through the room, tossing her up and whirling her over and over.

"Really?" she gabbled.

"Really. I can't believe you didn't guess I felt the same way about you."

"You did? You do? Why didn't you say something?"

"How could I? You might have been horrified. Anyway, I was too frightened of losing you."

Sliding her arms around Grace's neck, Lilith laughed. "That's exactly how I felt. So when did you know?"

"The moment I saw you take on Bill Marsden. How could anyone, man or woman, resist such a gorgeous firecracker!"

29

TAKING ANOTHER SWIG OF THE medicine she kept on top of the cupboard, her third in quick succession, Dilys was no longer sure when the stuff had lost its potency. She knew one thing though, the advice from the place she bought it from, of just one teaspoon three times a day, no longer did the trick.

"Ruby still in bed?" Jim asked, coming through to the kitchen and throwing his paper onto the arm of his chair.

Hastily wiping the corners of her mouth with the back of her hand she slipped the bottle into the pocket of her pinafore.

"Where else?"

"Given up on the job front has she?"

"Looks like it. Honest to God, you'd think her world had come to an end the way she's carrying on."

"She'll get over it, once she's on the boat."

Knowing he'd want a cup of tea, she filled the kettle and set it on the stove to boil. "Seems funny not having Alfie around."

Jim looked up. "It's only been a few days. Anyway, you'll be glad you don't have his washing any more, girl."

"Maybe. Have to say, she looked a picture, Alice did."

"So did you, all decked up to the nines."

"Wasn't so keen on her mother's outfit, though. Not even sure it was new. And as for that Beryl, well," and she huffed, "why on earth they even invited her I've no idea."

"Friend of the family, I suppose."

"Friend to anyone in trousers I've heard. And did you see the way she came on to the vicar? Bloody disgraceful."

"He is a single man," Jim ventured, flicking open his paper.

"Doesn't make any difference. And he wasn't any better. Call himself a man of God? He should have been concentrating on our Alfie's nuptials, not madam's cleavage."

"Can't say I noticed anything."

"Jim Doherty! How can you say that! I saw you having a gawp when you thought no one was looking."

"Must have been someone else girl. You know I've only got eyes for you."

And he turned a page.

"Lil seems happy enough in Southsea," she said after a while.

"Mmm."

"And that Grace, well, she comes across as respectable enough."

"She does."

"Nice of her to come to Alfie's wedding like that. Wonder if she's got a brother?"

When Jim looked up, she widened her eyes. "What wrong with that? She's going to have to settle down some day."

"I thought you wanted her out in New Zealand with us."

"I do. I was just thinking aloud, that's all. Anyway, it's good that she's got a place to stay all the while she's teaching and until she's finished college. You did say it was a nice house?"

"Very nice."

"Well, it is in a posh part of town. That helps of course. And her landlady? Lil says she very accommodating."

Jim was scanning the sports page. What was it this time? Portsmouth Football Club hoping for a better season than last year, despite getting to the FA cup for the first time ever? Or was it the dogs? Because if the list running on Saturday at the new greyhound track looked promising, she didn't need telling he'd be thinking about popping along. That is if Ruby could be persuaded to do a shift behind the bar.

"Yes, she's nice too," he said, vaguely.

"Good furniture in the room? Cos that matters, you know. She wants to be comfortable. Nothing clapped out or anything."

"Uh huh."

"You even listening to me?"

"Course."

That was the trouble with blokes, she thought. Flamin' useless when it came to noticing things. Like how their daughter had had taken to her lodgings and whether she was happy. It had only been a week, though, and she was going to try and get over on Saturday for a catch up anyway. That way she could see for herself.

Lil had seemed quite pleased at the thought of a visitor.

Dilys made it to the lav just in time. It was the medicine of course, for while it dulled the pain at first it also crippled her with the runs. But what choice did she have? She could hardly go back to the doctor's surgery. Not when she'd sworn she was better. Suppose he cancelled her certificate? No, she intended to see it through and hope for the best. There were times though she wished it could all be over and done with, like right at that moment, and breathless and perspiring and with the pain coming in crippling waves she knotted her fingers into her bunched up skirt and tried not to think about the fact she was about to throw up. For that's what the cramping did. Not content with squeezing her bowels like a vice, it went all the way back up to her stomach and did the same there.

This time it was really bad.

Dry retching twice, nothing came up. And why should it when she'd hardly eaten these past weeks. Still didn't stop her body having a go. A port and brandy was what she needed, and she'd get one as soon as she was back indoors. In the meantime, she had to get a grip. Take a few deep breaths. That was when she heard Jim shouting for her. Something about Lil having turned up? She eased forward, cocking her ear to the door but he'd obviously given up on finding her. Of all the time to choose. Not that she didn't want to see her daughter. Of course she did. But she couldn't let her catch her like this.

Getting to her feet she shut her eyes quickly, for blood was pounding in her ears and making her feel nauseous again. But if she didn't put in an appearance pretty smartish, they'd be calling her again. Stepping down from the lav and latching the door behind her, she made her way unsteadily across the yard and into the kitchen. Jim was in his armchair, of course. Lil was sitting at the table. They must have been talking about something, for they went quiet on seeing her.

Clutching the edge of the sink, she heard Lil's chair legs scrape the lino.

"Mum?"

From a long way off, she heard Jim's voice. "Doll?"

As the darkness closed in, and with the faintest of moans, she slid to the floor.

30

LEANING ON THE RAILING OF the third class promenade deck Ruby was thinking how far down it was to the wharf. No longer a hive of activity with stevedores shouting and signalling and derricks hoisting and swinging heavy freight and bulky cargo nets into the hold, now the only commotion was late arrivals paying off taxicabs. Those travelling first class sauntered on board to be greeted by a raft of officers and the steward that would personally direct them to their cabin. The rest, like the Doherty's before them, huffed and puffed under the weight of their luggage to receive only a brochure and a pointing finger at the top of the gangway.

Her second thought came with the cables unfurling from capstans and the Port Authority tugs taking up the slack on the starboard beam to draw the liner away from the quay. Smoke billowed from the single funnel, tainting and shimmering the air and with the *RMS Remuera's* propellers churning filthy seawater into froth there was a noticeable increase in the vibrations beneath her feet.

That was when bile rose from her stomach and coated the back of her throat.

Even had she wanted to, the time for any last minute rebellion was long gone. Seeing the last link with home soil being removed had dealt to that. But it was the mournful blast of the ship's siren that made it all seem so final. That and the rush of emotion from those on shore when the brass band on the wharf struck up *Rule Britannia*. Then the calls and shouts from loved ones had become a deafening wall of noise. Her father had drawn her mother to him, tightening his arm around her shoulders. Others were doing the same. Still more clutched hands. And on the dock as on board, parents held up children, sons and daughters stood closer than ever, friends shouted last minute instructions, to write, to take care, to remember them to others, until with the ship nudging further out into the channel and the gulls wheeling and screeching overhead, that last contact became urgent.

And in some cases, like that of her mother, unbearably frantic.

"Alfie," she screamed, tearing herself away to lean over the railing in a most alarming manner. "Alfie."

"Mum," she and Lilith both reached for her at the same time, though how her mother could see anything through her tears, Ruby had no idea. But it was their father she turned to, sinking into his arms as if all strength had left her.

"Come on now, doll," he said gruffly. "Bear up. Don't let the lad see you like this. Why don't we go and find somewhere to sit for a while?"

"No. I'm not going anywhere. I want to stay here."

"That's fine," he murmured into her hair. "I've got you. Lean on me. That's right. We'll stay right here for as long as you want."

Ruby was conscious of Lilith's hand closing over hers. "It's just so hard to say goodbye sometimes."

She nodded. She would never have said she and her brother were close or anything like that, yet her heart was breaking. And then there was Elsie, down there sobbing into a handkerchief. How were either of them supposed to survive without the other? They'd been best friends since infant's school.

"God, Else," she'd said, hugging her tightly before boarding, "whatever am I going to do without you?"

"I dunno Ruby."

"We've been together so long."

"Yeah. Forever."

"You will write, won't you?"

"Every week. You will write back though?"

"Of course."

"Maybe you might come back one day?"

"Definitely. And when I do," from somewhere she'd dredged a spark of the old Ruby, "I'll be bringing my wealthy husband."

"Can you bring his brother for me?"

"Goes without saying, Else."

As the ship nudged its way down Southampton Waters she blew her nose.

"I didn't see your friend on the quay," she said, after tucking her hankie in her pocket and leaning back on the railing alongside Lilith.

"No."

"That's a shame. It was quite a do, with the band and everything. Oh Lil," she said, only now seeing how pale her sister was, "I'm so sorry. I truly am."

And when Lilith turned away, her shoulders quaking, she put her arm around her and added. "There will be a teacher's college in Auckland. I'm sure of it."

"I'm sure too. Gosh, how ridiculous I'm being."

"You're not being ridiculous at all. Look, Dad's taking mum inside. You want to go too?" she asked, seeing others were thinking along similar lines.

"No. I'm going to stay out here a little longer."

"Then so will I. You know," she said, twisting to look up at the funnel and bridge. "This has got to be the worst bit. It can only get better from now on."

Her sister nodded. "I'm sure you're right."

Knowing there was little else to say, Ruby fell silent.

Passing the ruins of Netley Abbey and the grand buildings of the Royal Victoria Hospital, the *Remuera* steamed into the Solent on her slow and steady southeast course to round the Isle of Wight. That meant slipping between Portsmouth and Ryde, and that was when Ruby's throat welled again. Lilith too was staring long and hard as if wanting to imprint the sight of home into her memory.

"Funny seeing it all from out here," she said quietly.

Lilith didn't reply.

"You'll be back long before I will."

Her sister turned away as if it were all too much.

Having promised to be hot the weather hadn't disappointed and despite the salt-tanged breeze toying with her skirt and the fact she'd chosen her lightest outfit for her first day on board, Ruby's armpits were feeling disgustingly clammy. Taking off her straw hat and clutching the railing, she leant into the wind.

"Heaven's, look how brown the land is." She wasn't even sure her sister was listening, but that didn't matter. "It's all so very dry in this heat. I wonder if it will be the same when we arrive in New Zealand?"

She was thinking of her trunk in the hold which, thanks to her father's insistence that Auckland would be delightfully warm on their arrival, held more thin skirts, blouses and dresses than anything else.

"Right now it's winter over there," a voice came from behind her. "So no, the grass shouldn't be withered. Should be fairly lush, I'd say, though it could be covered in snow, depending on where you're headed."

Jacket hooked casually over his shoulder, the other hand plunged into the pocket of cream flannel trousers, perhaps more impressive was the hint of well-formed muscles beneath the cotton shirt. They'd been told they'd be mixing with interesting people, and not just those going out in the hope of making a name for themselves, but families going out to settle on the land. And of course, those on their way home. Wondering if the voyage might offer more than she'd allowed, she met his gaze squarely.

"Oh. You sound as if you've been there before?"

"I have. Grew up in Auckland before coming home to finish my studies a few years ago. What about you?"

Politeness dictated a response, but Ruby had no intention of advising all and sundry of her family's personal business. At least, not this early on. A smile would suffice since they were bound to run into each other again.

"Look!" Spying an outcrop of white rocks, and hanging onto her hat with one hand she grabbed Lilith's arm with the other. "Aren't those the Needles? Oh, and there's the lighthouse too."

"Our last sighting of old Blighty," her new friend said, following her gaze.

Feeling her sister tense, she replied coldly, "Thank you. I think we can work that out for ourselves."

"Ouch! I'll put that down to another example of the famous British reserve I've come to know and dislike. You know," he continued as if she hadn't given him the cold shoulder and nothing were amiss, "I think we're going to enjoy each other's company over the coming weeks."

"Really?"

"No doubt about it. The name's Ralph," and when she gave no indication of replying, he added, "And now, if you would excuse me, I think I'll go and unpack."

"Heavens! Two minutes on board, and already you have an admirer," Lilith said once he'd gone.

"Must be losing my touch."

"Why?"

"Well, he didn't exactly hang around, did he?"

"Did you expect him to? You were incredibly rude."

"Nonsense. Men like a challenge. You watch, he'll be searching the entire ship for me before nightfall."

31

EVEN WITH THEIR LEATHER SUITCASES tucked under the bed and out of the way there was little room in the two berth cabin when the steward arrived later that day to introduce himself.

"Just gunna go over a few important fings, ladies," he said, tugging on his white jacket and flashing a smile that had it not been for the fact he was no more than five feet tall, would have had the female passengers falling at his feet.

Fings, Lilith noted before asking where he came from.

"Battersea, miss. Could 'ave been born on the water, I could."

"And now you sail on the ocean, Harry," she smiled.

"Hexackerly. Right then. Shall we start wiv these 'ere life jackets?"

He passed over two cork and canvas vests and hearing Ruby complaining loudly as she tried to get the thing on, Lilith hoped for safety sake they would never have the need for them. It wouldn't be pleasant getting her into hers, even in the unthinkable situation she might be more terrified of not doing so.

"That's right ladies, one pad at the back, two at the front. Now tie the straps up nice and tight...lovely... good... right-oh, you can take 'em off now. Unless you want to keep 'em on for a special occasion?"

Ruby's scowl showed she for one couldn't see the funny side of his little joke.

"Now," he picked up again, but not before giving her sister a grin, "you got second sitting in the dining room. Gives yer a bit of a lie-in in the mornings. And if you wants a bit o' quiet we 'ave a library. And then there's always the Ladies Room. Men ain't allowed in there."

"Thank you. We'll be sure to find them."

Harry drew a small notebook from his pocket. "Ablutions," he continued. "Bathroom is down the passageway and to the right. Your bath time miss," flicking over the pages he stopped and glanced up at her, "is seven am. And yours, miss will be seven thirty."

"That will be fine," she said before Ruby could make any protest.

"This time of year it should be fairly smoove all the way to Curacao, where we'll be picking up fuel before heading into the Panama Canal."

"A journey of two weeks, is that right?"

"Right miss. Even so, if you ain't feeling well, just let me know, though unfortunately there ain't no cure for seasickness. Just ask Lord Nelson, he had it real bad. But I can bring you a cup of ginger tea to help settle yer stomachs. Other than that, you just has to get on with things until you gets yer proper sea legs."

"We'll remember that."

"Good. Lastly, see this 'ere bell?"

Two heads swivelled obediently.

"If you need anyfink, that'll get me. And don't forget," he said, stepping back into the passageway, "keep an eye on the notice boards. They'll be lots to keep everyone occupied over the next few weeks and yer don't want to miss out, do yer? Not two lovely ladies such as yerselves."

"Gracious," Ruby sputtered, once he'd gone.

"Gracious indeed."

"Well, I don't know about you, but I'm going off to find those notice boards he was talking about. You coming?" Having eased between the bunks to peer into the mirror over the washbasin, her sister was touching the tip of her little finger to the corner of her mouth.

"Might as well. I'll knock next door and let them know."

"Lilith," the reflection was stony and the tone flat, "we're adults. And that means we don't have to tell our parents everything we do anymore."

"It's hardly that."

"So what? You think they might worry about us. Look around you. We're on a ship. If they want to find us there's only so many places to look," she said, retrieving her hat from the bed and turning to the mirror once more.

"Now," she said a moment later, "shall we go?"

It took only a day or two for her sister to settle into shipboard life, so much so that even Lilith was hard pushed to know where she might be found at times. Deck quoits or tennis before luncheon, then perhaps a nap during the warmest part of the day. Mid-afternoon she was usually with her new friends in the lounge, or in a deckchair with her latest admirer enjoying the temperate breezes. And of course, there were dances in the evening. She, on the other hand, found it hard to show interest in anything. Even the lectures and talks in the dining-room came a poor second to the quiet corner in the library where she poured out her heart to Grace in letters popped into the mail bag in the Ships Office for collection at each port of call.

Their mother was even less sociable, and not just because of her condition and the worry she might be seen as unwell. A debilitating bout of seasickness kept her in her bunk and while their father was properly sympathetic, having his wife indisposed for most of the day left him free to spend his time in the smoking room and bar surrounded by others of like mind. And if not there, strolling the decks in his newly acquired linen jacket and boater hat - a must for the more temperate climate, he'd informed his family on returning from his shopping expedition, not a week before they'd sailed.

Now, leaning on the ship's railing she and Ruby, along with her father and a good few other passengers were mulling on their surrounds and trying to get to grips with the sheer scale of the endeavour to link two oceans with a canal.

"A marvel of modern engineering. Did you know a series of locks have been built to lift us up eighty-five feet? And that," he turned to them both, "is the difference between the level of the Atlantic Ocean and the level of the Pacific Ocean. Can you imagine that? A variance of eighty-five feet?"

"Amazing," Ruby agreed, although without anywhere near the same enthusiasm.

"The entire system is forty miles long, and you see those wire hawsers connected to the ship? Well, they're attached to electric motors that power us through this bit."

"Incredible."

"Even more impressive if you ask me, the electricity itself comes from a hydro-electric plant up there," he said, pointing up into the hills.

"Unbelievable."

Clearly not realising his audience wasn't anywhere near as enthralled with the facts and figures he was sharing, and knowing at any moment she would start giggling, Lilith had to look away as he carried on, "And between us and the next lock there's the artificial lake we have to cross. Even at full steam, it will take us twenty-four hours to do it."

"Just staggering."

"I couldn't have put it better myself." A newcomer was extending a hand to their father. "Ralph Macintyre."

Though his eyes had narrowed at the interruption, their father recovered quickly.

"Jim Doherty. And my daughters Ruby and Lilith."

Ralph swept off his hat. "I know. We've already met."

"Oh?"

Lilith's heart sank, for their father was looking decidedly unimpressed.

"As we were leaving Southampton. We just happened to be standing in the same spot as we passed the Isle of Wight. Isn't that so."

"It is," Ruby replied. "though I can't say I've seen much of you since, Mr Macintyre."

"Ralph, please. And no. Unfortunately, this is as much a working trip as anything else."

"Working?" their father questioned.

"All rather boring really. I'm making good use of my time on board to polish up on some engineering detailing which might end up having a bearing on a project I'll be involved with."

"Really?"

"Oh, nothing exciting. But it pays to keep abreast of these things."

"No sense in reinventing the wheel," her father agreed.

"Exactly."

"So, you're an engineer then?"

Her father's entire demeanour had changed.

"A civil engineer. Roads, bridges, tunnels. That sort of thing."

"Work that will always be in demand."

Oh God, Lilith thought, he's wondering if he might have found a potential husband for one of us.

Their father was nodding as if he and Ralph Macintyre were already kindred spirits. "And you are setting out for the Empire."

"Not exactly. I'm going home."

A look of surprise flashed over her father's features. "And yet I can't detect an accent."

"My parents are from Buckinghamshire. And while they haven't left their adopted country these past fifteen years, I've spent the last five in London, and I can assure you, living in a metropolis will soon cure any hint of a rogue dialect."

"And you were studying?"

"I was. And having qualified, and with a couple of years in the field so to speak, I'm on my way back to join the family firm."

"Ah ha! And that would be in…"

No longer amused, Lilith was mortified. For their father wasn't so much having a conversation as conducting an interrogation. At least that was how it seemed.

Thankfully Ralph didn't seem at all bothered.

"Auckland."

Hoping to prevent a new line of questioning, she placed her hand on her father's chest. But Ruby was already ahead of her.

"Father," her sister said, smiling sweetly at both men, "would you mind if Lilith and I left you alone for a while? This is all terribly interesting," she waved her hand at nothing in particular, "but the truth is, the sun at this time of day can be a little too intense."

Father? Lilith's eyebrows shot towards her hairline.

"Not at all. Off you go, both of you. And perhaps someone might pop in and see if your mother would like to enjoy this marvellous spectacle?"

As she allowed herself to be drawn away, their father was saying to Ralph, "I would think that this must be of great interest to you?"

"It is. And not purely from the construction aspect though of course that is simply astounding. But the human endeavour. The cost in lives."

"Indeed. I was only just reading…" his voice carried as Ruby pushed open the door.

"God save us!"

"I don't understand. Why did you drag me away?"

"Didn't you see the way he looked at me?"

"Who, Ralph Macintyre?"

"Of course Ralph Macintyre. Who else was standing with us? He's angling to get to know me better, and he wants it to be above board with Dad's approval and all that."

"Are you sure?"

"Don't be silly. Anyone could have seen it."

"Well, he seems nice enough."

"Nice?" her sister screwed up her nose as if confronted with an unpleasant smell. "Who want's *nice*?"

"Some girls would."

"Not me. Not when you can have *exciting*."

She nodded. "I suppose you're right."

"I am. And anyway, what have I got in common with someone who wants to spend his time studying when there's so much shipboard entertainment up for grabs."

Absolutely nothing, Lilith thought.

"Shame though," her sister shrugged, "because he's not bad looking."

"Well there you are then."

"Sometimes that's not enough." Nudging and giggling she continued, "Luckily there are plenty who do fit the bill. At least, if I were to let them. Can't see any reason to limit myself, though. Not this early on. And there's enough to go around too."

"Is there?"

It was hard to raise even one jot of enthusiasm. Not that she cared.

"There is. I bet even you could find someone you liked. Why don't you come to the dance tonight? Give it a whirl. And if Ralph Macintyre's there, why you can sit in a corner with him."

Their mother was in the Ladies Lounge, lying back in an armchair and fanning herself with a periodical she must have removed from a nearby stack.

"Heavens, it's hot," she said, looking up at their approach.

"You don't have to tell us. We've been outside with dad," Ruby dropped down beside her. "The deck is just baking, and everyone's frying and searching for shade."

"I'll be happier when things are back to normal. English people were never meant for weather like this. Look around you. We're wilting, every one of us."

Lilith did just that and her mother was right, there did seem to be a lot of red-faced and perspiring women in the salon.

"It'll be tolerable once we're in the Pacific and heading south. But how are you feeling?" she wanted to know.

"Much better."

"Good. Did you want to go outside?"

"No. I'm quite happy where I am, now the ship isn't rocking anymore."

Lilith smiled. "According to Harry, we've had a good sailing so far."

"Really," her mother's tone implied she doubted that. "Then all I can say is he wasn't on the same voyage. You have no idea how lucky you are. Some of us have been suffering terribly. Take Mrs McGrath over there - for heaven's sake don't look round, or she'll know we're talking about her."

Having already noticed the large bosomed, red-cheeked woman in a dress far too heavy and restricting for the climate, both girls quickly averted their eyes.

"Lost her husband recently," their mother continued in a hushed voice, "going out to live with her son and his family. Anyway, yesterday was the first time she was able to leave her cabin, poor thing. So you see, not everyone gets over this terrible seasickness as easily as you two did."

"We do know," Ruby assured her. "And don't forget while Lil only had it a few days, mine is still going on."

"But it hasn't kept you in your bunk like mum," Lilith thought it only fair to point out. "Nor does it seem to get in the way of your enjoying yourself."

"Only after I've stopped throwing up each morning. Anyway, you have to make the effort to be friendly on board a ship like this."

"Of course you do," their mother agreed, reaching for her youngest daughter's hand. "You never know who you might meet."

It seemed both parents had the same idea in mind.

Ruby gave her a sly glance. "I'd say most people have found their sea legs by now. The dining room is quite full up these days."

She knew her sister was referring to the number of single young men on the voyage who regardless of weather conditions never seemed to lose their appetites. That meant meal times were often a source of amusement, especially after breakfast when decisions were being made as to the day's activities. There would be joshing and joking as challenges were offered, whether it was deck cricket or press ups in the gymnasium, after which glances would flicker in the direction of the young ladies dawdling over their oatmeal. Looks to which Ruby was not averse to returning.

"Well, I'm glad to hear it. And I'm looking forward to us sitting down as a family tonight and enjoying dinner."

"Me too," Ruby said, though with about as much enthusiasm as she'd given to the Panama Canal earlier.

32

CROSSING THE EQUATOR, AND in the warm seas of the Pacific Ocean, they came across flying fish and large pods of spouting whales, sights that naturally enthused Jim Doherty.

You should see him, Lilith wrote to Grace that night, *it's as if the weight of the entire world has been lifted from his shoulders. Thankfully Mum is over her terrible seasickness, and seeing them strolling the decks together is such a relief. Now my only hope is that Auckland lives up to its promise and if that should happen and mum's other problem can be kept at bay, then my darling I will be back on the very next sailing. So keep an eye open for that flat we dreamed about, the one on the sea-front. I can't wait to take coffee with you on the balcony. Nor for the day we're able to shut our very own door on this censoring world and be truly one. Not that I can see society embracing our union any day soon!*

Lilith's letter was sent from the Pitcairn Islands, home of the mutinous Fletcher Christian's descendants and a place of palms, bananas, pineapples, papaya and other tropical vegetation, as proved when the islanders paddled out in their boats to offer fruits and curios to those on board.

It was also where Ruby chose to confide in Lilith.

"I didn't think about it at first," she said, sitting across on her narrow bunk. "You know how I am with my monthlies. All over the place. And then when I missed the next one and the one after that, I thought it was everything going on around us. You know, emigrating and all. That's why I wasn't bothered."

Lilith stared. "How many Ruby? How many have you missed?"

"Five counting this last one."

"*Five?* For God sake! Five? And you never once thought?"

"No."

Calculating backwards, she was thinking hard. If her last period had arrived in February… then who, other than her sister, was to blame for such an appalling situation.

"Do you know who the father is?" she asked.

Ruby's head shot up. "Of course I know," she snapped.

"Then who is it?"

"Does it matter?"

"It does to me. And if you want my help…"

"I can't see…"

"Well I can," she insisted. "So who is it?"

"If you really must know, it was Bert."

"Bert? The one whose ship went out to the Indian Ocean? The one you were talking about marrying?"

Ruby nodded.

"Have you told him?"

"Don't be ridiculous."

"Do you intend to?"

"Oh yes. That would be a good idea wouldn't it. I'll just sit down and write him a letter. *Care of HMS Cornwall, Dear Bert, sorry to tell you but you're going to be a father. Oh, and by-the-way, the baby's being born in New Zealand. Any chance you could pop over and make an honest woman of me?*"

Lilith winced.

"He's not interested in me or his child." Ruby continued flatly.

"How do you know?"

"Because he couldn't be bothered to tell me he was leaving when he did. And he didn't write either so I would say that speaks volumes, wouldn't you?"

"Even so…"

"Look Lil, Bert dropped me like a hot potato the moment we'd done it. Now do you understand why I've no intention of telling him? And yes," she went on, no doubt seeing the look on her sister's face, "we only ever did it the once. And no, despite what you might think of me, I've never done it with anyone else. Before or since."

It was enough to break Lilith's heart.

"Did he…?

"Did he what?"

"Did he force himself on you?"

"Did he what! Oh, don't be so silly! Of course he didn't."

"So you're…?"

"I'm what? Spit it out, Lil. Yes, I'm as much to blame as he is."

"I wasn't judging."

"Weren't you?"

"No."

Ruby was fiddling with a fold of her loose, white dress. "I didn't think it was possible to fall on your first time. Isn't that what they say?"

"Yes, well obviously you can."

"Obviously."

Lilith stood up. "So what are you going to do?"

"I have absolutely no idea."

"You'll have to tell mum and dad."

Her sister looked aghast. "Not yet. Not until we're in New Zealand. It'll give us chance to think of something."

"Think of something? What exactly is there to think about? You're having a baby, Ruby."

"You think I don't know that? You will help me, won't you? Please, Lil. I don't know where else to turn."

"What a mess. But we can't wait until we arrive to drop this on mum and dad. I'm sorry, but it has to be done now. You're lucky you're not showing, otherwise the entire ship would be talking about it."

When Ruby shrugged, Lilith rounded on her. "Don't you care? It's not just you, you need to think about. There's other's too."

"Like you, you mean? Scared of being tarred with the same brush, are you?"

"Yes, as it happens."

"Well that's hardly likely, is it?"

"What are you talking about."

"Think I haven't noticed?"

"Noticed what?" Lilith was genuinely perplexed.

"Well by my count, I'm not the only one with a secret."

She didn't need telling the blood had drained from her cheeks.

"You and Grace?" Ruby hinted.

"What about her?"

"You were awfully close. Like at Alfie's wedding? I saw the way you looked at each other. And now you do nothing but write her letters. That is when you're not sobbing yourself to sleep at night."

"She's a friend. That's all," her heart wrenched at the betrayal. "And I think you should be concentrating on your own problem. Not trying to cause trouble for others. Have you even given a thought to what dad's family is going to say when we get there and they find out?"

"Why don't you just come right out with it? Call me a tart and get it over with."

"It's not going to help, though, is it?"

"Might make you feel better."

"Well, it won't. God, how could you be so stupid."

"Maybe I can get rid of it."

Lilith was shocked. "What? And how do you intend to do that?"

"There must be a way. What about gin and a very hot bath? Isn't that the recommended cure where we come from?"

"And if it doesn't work? Or even worse, goes wrong?"

Her sister shrugged.

"No. We need to tell mum right now," she said. "She'll know what to do."

Suddenly Ruby looked less certain of herself. "You will stand by me though? Help me explain what happened."

"Oh, I'm sure she already knows exactly what happened." Then seeing her sister's face, relented. "Of course, I will.

Lilith couldn't decide which was worse, their mother's outrage or their father's shattered look. The latter she decided, when after hearing them out, he left the cabin without saying a word.

"Let him go," her mother said, her hand on Lilith's arm. "He'll need a while to get his head around this one. And as for you…"

To her credit Ruby was looking suitably chastened. But Lilith knew her sister. Give her a moment or two and she'd have had enough of being contrite.

"November, then," her mother said after a moment.

Ruby nodded.

"Doesn't give us much time, does it?"

Two heads shook.

"Thank God you're not showing."

"We've been through all that," Ruby muttered.

"Well, this'll put a stop to all those shipboard romances you've been having."

"Why?"

Her mother blinked. "Surely you're not expecting to carry on as you have been doing?"

"Why not? Unless you want people to start asking awkward questions about why I've suddenly become a nun."

"She's right," Lilith said. "We shouldn't draw any more attention to ourselves than necessary."

"But what will they say when they find out?"

"Who's going to find out?" Ruby said. "As soon as the ship docks we'll all go our separate ways."

"Maybe not quite *all*," Lilith reminded her. "Dad's got rather friendly with Ralph Macintyre, don't forget."

"As if he counts."

"We have to find a place to send you," her mother said slowly. "Perhaps Joe's wife can help. Though God knows what they're going to say when they find out. For all we know, he'll disown us on the spot. Then what?" her voice shook. "What we going to do then Ruby? We can hardly catch the next boat home, can we?"

"It's alright mum. We'll have figured something out by then," Lilith's arm was about her mother's shoulders.

"Why don't we just say I'm a widow?" Ruby wanted to know.

"And make this an even bigger mess?" their mother got to her feet. "No, you'll just have to go away as soon as we arrive."

The only one still seated, Ruby pouted. "But I don't want to go away."

"Then you should have thought of that before... before you did what you did."

33

BY THE TIME THE *REMUERA* sighted the most northern tip of New Zealand, seabirds had been flying around the ship for a while and aware of the significance, those who'd set out as strangers weeks earlier clustered at the railings as friends for their first glimpse at their new home. Overall the consensus seemed positive, with loud exclamations of how pristine everything looked, how wonderfully untouched. But steaming on and passing only small settlements and blocks of cleared bush there was a noticeable shift in third class as some began to raise the question of towns and cities that might offer employment, and more precisely, where they might be found?

"S'alright if you're looking to work the land, I suppose," someone said.

"Don't look very cultivated, does it. Too much wilderness."

"T'ain't flat either. Look at all them hills."

"What about crops then?" someone else put in. "Don't need flat land to grow stuff."

"Do when it comes to harvesting. Unless you want to do it by hand."

"You're right. Anyone seen any proper fields? One's with hedgerows?"

"It's all grazing here. Sheep. I read up about the place. You want to grow wheat and barley; you should have gone to Canada. Great big prairies of the stuff there."

"Be different in the towns. They'll be plenty of work. Government wouldn't have paid towards our passages otherwise."

"Got a point there."

Too late to enter port when they finally reached Auckland some nine hours later, and with the ship forced to anchor out in the harbour, Jim and Dilys spent their last evening under the stars, side-by-side in steamer chairs gazing across the water at the lights on shore.

"Well, here we are, girl. On the other side of the world," he said, reaching for her hand.

"It's colder than I thought it would be."

"Got to remember the seasons are back-to-front here. Still a darn sight warmer than a winter's night at home."

"Doesn't seem right, first week in September. It should be warm still. Not like August of course. But still enough not to need a coat."

"You wait until February. Be as hot here as it was up at the equator."

"See? That's not right either."

Jim laughed. "I suppose we'll get used to it."

"Won't get used to being away for birthdays and Christmas's though."

"Nothing to stop us celebrating, girl. And I bet you can still buy a goose and the ingredients for one of your puds. Bloody lovely they are with a dollop of brandy and swimming in custard."

"Always thinking of your stomach, that's you."

"It's the way to a man's heart, doll," he squeezed her fingers.

"So what d'yer reckon then."

"About what?"

"Ruby. What are we going to do?"

He sighed. "I'll talk to Joe, see if his missus might know of a place that'll take her."

"Won't look good though, will it. Straight off the boat and all that. And who's going to marry her now?"

"Don't upset yourself," his fingers tightened again. "Things have a habit of working out. You know that."

"Not this time Jim. We're not even sure if Joe's wife has any family out here. And even if she does, what's to say they'll want to help. Not sure I would if it was the other way around."

"Then she'll have to go into one of those homes for unmarried mothers," he said. "Bound to be one around somewhere. If I could just get my hands on that bloke…"

"Just as well you can't then, isn't it?"

"But walking away… leaving her just like that. Without as much as a see you later. It ain't right, girl. He's got responsibilities and he should be made to face up to them. Don't matter he's over there and she's over here."

Dilys stared up at the moon. And the stars. There were so many of them. And that bit there, like a glittering veil across the heavens? How many were caught up in that? Then there was the Southern Cross. Jim had pointed it out one night, telling her she'd never ever have seen it had they stayed in Portsea. It's on the New Zealand flag, he'd told her. Four bright stars, though there is another one, but it's a lot fainter.

"So it doesn't count then," she'd laughed.

"No. Only the best for where we're going," he'd replied.

"I spoke to him, Jim," she said softly. "He came in the bar."

When he eased his hand away she felt as if she'd disappointed him somehow. Even so, she knew he'd not over-react. Knew he'd wait for her to say her piece. He was fair like that.

"Came in looking for her," she was still staring up at the heavens. "Said his ship was leaving earlier than they'd thought."

Jim was nodding silently. As if he were mulling over the implications.

"I told him she wasn't in."

"Where was she?"

"Upstairs."

He let out a harsh breath.

"How was I to know," she asked.

"You weren't doll. Did he come in again?"

"No. He finished up his pint and went. And that was that."

"Nothing else?"

She took a moment. It would be so easy to say, no nothing else.

"Yes. He wrote her a letter."

"When?"

"I dunno. About four weeks later."

"And?"

"I threw it in the range before she could see it."

"Did you read it?"

"No. What do you take me for?"

For a long moment there was only the sound of waves lapping against the hull and the ever-so-slight rolling motion.

"Well, it's done now," he said. "So best we forget all about it."

Their father was in no end of a good mood when a little after sunrise they finally tied up alongside Princes Wharf. Unlike Ruby, who tossed angrily when he rapped smartly on their cabin door to summon them both to breakfast.

"Why does he have to wake at such an ungodly hour. I can't see what's the rush," she complained. "Even if we could get ashore, it's not as if anywhere's open yet."

"I don't think dad has shopping on his mind," Lilith said. Having been up herself for the last hour, she'd already tucked away her toiletries and was now folding the last of her blouses and cardigans into her suitcase. "Anyway, don't you want to say goodbye to all your admirers?"

"Did that last night," her sister mumbled, turning over in her bunk to face the steel bulkhead.

"What time did you get to bed?"

"Dunno. Two?"

Shutting the lid, Lilith pressed the locks home. "No wonder you're tired."

"Could you be a little quieter?"

"Sorry. But you do have to get a move on. Breakfast is early today and there's bound to be a rush."

"Just go without me. Oh, and bring me back a piece of toast."

When she got into the dining room it was just as she'd thought. It was packed, and with no one taking any notice of sittings on this last morning she was not overly surprised to see a familiar face next to her father.

"Good morning," Ralph said, dabbing his mouth with his serviette.

Returning the greeting, she sat down.

"Where's Ruby?" her father wanted to know.

"Caught up with her packing," she lied.

He raised an eyebrow. "Really?"

"Mmm," was all she could manage.

Having mopped up the last of his bacon grease Ralph was setting his knife and fork on the plate. "Your sister has made quite an impact these last few weeks."

"I wouldn't say that," she protested.

"It wasn't meant it in a derogatory way," he was looking at her. "More that she could always be relied on to lift everyone's spirits."

"Oh, I see. Yes, she certainly does that," and looking to change of subject went on, "Gosh, isn't it exciting, after all these weeks, we're finally here."

"We are indeed. And I was just saying to your father, we should arrange to meet up once you're settled," Ralph said.

"That would be nice," she replied, though if he was hoping to see Ruby as she guessed, he would be out of luck. At least for the foreseeable future.

"And will you be staying in Auckland now that you're back?" she asked before turning to a steward, and requesting a boiled egg and two slices of toast.

"Not at first. I'll be working from our Christchurch office down in the South Island. But I do hope to be back up around Christmas time."

Before Lilith could reply the empty chair opposite was pulled out.

"Heaven's! I'm sorry I'm late," her mother said, bestowing a beaming smile first on Ralph, then on her.

"There's plenty of time yet," Jim assured her. "Lilith's only just got here too."

"And Ruby?" her mother cast an eye around the salon.

"Packing apparently."

Lilith had to duck her head when Ralph glanced her way, for judging by the way his lips were twitching, he wasn't convinced either.

Oblivious to everything, her father was pointing his fork at her mother. "Ralph here was just saying we should all catch up again next year."

"What a lovely idea. It's always nice to see a friendly face," she replied. "Isn't it Lilith."

"It is."

"You must give us the address of your office in Auckland."

"That's easy. We're not far from here actually. But why don't I call on you when I get back up. The Tivoli Hotel, wasn't it?"

"That's right," her mother said, clearly surprised. As was Lilith. Exactly what had her father been saying, she wondered uncomfortably. But Ralph was already swallowing the last of his coffee.

"Well," he said, smiling broadly and dropping his serviette on the table, "I suppose I should be on my way."

"Are you being met," her father asked.

"Oh, I've no doubt they'll send someone from the office to collect me. Just have to get through customs first and to be honest, I'd rather beat the rush."

Her father stood, holding out his hand. "It's been good to meet you."

"You too. And good luck with the new venture."

"Such a nice young man, don't you think Lil?" her mother asked, as Ralph made his way to the door.

"He won't do for Ruby if that's what you're thinking."

"No?"

"No."

"Why's that then?"

"He's far too level-headed for one thing."

"Do you think so?" her mother was looking doubtful. "That's a shame. I thought he was rather nice myself."

34

WITH THE TRAMPS AND STEAMERS alongside Queens Wharf unloading cargo destined for merchants and shops, or to be sent further away by railway wagon, the smaller Princes Wharf was alive with human flotsam. Outside the custom's hall flat-bed trucks and carts were waiting for the trunks, boxes and crates requiring delivery to hotels around the city. Or, for those less affluent, the boarding houses of Parnell and Freeman's Bay.

"I had no idea it would be like this," Ruby grumbled, making her way unsteadily down the gangway.

No one answered for they were all too busy trying to keep their footing while managing their luggage. Only when they'd stepped down onto firm ground - or not so firm Lilith thought, since Harry had been right in warning them that having been at sea so long it would then seem as if the land itself was rolling - did her father gather them together.

"Right," he said, eying the long queue winding its way into the cavernous shed. "Customs first, and then let's see if Joe is anywhere to be found."

Waiting in line seemed to go on forever, and soon even she was fed up with fractious adults and children running riot and playing tag and taunting each other. Especially when the game involved pushing in and out of the queue. She kept a sharp eye on her mother for nervous of appearing anything other than in the peak of health, Dilys was smiling brightly and laughing off suggestions she took a seat until they were closer to the front. Though what she had to be worried about Lilith had no idea, for the sea voyage seemed to have worked wonders. No longer peaky and gaunt, instead she was looking healthier than she had in a while. Of course, it could be the change in diet for they'd a fairly wholesome one on board, though who could forget the oxtail soup? Served far too often, she was sure the taste would stay with her for years to come. Or did the improvement in her mother simply come from exchanging the unsanitary conditions and gloomy streets of Portsea for fresh sea air and sunshine? Who knew? But if her mother had turned a corner…

Lilith didn't dare hope that she might be back with Grace sooner than anyone had thought.

Shuffling forward, every inch gained was met with encouraging murmurs until finally her father was shepherding them over to the desk of a stern-faced and uniformed official. Producing their passports and after going through the rigmarole of answering questions and handing over documentation, followed by more questions and a thorough delving into their suitcases to ensure they weren't hiding goods on which duty was payable, they were freed to make their way through the magnificent port gates - only to walk into a excited crowd eagerly awaiting the appearance of friends and families from the mother country. Barely able to discern more than a few feet in front of her, and with no idea what her father's brother looked like - that is, if he had turned up to meet them - Lilith glanced at her mother. At the very same moment her father dropped the three cases he'd been struggling with, and pushing through the crowd, rushed over to a stocky, but well-dressed man.

"Joe!" he cried, throwing his arms around him. "God, it's good to see you. And look at you. All dressed up like a real business man! Still recognise you anywhere though," he said, faking a punch at the man's bicep before calling back over his shoulder, "Dilys. Girls. Get over here and meet your uncle."

Clutching her suitcase with both hands and trailing behind her mother, Lilith skirted a group of women on tiptoe straining to get a glimpse of the steady trickle emerging from the custom's hall.

"Dilys! My word!" Joe smiled warmly. "You haven't changed a jot since the day you married this old reprobate."

"Well, you certainly have," she replied, looking him up and down just as her husband had done.

A little taller than her father, he had the appearance of a man who had done well for himself, Lilith thought, dropping her case onto the pavement. Even she could see his suit had been fitted by a bespoke tailor, while his boots were clearly of the best leather. He also had the all-over pastiness of a man who spent his days in an office. But he seemed pleased to see them, and that was the main thing.

"And these two young ladies can't be my nieces," he turned from her father to her mother and back as if needing confirmation. "Why, they were children when I left."

"Indeed they are, Joe," Jim said proudly. "Lilith here," and with an arm around her shoulders he drew her forward, "is a teacher."

"No!"

"And this," reaching behind, he grabbed Ruby's elbow, "is my youngest. Ruby. You remember Alfie. My boy?" his mouth twisted. "Well, like I told you in my last letter, he's married now. That's why he's not here. But he's doing well in the dockyard."

"Glad to hear it. Have to say it's a shame, though. This is the right place for a hard working young man. Especially one looking to start a family. Well, never mind. Everyone, let me welcome you all to New Zealand, the land of the long white cloud."

Ruby glanced at Lilith, who in turn glanced at her mother.

"Maori translation," Joe said as if that explained everything. "Right! Shall we get moving?"

Leading the way out of the crush and raising a hand, he summoned the next taxicab forward off the rank. "I suppose you'll be wanting to see the hotel first. Once the sale went through last week, the owners left pretty much immediately. Gone down to Wellington, I understand. First thing I did was get a sign up in the window advising it's closed temporarily, and under new management."

"Good. But Joe, we've a lot to talk about yet. We need to get a few things sorted at least."

"And we're going to, tonight. In the meantime, I've a couple of things to deal with this afternoon, so I'm going to give you the keys right now. You can move in straight away, how does that sound? The bulk of your stuff will need to come up from the ship, but I can arrange that if you haven't already done so. And if it doesn't suit, then there's plenty of places nearby offering accommodation for a night or two. So I'll send a cab to fetch you at six. Bessie's been baking all week. She can't wait to meet you. Nor can the kids. Oh, and Jim," and she watched as her father was pulled aside. "It's no big deal, but I'd rather you didn't call me Joe. Not in public anyway."

"Oh?"

"It's just that I'm known as Joseph here."

Her father was clearly taken aback. But then he scowled. "Does that mean I have to be James?"

"Wouldn't hurt," and stepping back, Joe grinned. "James Doherty. Has a good ring to it, don't you think? Now, is that all yours?" he indicated the heavy cases.

Dilys was already waving Ruby towards the taxicab. "Come on. Let's not keep the man waiting."

Jim nodded.

"Then I think we could do with a second cab. I'll pay," he said, approaching the driver.

Peering from the window as they shot smartly across Quay Street and made a sharp left Dilys couldn't decide if she was impressed with her first glimpse of the city, or completely out of her depth. Busy with trams, carts, trucks, motorcars and pedestrians all going about their business, her first thought was it wasn't so different from Commercial Road at home. The buildings, mostly four stories high and embellished with all kinds of splendid detailing, were just as impressive as any she'd seen, if not more so. But never in her wildest dreams had she imagined verandah's covering the entire width of a pavement, though she supposed it meant you could walk from one end of a row of shops to the other without the worry of getting wet in a sudden downpour. What did come as a relief were the easily recognisable establishments they were passing. A shoe shop, the Union Bank of Australia, and the premises of Alex Howey Walker dentist, then a department store, a bookseller and a chemist above which she guessed and looking up, were offices.

"You good, doll?" Jim reached across the leather seat for her hand.

She nodded.

"Wonder what the girls are saying to each other," and he craned his neck for a glimpse of the taxi behind.

"Probably like us, just trying to take it all in."

Glancing at his other hand and the fingers tapping a steady rhythm on his thighs, she realised he was nervous.

"Any idea how far we've got to go?" she asked.

"Not much further I shouldn't think. I got the impression we're going to be close by to everything."

The taxi slowed and after waiting for an oncoming tram, turned right and chugged up another busy street.

"More bloody hills here than at home," she murmured.

"Good exercise for you then, getting back down to all these shops we're passing."

He'd hardly spoken before another right turn was made as if to take them back on themselves, albeit a couple of streets over, and drawing to the kerb and stopping outside a building with a large sign in the window, the driver twisted around.

"This is it, mate," one hand still on the steering wheel, the other was on the back of the passenger seat.

Dilys stared out. Jim leaned over her shoulder.

Neither said a word.

Two storied and seemingly of substantial construction, the outward appearance overwhelmed with architectural flairs and finishes. Imposing arched windows, six on the upper floor alone, were flanked by ornamental pillars and fluted columns topped by highly decorated capitals. Swags, scrolls and rosettes of plaster foliage were in abundance, as were lintels and cornices and crowning it all; a grand parapet. Divided into three, the two outer parts held plaques and yet more garlands. The centre section contained the hotel name in huge, embossed lettering.

Having opened their door, the driver was lifting their cases onto the pavement. Parked close behind, the girl's cabbie was doing the same, and extracting herself from the vehicle Dilys found herself beside Jim.

"You got the key?" she questioned as the girls came up.

"Right here," and with an exaggerated flourish he produced the bunch Joe had given him.

"Well then…?"

Slipping one at random into the lock of what would seem to be the main entrance, he tried turning it. "Not this one."

He tried a second before shaking his head again, and looking over at the girls Dilys saw they'd clasped hands. Amazing really, they could bicker like nothing on earth when the mood took them, but when push came to shove…

"Here we go," Jim exclaimed.

She held her breath as he put his shoulder to the door. Then everyone wanted to be the first to get a look at the place. He was having none of it, though.

"Your mother first," he said firmly.

Stepping over the threshold and into the carpeted foyer, the girls close on her heels, she stopped and sniffed. The lingering smell of stale beer was only too familiar. It was also strangely comforting.

"Here's a bar," Ruby said, having opened the door to the right.

"Then this must be the entrance to the hotel since there's some kind of reception desk," Lilith added, peering around a set of glazed doors.

"So those stairs must go up to the bedrooms?" Dilys questioned.

"Now wait a minute everyone," Jim called out, seeing his family about to wander off in different directions. "Mighten it be a good idea to get our stuff in first?"

"I can't be lifting heavy cases anymore, it's not good for me." Ruby threw back, more interested in what might lie around a corner. "I think I've found the dining room. So would this be the kitchen?" and she disappeared altogether.

Stepping outside again Jim muttered, "Better off doing it myself."

Dilys had decided a private tour the hotel was called for. Alone, so she could take it all in without any interruptions.

Eight bedrooms of varying size on the upper floor, four at the front and the rest overlooking the side alley, were serviced by a fully equipped bathroom. That was a refinement she'd not expected. And while the furniture and carpets were clearly past their best, anyone could see they'd life in them yet. Opening a door at the end of the hallway she discovered another passage and a sitting room and three more bedrooms, obviously intended for the owner's use. A set of back stairs - though nowhere near as grand as those at the front, since they lacked both carpet and the luxury of mahogany bannisters and railing - led down to the hotel's kitchen.

She wasn't sure how she was feeling right at that moment. Excited, yes she would have to admit to that. Nervous? Very, for until then she'd no idea what they were coming to. Now it was all too real.

35

DROPPED OFF IN A LEAFY and clearly affluent suburb that evening, Dilys considered the lighted windows and porches of the substantial stand-alone houses, with their wrap-around verandahs and well-maintained front gardens.

"Funny not to see brick, isn't it," she murmured. "All this timber boarding, well it's not exactly English, is it?"

"Oh I don't know," taking her arm and enclosing it in his own Jim gave it a squeeze. "Seen plenty of ship-lap in my time."

"Ah, but that's poor man's cottages. Not big houses like these."

"Suppose it's what you build when you're not in England, doll. Least it looks as if people round here have got a bit of money."

She couldn't deny that.

"It's rather nice," Lilith said, looking up at her uncle's house.

Ruby was doing the same. "Do you think we'll be living in a place like this one day?"

"Can't see why not," her father stepped up and unlatched the gate. "Could be most folk around here were immigrants like us, at one stage," and standing back he ushered the women through and shooed them up the path to the front door.

"We don't stand on ceremony here," Joseph beamed, having flung open the door before the knocker was even lifted. "Just come right on in and make yourself at home."

Having thought the evening would be a little more formal, her brother-in-law being well-off and all that, Dilys was amazed to see him without a tie or jacket. She'd made Jim put on his best suit while she had on one of the nicer outfits he'd insisted she bought before leaving Portsmouth. His wife, on the other hand, did not disappoint, for the dress she was wearing was quite lovely. But then clothes, Dilys had always felt, never failed to look good if you had a bit of height and while Bessie was not excessively tall she had a good two or three inches on her. Which wasn't hard, she thought. She even found herself looking up to the girls these days.

"Come in," Bessie echoed her husband. "Let me take your coat. It certainly is colder than usual this evening."

Not wanting to appear easily impressed, Dilys gave the hallway and staircase the barest glance, at least on the surface. Later in bed, she'd tell Jim the bannisters were poshest she'd ever seen.

"And that newel post? Well! have you ever seen anything so lar-di-dah in an ordinary house? And the wallpaper? You must have noticed that. All I can say having seen the inside of his house is he must be worth a bit, your brother."

Clearing his plate of the perfectly cooked lamb and potatoes - Dilys would only later discover Bessie had spent most of the afternoon fussing over that and the equally anxiety-laden apple crumble that followed - Joseph Doherty eased back from the table and loosened his belt.

"So what do you think of our little investment?" he addressed his brother.

Jim nodded thoughtfully. "I think it can work."

"I do too. It's a little run down," he said, dumping his napkin onto his side-plate, "but that can soon be fixed. It's the location that makes it a good proposition. Close enough to the port to pick up that trade, it's also well situated for those coming into the city for business. Commercial travelers and the like."

Jim was nodding. "You've checked over the books?"

"First thing I did," his brother assured him.

"It needs a good scrub from top to bottom," Dilys put in. "And not just a flick over with a mop either."

"Nothing we can't do of course," Jim said quickly.

"Just saying," Dilys glared back.

"I've got the addresses of everyone the previous owners employed, in case you might be thinking of offering them their jobs back. I did ask if there was anyone you should steer clear of."

"And was there?"

"Only one. And apparently he's gone on to pastures new anyway."

"What do you think doll? Should we talk to them? Or start afresh?"

"Might pick up some useful information if we ask them to come in for a chat."

"You could be right," he nodded before turning back to his brother. "Stock?"

"Very little. I gather they let the place run down knowing they were leaving."

"So that'll be an expense."

"On account though."

"Thirty day's credit? Won't that be a little difficult to get, given we've only just arrived in the country?"

"I'll vouch for you. Stand surety if necessary."

Joseph's wife gave a little cough. "I hope we're not going to discuss business all evening?" she said to her husband. "Not when there are more interesting things to talk about. Like England."

"You're right, Bessie" he agreed indulgently. "Bad form and all that. But look, how about if Jim and I pop into the drawing room for a quick smoke? Leave you ladies alone for ten minutes or so, and meanwhile," he focused on his two young sons, "you boys can go and get ready for bed. How does that sound?"

Bessie rolled her eyes at the youngsters good-natured grumbling. "You heard your father," she said.

"That was delicious." Dilys complimented her newly-found sister-in-law once the children had disappeared. "I have to say I was a bit worried about what we'd be expected to eat in New Zealand."

"Joseph does like his roast and two veg, as he calls it," Bessie laughed. "Drives me mad sometimes, but everything has to be like his mum makes. Not that I've ever met her of course."

"Jim's the same, isn't he girls? Plain food and nothing fancy. I don't think I could cook anything needing a recipe."

"The pudding was especially lovely, Aunt Bessie," Lilith agreed.

"We do eat a lot of fruit, I must say. And there's always more coming into season."

"It seems so very back-to-front to me, the seasons I mean," Dilys smiled. "I'm sure I'll never get used to it."

"You will," Bessie offered before asking, "Would you mind if I cleared the table? Then we can go and join the men."

"Let me give you a hand."

More than anything Dilys needed to make a friend of this woman.

In the scullery she was looking for a place to stack the dirty plates and dishes, and a bin.

"Where do you put the scraps?" she asked.

"Oh, don't bother with that. We have a girl in every morning. She'll do it all."

"Oh," Dilys said, feeling even more out of place.

"I will tell you, it took me a while to get used to someone running around after me, but Joseph insisted it was essential in a house this size. And while we could get a cook as well I'm loathed to give up my kitchen completely. After all, what else would I do if I wasn't shopping and preparing meals for my family," she said, reaching into a cupboard. "Fancy a small port?"

Dilys returned the conspiratorial smile. "Wouldn't say no."

"What about the girls?"

"Probably not."

Taking the delicately stemmed glass, Dilys asked casually, "You said earlier you aren't from Auckland?"

"No. I'm from up north. A little place called Whangarei."

"Oh, and do you still have family there?"

Bessie nodded. "Two sisters. Both married. And Mother and father, of course."

"So you were born there?"

"No, I was born in Kent, of all places. My father brought us all here when I was still an infant. So I suppose you could say that while I'm English at heart, New Zealand is the only place I've ever really known."

"Oh."

Bessie smiled. "It's going to be very strange for you at first, but if it's any consolation I've been looking forward to having family here in Auckland. Joseph can be so very busy at times. Not that I'm complaining. But it will be nice to have someone to call on for a chat."

"There, that wasn't so bad, was it," Jim said, sitting on the edge of one of the Tivoli Hotel's guest beds and pulling off his shoes.

Dilys was at the dressing table, brushing her hair. "Bessie seems very nice," she admitted.

"And Joe appears to have his head screwed on right."

"Joseph," she reminded him.

"Hmm. It's going to take a bit of getting used to, that will."

"Best you do. So what you got planned for tomorrow, because those packing cases need emptying and shifting if we're to move in properly. Can't be using up two paying rooms like this."

"Thought you and the girls would do all that."

"We will once the heavy stuff is out the way."

"Hmm. Well, Joe and I are off to meet a few useful people in the morning. Brewers, wine merchants, that sort of thing."

"Oh?"

"Need to make the right contacts from day one, girl." Dropping his braces, he stood to undo the buttons of his trousers. "He's putting a half page advertisement in the local paper. Grand opening Friday. New management."

"Thinking big then?"

"And why not? We just need to be ready."

"It'll take more than just us to get this place up to scratch for the end of the week."

"You'll have help; I'll see to that. Oh, and you'll never guess what else Joe said?"

"What?"

"Pubs round here close at six o'clock."

She stopped, horrified. "How on earth are we going to cope with being up all night? We'll need even more staff to cover all those hours, and that'll cost."

"Not six in the morning, doll. Six at night."

She frowned. "But why would a landlord shut his doors just as the evening was kicking off. You must have got it wrong."

"Couldn't believe it myself."

"And?"

"It's true. It's a way of life here. Blokes crowd in between knocking off work and going home and drink as much as they can in the short time available. And it's not a pint here and there either. According to what Joe said, it's jug after jug as quick as you like, and all filled from a hose of all things."

"But that's daft."

"That's what I said. Apparently they have a sort of prohibition here."

"Did he say anything else?" she asked, her tone suddenly frosty. "After all, we've come all this way and suddenly it's not looking as rosy anymore."

"I wouldn't say that. At least I wouldn't say it just yet."

"So, what other rules are you going to spring on me," she insisted.

"No serving food with beer for one."

"But - "

"No buts," he said smugly, unbuttoning his shirt. "You have a dining room now. That's the place to make the money."

"What else, Jim Doherty?"

"That's it really. Oh, and no music."

"Not even a piano for a singsong?"

"Not even."

"Bloody hell," she swore, "No drinking after six, nothing to eat and no singing. It's going to be a pretty miserable place."

"According to Joe, owners here are more interested in buying up other pubs rather than do anything about changing things in the ones they've got. Not only that, it's not easy to get a licence either. We'd have found it bloody hard if it weren't for him," and throwing back the frowsy sheet and blanket he jumped into bed.

"Jim," Dilys began.

"What doll?"

"You spoke to him yet about how he's made all his money?"

"Bought himself a few properties, or so I gather."

"What sort of properties?"

"Ones people rent from him."

"Oh. Like us."

"Not like us at all. We're partners in this investment, and one day in the not too distant future we'll own it outright."

"'Course. I was curious, that's all."

"Well, don't be. Just be glad he's here, and so are we."

36

THE FOLLOWING MORNING, SLEEVES rolled up and pinny on, Dilys was overseeing Lilith and Ruby and two local girls Joe had sent over.

"Just to get the place ready," he'd said, turning up himself an hour later. "Of course, that's not to say they won't be interested in a more permanent arrangement. You'll need good workers, and ones you can trust if you get my drift. Nothing worse for a guest than having their belongings rifled through. Meanwhile, you might put a notice in the window stating exactly what you need."

"We'll do that. And while you're here, where's the tables and chairs in the public bar then?" she asked. "Did the previous owner take them with him? I suppose that means we'll have to replace everything with new."

Even as she asked Joe was shaking his head. "There never were any Dilys. Men drink standing up here."

"What about women? Surely they prefer to sit down and get comfy?"

"Not in the public bar they don't. They're not allowed in."

She stared. "Women aren't allowed in the bar?"

"That's right."

"So where do they go?"

"In the small private bar round the side."

"So a husband and wife can't have a drink together."

"They can. Just not in the public bar."

"That's not right."

"Way it is, though."

Her brother-in-law grinned, "Ah, and here's the new landlord," he said as Jim walked in wiping his hands on a towel.

"'Morning Joe. Just been down the cellar," he said.

"All good?"

"Seems to be. I've been looking to see how things should be arranged."

Joseph nodded. "We'd better get off then. That is if you want any chance of a delivery tomorrow."

Wrapped in one of Dilys's pinafores, and balancing on a stool behind the counter, Lilith was cleaning shelves. Below her, Ruby was going through the motions of washing glasses.

"This is going to ruin my hands," her sister complained.

"You could always join her," Lilith jerked her head at the girl on her knees, scrubbing.

"No thank you very much. That floor hasn't seen soapy water in years."

"Nor have the windows judging from the grime in that other one's bucket."

"You know; I shouldn't be working at all. It's not good for someone in my condition."

"Ruby!" she spluttered. "Why not say it a little louder and let all of Auckland in on the news."

"So what? It's not as if they won't know soon enough."

"Shhh. Mum's arranging something."

"I'm not being sent away."

"You can't stay here," she was shocked. "What about your good name."

"What good name? No one here has any idea of my existence and that's why I don't see why we can't all pretend I'm a widow. After all, who would know any different?"

"Uncle Joseph and Aunt Bessie for one. Anyway, you'd have to keep the child in that case."

"Don't be silly!"

"If you've just buried your husband you can hardly put his child up for adoption. It would look far too cold and heartless," she hissed, before glancing at the two. Thankfully, neither seemed to be listening to the conversation.

Ruby said nothing.

"And being a widow," she added quietly, "would also ruin your chances of a good marriage."

Even so, her heart wrenched when tugging her dress so that the folds fell loosely and disguised any evidence all was not as it should be, her sister silently reached for another glass.

"It'll be fine, you'll see," she added.

"Easy for you to say."

37

HAVING INVITED BESSIE ROUND TO see the changes made to the Tivoli Hotel, Dilys was trying to bring the conversation around to Ruby's predicament.

"Thanks to those girls Joseph sent around we managed to get most of the hard work out of the way in the first three days," she said, over a pot of tea in the newly scrubbed and polished dining room. "After that is was just pottering really. My two did well, especially Lil, and it can't be easy for her, her being a teacher and all. We're on the lookout for a training college so that she can study for her full qualifications. I don't suppose you know of one?"

"I don't. But why don't I ask at the boy's school? Someone there is bound to know."

"I'd appreciate that," and she sighed, "if only everything could be as simple and straightforward."

Just as she'd hoped, Bessie looked concerned. "Is something wrong?".

"I shouldn't burden you. After all, we hardly know each other."

A hand was placed on her arm. "Don't think that way, Dilys. We're family now."

Setting her cup down on its saucer she took a moment. Then, almost as if the admission had been wrung out of her, said, "We do have a small predicament. It's all very unfortunate, and of course, if we were still at home I could have made a few discreet enquiries and arranged things in a suitable manner. But here…" and she lifted her hands helplessly.

"Can I be of help?"

"I don't wish to put upon you."

"Please."

Bessie had moved closer.

Dilys sighed. "I doubt you've ever had experience of anything so…" she searched for a word, the first that had come to mind was *horrendous*.

"Try me. You never know."

"It's Ruby."

"Your youngest?"

"Yes. There was an unspoken agreement. An unofficial promise of marriage, you might say. A rather nice young man. In the Royal Navy as a matter of fact. But before a date could be set and anything finalised with his family, the ship he was serving on had to sail. Left us with no time for anything."

"Oh! What a shame. And poor Ruby. She must be heartbroken."

"She is," and she bowed her head as if burdened by her family's sorrows.

"And Lilith? She didn't leave a beau behind?"

"No."

"Thank goodness. A broken heart is not the easiest thing to mend."

Realising her sister-in-law had misunderstood the extent of the problem, Dilys tried to bring the subject back on track. "Unfortunately," she said again, "Ruby was a little premature is a certain matter."

Bessie looked blank.

"She had... um... relations she shouldn't have had. Not before a wedding night anyway."

"Ahhh! Oh dear. How very unfortunate."

"It is. And of course, such a situation would be disastrous under any circumstances. But here, where we know no one, as I've said..." and she reached for the handkerchief tucked up her sleeve.

"I'm sure we can find a solution."

"Do you think so?" she allowed her expression to show hope.

Regardless they were the only two in the room, Bessie leaned even closer. "How far along?"

"Seven months."

"Gracious! I'd never had guessed. She certainly has kept her figure."

"Yes, she's been incredibly fortunate in that respect. A decent girdle's helping too. God knows what she'd be looking like otherwise."

"I suppose so. Can I ask, what you are considering?"

Dilys had scrunched up her handkerchief. "I have no idea."

"Well, there are always orphanages?"

"I would prefer to have the child adopted out. If that is possible, of course."

"Yes, I think that would be the best solution. Some of those institutions can be very austere, so I've been told," Bessie nodded thoughtfully.

"There's the other thing as well."

"The other thing?"

"Yes. Jim and I think it would be for the best if she could go away somewhere, just until she's had the baby. Then, when she comes back afterwards no-one will be any the wiser."

"Oh I see. Well, yes. That would be a good idea. You wouldn't believe how parochial Auckland can be when it comes to people knowing your business."

"Like I said, if we were back home…"

"Don't worry, I'm sure we can come up with something."

Dilys tried to contain her relief. "I would really appreciate it if you could."

"Give me a day or two to think on it. There is a family I know of in Whangarei. A good family who have fallen on hard times, and for a little financial inducement, they might be persuaded to offer her accommodation throughout her confinement. It might be a good idea though to stress the situation. That Ruby's background is impeccable and that she herself might have been a little -" she stopped and with her head on one side, asked, "would you say the term naïve might cover things?"

"Certainly," said Dilys, thinking *naïve?* Ruby? That would be the day.

"Then that's what we'll say. Poor Ruby rather naively allowed her young man to take advantage of her. Through no fault of her own of course. And we should also make it clear that other than this single fall from grace, the young man in question is also of good standing, but that circumstances have dictated the couple are separated. So along with her family, she has arrived in New Zealand to pick up the pieces and start again."

"That sums it up rather nicely," Dilys agreed.

"Excellent. Then leave it to me to make the arrangements. It would probably be better to come from someone they know."

"Bessie, I am unbelievably grateful for your help. And your understanding. This has been a nightmare for Jim and me."

"Think nothing of it."

"Well, I hope one day I can repay you."

"What else is family for?" Bessie shrugged.

38

NEVER HAVING RECEIVED MANY LETTERS in her life Lilith was only just learning how unbearable waiting for a postal delivery could be. The dry mouth and nervous fluttering in her stomach on waking, that this just might be the day, became second nature. As did the loafing around aimlessly and jumping at the slightest noise. Then, on hearing the heart-stopping rattle of the letterbox she'd get up from the table, or stop whatever chore she might be doing as if it were nothing out of the ordinary.

"I'll go," she'd offer, walking steadily to the front door and retrieving the envelopes from the mat.

The crashing disappointment on discovering none were for her would leave her listless and morose for hours. No one could bring her out of such a mood, though her mother and father tried. And with no idea of the cause, and believing she was missing her vocation, their solution that she applied for all available positions in any Auckland primary school regardless of how far away it might be, wasn't any help at all.

"Your mother and I can manage," her father assured her, on more than one occasion.

She knew that wasn't true for while her mother might have rallied at sea, the improvement hadn't continued on dry land. Some days she looked as haggard as she'd been in Portsea.

And then five letters marked with her name arrived at once.

Heart surging at the distinctive writing on four of the envelopes, the fifth one which she knew to be a lengthy correspondence from Nora giving all the gossip on her wedding to George, though not that it would also enclose a drawing from Lilith's old infant's class, was barely acknowledged.

Slipping all but one of the precious letters into her pocket, she returned to the kitchen and dropped the remainder of the mail in front of her mother.

"Look," she said, holding up the single envelope and beaming from ear to ear. "It's from Nora. Would anyone mind if I go up to my room and read it in peace?"

"Doesn't bother me," Ruby said. "Nothing from Else I suppose?"

Lilith shook her head. "Sorry."

"And only bills for your father," her mother commented, flicking through the rest. "Come down when you're ready. I'll make a pot of tea and you can tell me how she's getting on."

"I'd have thought she'd have written by now," Ruby muttered.

"Who? Elsie?" Lilith questioned, before adding, "Have you written to her?"

"Yes. On the ship."

"Just give her a chance. You know how long it takes for things to get here."

"Uh huh. But you got yours."

She hurried upstairs without replying.

Closing and locking the bedroom door, she hurled herself onto the bed in a fit of light-hearted giggling. Four letters, and lying on her back she fanned them out as if they were a hand of playing cards. Four! Oh and Nora's of course, she thought, guiltily setting that one aside.

Putting the other's in order of the date on the postmark, she eased the topmost one out and using the kitchen knife she'd brought up for that reason, nosed the blade under the flap.

My darling Lilith,

Only the second day, and I am so utterly lost without you.

Closing her eyes, she willed away the lump in her throat. Oh, to be with her right now. In that room with the bay window overlooking the road, and settled in the cosy armchair. Grace would be propped up on cushions by the hearth as she so loved to be, reading some article or other. Every now and then she'd stop, exclaim aloud, then return to the page to share the sentence or paragraph that had caught her attention…

It was never going to be easy, we both knew that, but last night I had to force myself to sleep and even then I had to pretend you were nestled against me, as on the too few nights we were given. I miss you, my darling. I miss your gentle smile and your ferocious and boundless enthusiasm in equal amounts. I miss every touch, every caress, and I especially ache for the brushing of your hand against mine. How you love to fly in the face of convention.

But let me save those thoughts for later. Instead, I will start with the latest news, such as it is…

Lilith read right to the end, to the flourishing loop of the single *G*, and then without pausing, slit open the next envelope. Tugging out the pages she devoured those too as if long starved of words.

Only when she'd digested all four did she lay back and allow the tears fall.

39

IF RUBY THOUGHT THE LONG, slow train journey north to Whangarei excruciating, sitting sideways on a bullock-drawn wagon as it juddered from side to side and regularly dropped into deep ruts only to tilt perilously and climb out again, was far, far worse. Clinging to the edge of the planked seating she truly thought she might have the baby then and there, and hoped that wouldn't be the case for not having seen a soul in ages who would come to her aid? The hills and valleys were unrelenting, and with little more than the odd farmhouse dotted around it was looking more and more likely the only company she could expect would be the family who had negotiated her keep in exchange for their care, and silence. Surely there must be a town close by? A place busy with people and dress shops, and the bright lights of the pictures? Or was this it? Utter desolation. Dear Lord, she prayed, don't let this be all there is. She'd never survive a week, let alone two months.

Another bone-jarring lurch shifted her and her suitcase a little more to the back of the wagon and gritting her teeth she cast daggers at the wide-brimmed hat and hunched and rounded shoulders of Mr Steiner up front. A dour man, and uncaring what the world thought of him or so it seemed, he'd been leaning against a pillar as the train pulled in and while she hadn't expected a brass band reception she felt he could at least have managed a smile before gathering up her luggage and striding off with the expectation she'd take it upon herself to follow.

Turning her gaze back the way they'd come, she could only hope his wife was more accommodating.

When the bullock lifted his head and sniffed the air, and the two mangy-looking dogs trotting alongside lost interest in whatever might be found either side of the track and surged ahead, Ruby took it as a sign they must be nearing the end of the interminable journey. Sure enough, after rounding a corner of bush and passing between two rotting gate posts, she had her first view of the place at which she was to remain for the next two months. The grey barns and sheds and fenced-off animal pens only served to fulfil her worst fears, since they had as unfriendly an air as their owner, while the house, a single storey villa with the remains of what must once have been highly detailed fretwork around the porch didn't seem any better. With the wagon drawing closer a woman stepped out from the doorway and guessing this might be her hostess, Ruby stared curiously, for at first glance she seemed so much younger than her miserable husband.

"You might welcome her," Mr Steiner instructed the woman, jumping down from his perch and moving to the bullock's powerful shoulders to unfasten the yoke.

"You must be thirsty after your journey," the young woman said instead. "I have lemonade inside."

Standing and massaging the small of her back it took less than a second to realise no one would be helping her down. So be it, she thought, and with one hand on the roughly hewn side of the cart, she placed a wary foot on the metal stirrup and jumped the eighteen or so inches to the ground.

Clearly, the house had seen better days, and some of the timbers showed worrying signs of disrepair. Making her way up onto the porch Ruby glimpsed what was surely the Steiner's bedroom to the left of the front door, and wondered what might be behind the door to the right? A sitting room perhaps.

"That's your room," the woman set off down the dismal hallway. "Back here's where we live. Not what you're used to, no doubt."

Ruby blinked.

"Pardon?" she said, following dutifully.

"New Zealand."

"No."

Stretching almost the full width of the rear of the house the room was sparsely furnished. A range and a sink took care of the basic necessities, but there was no modern stove or any other convenience, nor anything to give the place a lift; like curtains. Nor was there a corner cabinet of china knick-knacks like the one her mother had insisted came with them. The same one two hefty Maori men had struggled to get up from the port and into the Tivoli's back room.

Having upturned a glass from the draining board, the young woman filled it from a jug and slid it across the table towards her.

"Thought not. Been told you've just arrived."

"Yes, that's true."

The drink was deliciously sweet and given the heat and the dreadful journey she'd had to endure it was all she could do to stop herself knocking it back like a dockie sinking his first pint of the evening. Instead, sipping delicately, she supposed right at that very moment Mr Steiner would be unloading her trunk, and wondered when she would be shown the bathroom? Or at least somewhere to freshen up? She was, after all, a guest.

"Like your dress."

Taken aback at such directness, she looked down. Hardly the height of fashion to begin with, now the seams had been let out it was shapeless beyond belief. But in a pinafore and washed-out jumper, and with her long hair dragged back into an old-fashioned knot at the back of her head, her hostess wasn't looking any better.

"I bought it a while ago. In Portsmouth. Which is where we lived before we came here."

Her hostess said nothing.

"Have you ever been to England," Ruby tried, before realising how ridiculous the question sounded.

"Never been further than Whangarei."

"But surely you've been to Auckland? For shopping and such?"

When the young woman shook her head, a small sound escaped Ruby. Partly shock, partly resignation.

She was nodded towards a badly painted wooden chair.

"You can sit down if you want."

"Thank you. Look, I'm sorry, but I don't know your name. Unless you want me to call you Mrs Steiner?"

The woman sat opposite. "Olympia."

"Gosh! What a beautiful name. I'm just plain Ruby I'm afraid."

"I know."

"Do you have children?"

Olympia gave her a strange look. "Mr Steiner does."

She waited, but there was no further elaboration.

"Boys or girls?" she asked, for if this is how conversations took place in this part of the world they'd be here all day.

"Two boys. Almost men really."

And just as Ruby was about to pose another question Olympia added, "They're out in the orchard. Picking."

"So you grow your own fruit?"

"And bottle it. Most goes off to market the moment we've got it off the trees."

Ruby felt like cheering. Now, if only they could keep up the rhythm she'd soon find out all she needed to know.

"And do you have animals as well?"

"We've got sheep. They stay up in the hills. We got chickens too if you want to count them."

"I've never been to a farm before," Ruby said.

Olympia looked at her but said nothing.

"Born and bred in the city, that's me."

"You must like Auckland then."

"I haven't really seen much of it. We only arrived two weeks ago and we've been settling in since then. Do you go to the pictures much? I used to go all the time back home."

"I've been a couple of times. Before I was married, that is."

"So how often do you get into town? I suppose you'd go to Whangarei, wouldn't you? Though it seems a long way."

The expression on the long, pale face didn't alter. "I don't get into town. Not unless it's for something special."

Ruby could almost hear doors slamming and keys turning in locks.

"Perhaps we can change that, then," she said, hoping her smile would mask what was fast becoming panic. "At least while I'm here. Do a little shopping or find a nice café and have tea?"

The fixed gaze was disconcerting.

"I don't think we'll be doing that. Not…" and Olympia's eyes lowered to Ruby's stomach and the gentle roundness beneath her dress.

"Oh. No, of course not."

She couldn't breathe. What had her mother done to her, sending her to such a place? And Aunt Bessie too, since this was as much her fault, if not more.

She'd never have agreed to it had she known what was in store. Never. How was she supposed to cope for the eight weeks or more? It was impossible. Not only that, the very idea of keeping her so far from civilisation was inhumane - and they'd certainly kept that nugget of information to themselves. Not once had anyone told her she would be exiled to the back of beyond without a car or a streetlight or a row of shops in sight. Well, she wouldn't stay. No one could make her. She'd write to her mother that very afternoon, tell her it was all a dreadful mistake and get her to send the return train fare immediately. Something else would have to be worked out, that was all.

"Do you need to lie down?" Olympia asked.

Lie down? Ruby wanted to shout at the young woman opposite, a woman who so far hadn't moved a single facial muscle. *I want to go home. Right now.*

"No thank you," she said, inhaling deeply. All this upset was having a terrible effect on her bladder. "But if you could point me in the direction of the facilities?"

"Facilities? Oh," the pale face cleared. "Just across the yard," and she pointed towards the back door.

40

PUTTING THE LAST OF THE clean cutlery away in the sideboard, and before switching off the electric light and shutting the door, Lilith took a quick glance over the linen-draped tables to ensure everything was ready for breakfast in the morning. Serviettes were folded, china was stacked. All was as it should be.

"We were certainly busy in the dining room tonight," she said, dropping down into an armchair.

Her mother was at the kitchen table, the contents of three empty till drawers in front of her, and having separated out a pile of notes she was concentrating on stacking coins into equal piles. Her father sat opposite, watching.

"I hear we got another room filled this afternoon," he said, putting a cigarette to his lips.

Lilith nodded. "A salesman up from Wellington."

"Booked in for three days, isn't he? One room to go and we're full."

"That's right."

"Worthwhile, doll?" he said to her mother.

"Give me chance. How can I keep an accurate tally with you two rabbiting on?"

When her father turned in Lilith's direction, grinning and rolling his eyes, her lips twitched. Sometimes she wondered what would have happened if she'd met a man like him, one full of roguish good-humour, a one-woman-man. Would things have been any different?

But she hadn't, and now she didn't care anyway. Not since Grace had come into her life.

"Now then," her mother looked up a few minutes later. "Pass me the account book Jim, then you can put the kettle on."

Lilith didn't dare look over, not if she was to keep a straight face, for in return for her willingness to take on the hotel her mother had insisted on a new regime. One in which the entire workload was shared a little more evenly, and while her father had been only too happy to go along with it at first, she knew he was hoping the day was not far off when things would return to normal, and he would be waited on hand and foot again. Trouble was, she didn't believe her mother would let that happen. Not now she'd got the bit between her teeth. It was astonishing how naturally she'd had taken to running a hotel, almost as if she'd been born to it. Of course, she did have staff. Of the two original girls brought into clean, one had asked to be kept on and since then they'd employed a cook, a chambermaid and three barmen, the last working in shifts. On top of that, she and Aunt Bessie were as thick as thieves these days, and it had been her suggestion to approach the recently formed staff agency in Karangahape Road and try to negotiate a discount on the finder's fee. A success they'd celebrated by taking tea at Smith and Caughey after visiting the store's china department and purchasing a rather fine Royal Doulton soup tureen.

"I've always wanted one,' she'd told Lilith a touch defensively, having removed it from its packaging and placed it in the centre of the buffet, "and now we have a public dining room we should be thinking about appearances."

And she'd stood back to admire the piece.

Now the account book was slapped shut.

"Well?" her father asked.

"Could be better."

Lilith and her father exchanged glances again, for there was no praise for hard work not even a begrudged appreciation, regardless takings might be on the up. It was the same every evening. As if her mother feared a level of complacency would settle over the place if she didn't keep a tight rein on things.

Dilys couldn't believe how their lives had changed. And to think she'd been so against coming out in the first place. Not that it had been plain sailing, especially in the first week when Jim had been more than a little reckless with their savings - and Joe's money come to that. Look at the new sofa and chairs he'd gone out and bought for their back room. It was everything she could ever have wanted being gold and brown plush and so very up to the minute with the curved arms and all. Then there was the rug he'd turned up with a day or so later, saying it was just what was needed to make the place really look like home. But all that paled beside the accounts he was running up. Wines, spirits, beer, cigarettes and tobacco, that she'd expected. But the lines of credit he'd gone out and got at the butchers and grocers Joe had recommended? That was something she hadn't been comfortable with. After all, getting stuff on tick just wasn't in her nature. But as Bessie had said at the time, if they were to fill the dining room every day they'd need regular suppliers and what with wages to find on top, how else would they get started? And then, to everyone's surprise, Lil had stepped up and taken charge of the accommodation side of things, first by recording all the bookings and then overseeing the cleaning and ensuring everything was in place when guests arrived. No one had asked her to, she just seemed to slip into the role. And it kept her busy, that was the main thing, since she'd not bothered looking for a teacher's college to get that qualification she needed. Sad really. It had been all she'd wanted for so long. It wasn't all good though, for she was dropping hints about going home next year and no doubt that was something to do with those letters she kept getting from her friend Grace. They were coming regularly now and filling her head with thoughts of all the political stuff she used to go on about.

She sighed. You had to let them go, of course you did, but it didn't make it any easier.

And then there was Ruby, and who could tell what would happen when she got back from Whangarei. Please God, she would be her old self, as lazy as they come and full of big ideas about finding a wealthy husband. She was nervous though, for some girls never got over having a kiddie and giving it away. Hadn't she seen itself herself back home? Young women pretending they didn't give a fig, hanging around the pubs on the Hard hoping to catch someone's eye. Someone who couldn't care less about a colourful past. Good time girls they were, and everyone knew it. And what about those who hadn't had a say in getting up the duff in the first place? How many went all the other way and shut themselves off altogether, in spirit if not in body? Some even ended up in the asylum for a while. It was just the way it was. But it would be different for Ruby. She could start again since no one in Auckland knew her, and so there was no one to ask where she'd been these past weeks.

Gathering up the account book and her pen Dilys went over to the bureau - another one of Jim's purchases, though why they had any need of such a flash piece of furniture in the back room she'd never know - and opening the lid, placed the two items side-by-side in a pigeon hole. Pleased with the way things were going, since they didn't just have this month's payment to Joe in hand, but next month's too, she was quietly optimistic that Jim could be right, and that maybe, just maybe, he and the girls might end up in a house like his brother's one day.

41

DROPPING HER LEGS OVER THE side of the bed Ruby leant back on her hands and lifted herself upright, bottom first. Then, waddling over bare floorboards to the chair she threw on her ungainly smock dress. The same one she'd worn yesterday and the day before. What was the point in doing otherwise, she told herself, one hand on her back and with the baby's weight pressing down hard on her bladder?

Appearing in the doorway Olympia was carrying clean linens. "How are you feeling?"

"Like an elephant. No, make that two elephants."

"Not long now."

"I'm sure you said that yesterday and yet here I am, still the same."

"Do you want breakfast?"

"No. I'm not in the mood."

"It's a lovely morning. Why don't you sit on the porch for a while?"

"You don't think I'd go straight through? And I'm not just worried about the boards that are already weak."

Olympia laughed.

"You wouldn't find it so funny if you were in my shoes," Ruby threw back. "Now if you don't mind, I need the toilet. And fast."

She was halfway across the yard when the pain hit, so sharp and intense it knocked the wind right out of her. She made it the rest of the way at an ungainly trot, and with both hands supporting her heavily bloated belly.

"Flamin' hell," she swore, shoving open the door of the long-drop.

With summer around the corner, the stench was nauseating but nowhere near as bad as it would be later that day when the sun was high in the sky and beating down on the corrugated iron roof. At least she no longer had to pinch her nose and breathe through her mouth when doing her business, though she wasn't sure if that was a good sign or not. What she did know was that she couldn't wait to get back to civilisation and the wonderful indoor plumbing of the Tivoli Hotel. Did the rest of her family have any idea how spoiled they were? Even the lav back at *The Saracen's Head* was streets ahead in comparison to the cutout plank she was sitting on, and a flamin' deep hole in the ground. And it didn't end there. Instead of a cistern of water for flushing, there were the sweepings from the wood shed. In a bucket, no less. Wondering what Elsie would say if she could see it all, she let out a laugh before throwing a few handfuls of sawdust and chippings down the hole and lumbering out to hold her hands under the pump.

"I think I've just had a contraction," she said, coming back into the kitchen and easing herself down at the table.

Olympia looked up, her face eyes wide with excitement.

"Do think Mr Steiner should go and fetch Mrs O'Leary?"

"I don't think so. I only had the one, and I feel fine at the moment. Besides which, I wouldn't want to send him on a wild goose chase."

"No, I suppose not."

"Don't look so glum. It'll be here quick enough."

"Not quick enough for me," Olympia smiled.

Had Ruby foreseen two months earlier that they would become friends, and good friends at that, she wouldn't have believed it. Not back then. They were far too different for one thing and anyway, all she'd wanted was to get back to the bright lights of Auckland. Her mother's stubborn refusal to send the train fare had put an end to that, and seething and plotting how to get her own way, the change in their relationship hadn't happened overnight. It was more a gradual thawing with each woman knowing they had little choice but to make the best of things. Until the day Mr Steiner chose to let his sons ride up into the hills to check on the sheep without him.

That morning, she'd walked into the kitchen to see him sitting at the table. Olympia slipped into the chair beside him.

"Is everything all right?" she'd asked, pulling out one opposite.

"Mr Steiner would like to talk to you," Olympia said in a quiet voice.

Wondering what she could possibly have done wrong, she sat straighter. "Oh yes?"

"It's about the baby," he said, not looking at her. His big hands were flat on the table.

"Yes," she said again.

"You're putting it up for adoption once it's born."

"That's right."

He glanced at his wife and as if compelled, Ruby did the same.

"We were wondering if you might consider us as parents," Olympia said.

Her mouth opened, ever so slightly. "You?"

"Yes."

"Well…I…"

"You were hoping for someone with a little more money, I expect," Mr Steiner sat back, his expression neutral. "That, and a large house. Large garden, too."

"No…that is yes…that is, of course I want the best for the child."

Olympia smiled, "We have none of those things, as you know."

Ruby nodded.

"We have spoken," Olympia continued, after another quick glance at her husband. "And we would like you to know what we can offer. Mr Steiner has two grown boys. I have no children of my own -"

"But you've only been married three years," Ruby cut in. "There's plenty of time for you to have two, three or even four."

"There is," Olympia agreed. "But you are having a little one who will be needing a home immediately. And that is what we would like to give him. Or her."

Ruby gazed from one to the other. Mr Steiner's receding hair and weathered complexion made him look so much older than he really was. But Olympia was blooming, with a heightened colour in her cheeks and a new sparkle in her eyes.

"You wish to go through a formal adoption?" she asked slowly. "Just so I have it right."

The Steiner's exchanged glances yet again, and once more it was Olympia who spoke.

"We could. Though that would take time, or so I believe. And in the meantime, the child will be put in an orphanage." She paused before adding, "and who knows how it will be treated there."

"So what are you suggesting?"

"An alternative. That the birth is registered in our name, and not yours."

"But…" Ruby was having trouble taking it in, "isn't that illegal?"

No one spoke.

"People would know," she tried again.

"Who would know?"

"I don't know. People. In the town," she was shaking her head. Was it possible? Could it work? Heaven's, it would solve a lot of problems all round. She'd simply hand the child over and be gone.

"No one knows you are here," Olympia said reasonably. "And since I haven't left the farm all winter, who's to say I'm not the one who is pregnant?"

"The midwife," Ruby said triumphantly. "She will know which of us gave birth."

"Mrs O'Leary? She will. But she won't be there when Mr Steiner registers it, will she?"

"Think on it," Mr Steiner said, rising from the table. "I give you my word the child will be brought up well."

"I'm having trouble getting my head around this," Ruby said to Olympia once the door had closed behind him. "I've never heard him mention he wants more children."

"If you want the truth, Ruby, it's me who wants the child."

She'd already guessed as much. "And he's prepared to let you have what you want?"

"Yes."

"He will stand by his word and treat the baby well?"

"He will. He's a good man at heart."

"Just needs to smile a bit more if you ask me," she said dourly.

"I promise I'll work on that." Eyes dancing, Olympia was biting her lip.

"Well, as we say back home, you could knock me down with a feather."

"So you think you might agree to it?"

Pushing back her chair Ruby rose from the table and went around to pull the other woman to her feet. "You're going to be a good mum," she said, hugging her as tightly as she could.

"It's like my marriage." Olympia offered later while brewing a pot of tea. "Works in both our favours. Mr Steiner gets what he wants, which is a female about the place to cook and keep the place tidy for him and the boys. I get what I want."

"Somewhere safe," Ruby agreed, having already heard Olympia's story.

"Exactly. Somewhere I don't have to worry about my old dad coming home drunk to the eyeballs and wanting his way with me."

"Does Mr Steiner know about that?" she asked carefully.

Olympia nodded. "Of course he does. That's why he doesn't pester me in the bedroom. And do you know something? I think having a baby here will help make up for his wife dying."

"Really?"

"Yes. He still grieves, you know."

"He must have loved her very much."

"I think he did. Strange how things turn out, isn't it?" she mused. "Almost as if she sent you to us."

"Well, he could have been a bit more welcoming at the start."

"You know it's just his way."

"It wasn't that. It's because I wanted to leave within five minutes of getting here."

"You were very cross."

"I was, wasn't I. I still think he would have been glad to see the back of me, though."

"Well, I wouldn't have."

"We've had some laughs haven't we?" Ruby chuckled.

"Oh yes. Like calling the dunny 'the facilities'. I had no idea what you were talking about."

"You should have been in my shoes when I found out there was no proper plumbing here."

"And what you said to Marshall? About going into town for some fun?"

"I meant him, not me," Ruby protested through her giggles. "Heaven's, he's only sixteen."

"But he didn't understand that, did he?"

"No," lacing her fingers over her stomach she giggled again. "He thought I was going to lead him astray. In my condition! And the look Seymour gave me…"

"He's very protective. He thinks he has to look after his younger brother," Olympia grinned.

"How do you think they will take to the idea of a baby around the place?" Ruby was suddenly serious.

"Once they get over the shock, I think they'll be fine."

"Have you thought about it though? It won't be just the three of us knowing the truth. They will too. Do you think they might tell anyone?"

"Why would they?" Olympia shrugged.

"Well, from my point of view I know this baby is going to be well cared for and well loved. He will be your son," and reaching over she took Olympia's hand in hers, "or she will be your daughter. Either way, I know it will be in the safest hands possible."

"It will," Olympia breathed. "So if you could possibly hurry up and bring him or her into the world…

When the pains came that evening they were dreadful beyond belief, and lying back against a pillow with her knees apart and her old nightgown bunched up on her swollen stomach, Ruby screamed.

"I can't do this."

"Of course you can," Mrs O'Leary assured her as if she were nothing more than an unruly child with an unappealing task. "Just breath with the pain."

"No. I. Can't!" and with another hideous contraction ripping apart her insides she clenched and twisted the soft rope tied to the bed-head for just that purpose.

Standing to one side Olympia clutched her own stomach.

"This is dreadful. I had no idea," she whispered

"Sure and it's nothing. Wait until the baby's head appears."

"I can hear you both," Ruby managed between groans. "If only I'd known."

"You'd have what? Not let the fella near yer? They all say that, and then they go and do exactly the same again. And nine months later…" Busying herself with spreading newspaper on the sheet beneath Ruby's legs Mrs O'Leary let the end of the sentence hang.

"Not me. I'm never doing this again."

The midwife laughed. "Once the little one's out you won't remember any of it."

"Oh, won't I?"

"No. It's nature's way. Otherwise, you wouldn't be having more children, now would you?"

"Didn't you hear me," Ruby spat. "I'm not going through this again."

"Ah, she's just ravin'," Mrs O'Leary assured a rather worried looking Olympia who, having soaked a cloth in icy water was placing it on Ruby's forehead. "Now if you'll move over there I'm going to check and see how things are going."

Easing Ruby's legs further apart and leaning and squinting, she nodded happily. "Not long now."

Olympia was fetching more hot water when there was a long, drawn out scream, and rushing back with the enamel basin, she hurriedly set it down on the chest of drawers and went over to the bed to grasp Ruby's hand.

"It's coming," she said, her eyes wide and fixed on the place between Ruby's legs and on Mrs O'Leary's busy hands.

"You think I don't know that?" Ruby replied breathlessly.

"Sorry."

"Push girl."

Grunting and panting Ruby bore down. And again. And again.

"I can see the head," came the pronouncement. "Now you," Mrs O'Leary said, looking up and glaring at Olympia. "Massage her belly. Go on girl, get on with it."

Hastily rolling the soaking nightgown further out of the way, Olympia nervously placed her hands on the hugely swollen stomach and kneaded for all she was worth.

"That's it," Mrs O'Leary encouraged. "Good. Now Ruby, push again… good… once more."

And with one mother grunting and sweating and digging her heels into the mattress, and the other frantically massaging and coaxing, a blood-smeared, purple infant emerged into the world.

42

"SO HOW MANY DO you reckon then?" Dilys asked dully, pen hovering over a sheet of paper.

Lilith tried to act as if nothing was out of the ordinary. But it was. Her mother had always been so strong, so dependable, even her father knew that. But now she couldn't even decide on what they were to eat for Christmas dinner. She looked so tired, so washed out. As if she hadn't had a good night's sleep in weeks. She'd heard her too, getting up not just once these past nights to go to the bathroom, but sometimes twice. If only she'd talk to her, tell her exactly what was wrong, but if she dared bring the subject up all her mother did was snap. And her father didn't seem overly concerned, so perhaps she really was worrying over nothing.

"Tully, Appleside and Wickes," she replied, ticking off the individuals who seemed to have taken up permanent residence in the hotel. "That's three, so I think we need to work on having six rooms booked out in total and that'll cater for any last minute enquiries."

"So, thirteen then? And us of course."

"Round it up to fifteen then, just in case. We can always use up the left-overs on Boxing Day."

"Don't forget, we're going to be at Joe and Bessie's."

"Oh, of course. Well, the day after, then."

"And all the way through to the New Year if we're not careful. So, goose or turkey?" her mother asked next.

"Hmm, turkey's more expensive."

Her mother nodded. "Goose then. And vegetables?"

"New potatoes are in season. And peas of course."

That brought a spark of life.

"Doesn't seem right, Christmas dinner without sprouts and a bit of swede and carrot mash. And have you seen the price of oranges? Scandalous, if you ask me."

She agreed. "We should grow them here, rather than import them from Australia."

"There's a lot we should be doing here. So are we done?"

"I think so."

Elbows on the linen covered table, Lilith looked around the empty dining room. When they'd arrived the room had been shabby and dreary. Now, three months later and thanks to copious beeswax, hot soapy water and elbow-grease, the woodwork shone and the claret-coloured chair cushions and curtains were almost as good as new. But that wasn't all. There were fresh flowers on the sideboard too, a small detail but a worthwhile expense in her view.

"Do you think everyone will go away for the holiday like Uncle Joe says?" she asked suddenly. "The railway company seems to think so. I've even heard there'll be more express trains laid on to take people to the seaside."

"If that's true, we'll be pretty quiet over the next few weeks," her mother was also looking about. "On the other hand, it doesn't seem as if there's a lot of money around, from what blokes in the public bar are saying."

"Do you think we're in for hard times then?"

"I hope not. I thought we'd left all that behind. And talking of home, have you heard from your friend lately?"

Lilith started.

"Not recently. Her last letter arrived a couple of weeks ago," she said, conscious of a burning sensation in her cheeks.

"How's she doing?"

"Good. Yes, good. Still going to all her meetings."

"Funny you being mixed up with a revolutionary." Her mother smiled, for the first time that day looking more like her old self. "Mind you, I always said you had more fire and brimstone than all this family put together. You ever thought about taking up a cause on this side of the world?"

She shook her head. "I don't really know the place well enough."

"Strikes me women all over the world get a raw deal sometimes. Or am I wrong?"

"No, you're not wrong, but I've read New Zealand is one of the more forward-looking countries. Maybe

I'll give it some more thought in the New Year. But mum…"

"And in the meantime," her mother interrupted, "have you decided what you're going to wear to the Christmas dance at the town hall? You can't let Ruby hog the limelight all the time, especially since you're just as pretty as she is."

Lilith tried again. "Mum…"

"No, I don't want to talk about it. Not if it's to do with your going back home."

Her mother's face had clouded over again, and her mouth was little more than a thin line.

"We'll have to talk about it one day," she said gently.

"But not now. And not this side of the holidays. So what are you going to wear?"

It was her turn to look uncomfortable. "Oh for heaven's sake! I don't even want to go."

"Don't be like that. It'll be fun. And good for you to get out and meet some nice young men," her mother said, before adding, "men like Ralph Macintyre. He must have some friends, and you know your father thinks very highly of him."

"Dad's made that abundantly clear," Lilith muttered. "It's just a shame Ruby doesn't feel the same way. Poor Ralph."

"I know," her mother sighed. "Well, hopefully she'll soon come around and see what a catch he is. And he does seem a patient man."

"He'll need to be with her." Lilith retorted.

"Now don't be like that. She's been through a lot, has your sister."

"Only through her own fault."

"Oh Lilith, stop being so judgmental. It's not like you. Not like you at all. You need to give Ruby a bit of understanding and try and help her forget."

"What? Having a child and giving it up for adoption?"

There was a strained silence, for it had been agreed all-round the subject was never to be mentioned. Ever.

"Yes I do," her mother said eventually. "Even though she's getting on with things, something like that will stay with her for the rest of her life, one way or another. Now, I'm off to the kitchen to have a chat about this Christmas dinner we're putting on. I suggest you go upstairs and have a look through your wardrobe, because if you want something new to wear you've only got a few days left to find it."

Lilith sighed. If only Ralph Macintyre hadn't shown up again. But he had, and as large as life and in the private bar, of all places. Up from the South Island to spend Christmas with his family, he'd told her his intention was to enjoy everything Auckland had to offer while he was in town. And in the company of the Doherty sisters.

So far they'd had been taken tea at the Esplanade Hotel in Devonport, a trip requiring a thirty-minute ferry journey in each direction, enjoyed a production at the new St James theatre, and strolled along the seafront at Kohimarama during which she had to admit, he gave them a pretty interesting talk on the volcano dominating the harbour. Now he was escorting them to the festive ball, the highlight of the years' social calendar, and while tickets had been snapped up in a frenzy, she had about as much enthusiasm in attending as she would have dipping her toe into a vat of boiling oil.

Ruby, on the other hand, was indifferent, chilly even as she was about most things these days. Oh, she'd go, with her platinum blonde hair professionally styled and wearing something stunning and expensive - though where she got the money to spend on her outfits, Lilith had no idea. But what did that matter to her sister, as long as the ladies were green with envy and the men drooled.

And Ralph? To be honest she wasn't quite sure what he was getting out of the whole exercise other than perhaps the good-natured ribbing of his friends. For he was no nearer winning her sister's heart than he'd been on the *Remuera*.

43

HAVING CLOSED UP FOR THE evening and after draping swags of ivy around the hotels reception lobby, Lilith was in the private bar dotting about more foliage and wondering whether or not there would be carol singers knocking on the doors every night until Christmas itself. That's what happened in Portsea where regardless how little money they had, the regulars of *The Saracen's Head* dug deep into their pockets to reward anyone prepared to brave the cold, dark wintery weather. In Auckland though it was warm and not only that, broad daylight until eight o'clock.

Stepping back from the mantelpiece and tilting her head she was just thinking that perhaps it was all a bit too much when Ruby wandered in.

"Don't know why you're bothering," she said, coming up beside her and fingering a thin spray of pine needles.

"Of course we have to bother. It's Christmas. And it's expected."

"By who. Not the people around here."

"You're wrong. Everyone celebrates in one way or another. I just want it to be nice for our guests and our customers."

Ruby shrugged. "So it's business then, is it? Like those flowers you keep buying, that no one notices."

"Do you have to so miserable? Anyway, what are you up to? Going somewhere special?" she asked, for no one could ignore how her sister was dressed.

"Point Chevalier, if you must know."

"Dixieland. The cabaret," Lilith filled in. "With anyone we know?"

"Depends who's going to be there."

"Ruby, this can't go on."

"What, sister dear?"

"The drinking. And using people for your own ends."

Ruby studied another arrangement. "I have no idea what you are talking about."

"Really? Look at you. The dresses, the jewellery."

"Jealous?"

"No. Just worried about you."

"Then don't be."

"That's not so easy. Come on, we're family. We have to stick together if we're going to have any chance of making a go here."

"So you want to make it work, do you? And are you prepared to stay here with the rest of us then? Or are you going to pack up your stuff and go home as if this was just a holiday."

"That's not fair. You know mum and dad agreed my studies are important."

"That was then."

"And what's that supposed to mean?"

"I would say things are different now."

Lilith stopped. "Would you? In what way?"

"Only that mum is sick. But I would have thought that was obvious."

"You've noticed it too?"

"Hard not to really."

"She was like it back home but thought she'd come right on the boat. Seems she just rallied for a while."

"You think she's dying?"

"Ruby!" she was horrified, though a moment later realised it wasn't that at all. It was more shock at having her own fear put into words. "Ruby don't. I can't bear it."

"So you think so, too."

"No. I won't think that way. I can't."

"Then you'll just have to be like me, won't you, and get on with things while you can. That's why I'm doing what she wants. Getting out and about, and who knows? One day soon I might find a suitable husband. That'll cheer her up."

"But not this way." Lilith touched her sister's arm. "Not by mixing with people in nightclubs."

"There's another way for people like us?"

"What do you mean, *people like us*?"

"Homies. Isn't that what we're called? New arrivals in this land of plenty? After all, it's not like we grew up here and have a ready-made circle of friends, is it?"

"What about Ralph. He thinks the world of you. And mum and dad like him."

"He's not my type."

"How can you say that?"

"Easy. You know what I'm like, and you know what he's like. We've nothing in common. Nothing," she stressed.

"That's a bit strong."

Had she not been staring at her sister Lilith would never have caught the expression that flickered over her face. Either way, it was gone in an instant.

"I'd eat him for breakfast," Ruby mocked, turning on her high heels and walking away.

"And he's too nice for that," she finished.

Accepting the glass of champagne from the gentleman beside her, a man she barely knew after all, Ruby gave a tight smile. They were such strange creatures for no matter how ungracious she was, they still chased after her. In fact, the more aloof she became, the more eager they were. She had no idea why it should be that way and to be honest, she hardly cared. Not anymore.

She knew it wasn't normal, this dark mood that came over her, settling like a lump of granite in the pit of her stomach. Nor was it usual to want to lash out when she was at her lowest. Surely she should be over it by now? She'd been home well over a month, and while she knew handing over her baby had been the right thing to do, she hadn't expected the feeling of utter despair that descended afterwards. Nor that it would stay with her as long as it had.

It could have been worse of course. Had a stranger not struck up a conversation with her on the train back to Auckland she'd never have found her way into to the city's booming nightlife for Betty, as she'd introduced herself, was a waitress at one of the most popular jazz clubs.

"Come along. See for yourself," she'd said, lighting up a cigarette. "It's all money and glamour, and the place to be if you're looking for a little fun."

"Who isn't?" she'd replied out of politeness.

With little to lose, and somewhat curious, she'd done so a night or two later.

"You should apply for a job here," Betty said, seemingly pleased to see her and suggesting she sat close enough to the bar that they could chat between customers. "Pay's not bad but it's the tips that make it worthwhile. That and the hours."

But Ruby wasn't looking for work to pass the time. She was after something else, and it wasn't long before she was approached and a drink suggested.

It had been easy after that.

Now her date leaned in to ask, over the blare of the orchestra, "Care to dance?"

The back of his finger was trailing down her arm.

"Not this time," and she stared pointedly at the morass of dashing young men and frivolous butterflies hanging onto their partner's necks.

Her date tried again. "I see Sybil's over there. And with Johnny too. Shall we join them at their table?"

"If you wish."

"I'll bring over the fizz."

"Darling," Sibyl's arms were wide apart as if any moment she might burst into song. "Love your dress. Simply gorgeous isn't it Johnny," and she cast fawning eyes at the man sitting beside her.

"Completely."

Ruby didn't like Johnny. To be honest, she didn't much care for hard-eyed, snooty Sibyl either. But they were part of the smart set and while she had no wish to become a member of their clique, she could hardly drink alone.

Johnny was talking loudly about a house-party he'd been invited to. "Taking the old car, so room for one more," his eyes flicked her way, "should be heaps of fun."

"I'm sure it will be," she replied, "but another time."

Sybil raised her glass. "To fun," her laugh was a touch too brittle, "and lots of it."

"Hear, hear," Ruby's date joined in, reaching over to top up everyone's drink.

Sipping her champagne Ruby watched those on the dance floor. Not everyone was a socialite that much was obvious, but that didn't mean society mixed in every way, regardless New Zealand was supposed to have shunned the long-established class system of the old country. Only a fairer distribution of wealth could really bring such a thing about, but at least it made things easier to get a foothold. Back in Portsea it would have been impossible.

The conversation around her droned on and while she tuned out most of it, every now and then a word or phrase caught her attention. That was why she turned to see who Sybil was gossiping about with such salacious enjoyment. Sitting at a nearby table the young woman dressed in the very latest fashion and with long and clearly expensive diamanté drops in her ears appeared to be a good thirty years younger than her male friend. Not that it seemed to bother either of them since they were quite wrapped up in each other.

"She's a whore," Sybil said, her eyes glittering maliciously.

"And how would you know that, my precious?"

"Everyone knows it. She's his little plaything. Has been for about a year now."

"You still haven't answered my question." Johnny knocked the ash off his cigarette.

Sybil pouted. "Myra told me if you really want to know."

"Then it must be true, I suppose," he rolled his eyes. "What do you think, Ruby? Does our friend over there look like a loose woman to you?"

Ruby stared. First at him, then at Sibyl. "No more than any other woman here."

Having narrowed his eyes Ruby's date was squinting at the young woman, "Now you come to mention it, I'm pretty sure I've seen her at one of Kitty Malloy's extravaganza's."

"Kitty Malloy's?" Sybil brightened. "The bordello in Freeman's Bay? Oh how terrible risqué. I've heard so much about those parties. My God, they're almost orgies aren't they? Do tell. Maybe I could go, one day? Wear a mask and all that so no one would know who I was?"

Johnny smirked. "You might be a woman of the world, my heart," he toasted her, "but I'm not sure even you should go that far."

"Spoilsport! There's very little that can shock me. Heavens! you should know that!" and she broke off into peals of laughter.

Ruby needed another drink.

44

WHEN TWO NIGHTS LATER LILITH and Ruby descended the front stairs in all their finery, the barmen had shut the doors for the evening, the customers had left for home, the floors had been swept and the glasses and crockery washed and back on their shelves. Waiting in the hotel lobby Dilys caught her breath. How on earth had she and Jim produced such marvellous creatures? Ruby, so polished, so poised, and of course so utterly fashionable in beaded chiffon. And Lilith, an enigma in dove grey silk.

"Come on, give us a twirl," she said as if needing to break the spell.

In the middle of the foyer, Lilith did just that before asking, "Has Ralph arrived?"

"Not yet. But don't worry, I'm sure he won't be long."

Ruby was already heading in the direction of the private bar.

"Let's not complain," she said over her shoulder, "after all it gives us time for a quick drink before we go."

Dilys glanced at Jim, who shrugged as if to say *where's the harm?*

Having slipped behind the bar Ruby held up a bottle as the others joined her. "What's your poison?".

"Wine. But only a half glass for me," Lilith said. "Have you decided what to take with us?"

"Champagne, of course. What else?"

"This prohibition is ridiculous. Fancy not being able to sell drinks at a dance. Couldn't see anyone standing for it at home," Dilys said, thankful for the chance to sit down at a table. Her aches and pains were constant and unrelenting now, and she was looking forward to a soothing bath once the girls had gone.

"Well, that's the law here. But you can't stop people drinking so the whole thing is rather pointless."

"I think the idea is to curb it, not prevent it altogether," Lilith said mildly.

"Really," Ruby raised an eyebrow. "I hope no one has any intention of curbing me tonight."

"As if anyone would dare," she answered tartly.

Dilys stepped in quickly, "Either way, I'm sure you're both going to have a good time."

"You know, you could have come with us," Lilith said.

"Don't be silly. At our age?"

"Speak for yourself, girl." Standing behind her Jim guffawed. "Plenty of life in this old dog."

"You wish."

"Ah ha. Sounds like your escort has arrived," he said as everyone looked up on hearing the front door open. "Now girls, play fair and share the poor man equally."

Dark hair slicked back, black tuxedo and of all things; an emerald green polka dot bow tie, Ralph breezed in and strode over to shake Jim's hand, before turning first to Ruby, then to Lilith.

"Not late am I?" he grinned.

Anyone could see he was bowled over by their appearance, Dilys thought. Now if only Ruby would give him a little encouragement.

"Not as far as I'm aware," her daughter said coolly.

"Of course you're not," she assured him. "Why the girls have only just come down."

"Good. Well, I hope no one minds but I met Freddie here in town earlier and when I found out he was going to the ball too, I suggested we all went together."

Dressed in a similar fashion, though with subtler neckwear Freddie stepped forward.

"I trust that's acceptable to everyone," he said, shoving his hands into his pockets as if not knowing what else to do with them.

When Ruby merely looked down her nose and offered, "It's fine with me," Dilys wanted the floor to open up and swallow her.

"What are we going to do with her," she said to Jim, once the foursome had left in a taxicab.

"I dunno girl. But she's not herself."

Dilys retorted. "She hasn't been herself since she got home from Whangarei. She should have snapped out of it by now. Do you think she needs to see a doctor?"

"No, not yet. Just give her a little more time," Jim said, slipping his arm around her shoulders. "You know what she's like when people fuss over her."

"Don't I just. Maybe you're right. Maybe I'm expecting too much, too soon."

With the girls gone and Jim downstairs listening to the radio, Dilys was able to bathe in peace, a treat she'd never known in Portsea where an all over wash meant a tin bath in front of the fire. A proper soak in private, and in a full-length cast iron bath with claw-feet at that, was a luxury she'd come to relish and not just because she'd discovered hot water relieved her aches and pains for a while. It was more that in locking the bathroom door she could keep out all the other demands, for there was always someone or something wanting her attention. Not that she was complaining since she liked to be busy. It took her mind off other things. Like Ruby. She worried more about her youngest than the other two put together. It was natural really. Alfie was never any bother, even growing up, and Lil was the same. Ruby was her baby and perhaps that was why she was a little more lenient with her. Spoiled her even, slipping her money every now and then so she could treat herself to something new to wear when she went out. She had an inkling Jim did the same. Didn't seem to lift her daughter's spirits, though. She was just so moody these days and not herself at all. If only she could move on and put the whole sorry mess behind her, after all it wasn't like she'd formed any attachment to the baby or anything like that. In fact, after letting everyone know she was pregnant she'd barely spoken about it again, and she certainly hadn't argued when the decision was made to have the child put up for adoption. At the time she'd thought it a good sign, meaning Ruby wanted to get back on with her life. But somewhere along the line, something had changed. And the amount of drink she was putting away didn't bear thinking about. She needed a husband, and a good one at that. Like Ralph Macintyre. He'd take care of her if only she'd let him. Instead, she treated him as if he didn't exist. It was a concern, all right. And who knew what she got up to in those nightclubs she liked to go to? Having read about the goings-on in the newspapers she knew it couldn't be good - not that she thought Ruby would let another man near her. Not in that way. But if she wasn't careful she'd end up with a reputation and then who'd want to marry her?

She'd have a quiet word with her, woman to woman. And soon. It wasn't as if she had any choice, for most days there was no easing the pains in her back and stomach anymore, no matter what she took. And she was tired, oh so tired. She daren't go to a doctor in case he reported her to the authorities for not being truthful on her application, but at least there had been no more episodes like the one at home when she'd fainted in front of Lilith, that time she'd come round. It had been touch and go, since Lilith had cried out for Jim and the two of them had gone on and on about taking her to hospital for a check-up. She'd managed to calm them down, saying as how she hadn't eaten that day and it had made her light-headed. She was on her guard now and making sure to eat small amounts when everyone was around the table. But with no appetite even that was hard sometimes. Looking down at the ribs sticking through her flesh and the jutting bones of her pelvis she cursed them as if they were the cause and not a symptom. The weight was falling away from her thighs too. Dear God, she didn't want to die. Not yet. There was far too much to do. Who'd take care of Jim? For all his blustering, he'd never cope. And the girls, they needed her too.

If only she could keep going a while longer, until her daughters were married at least. In her heart, she knew that was unlikely. The thing eating at her insides had other ideas.

45

"I'M WORRIED ABOUT RUBY," Lilith said, watching from the doorway as her mother squared up the linen cupboard.

"Why?"

"It's the way she's acting. The way she behaved at the ball last night."

"And how was that?"

"I know she's unhappy," she began, knowing she should choose her words carefully. "It's the way she treated Ralph. Treated all of us really," she said.

"And how was that?"

Her mother was waiting.

"Look, forget I said anything. She drank a little too much, that's all," she said. "Now, should you be doing this? Wouldn't you rather have a lie-down?"

"No, I wouldn't. I want to know what happened."

Regretting having ever brought the subject up, she ploughed on. "Well, she does seem to know a lot of people, considering we've only been in Auckland a short while."

"Men?"

She nodded, before adding quickly, "Don't get me wrong, she didn't throw herself at anyone or anything like that. But quite a few people stopped to talk to her and make arrangements to catch up."

"And?"

"They were clearly the fast set. You know, champagne and caviar, all that. Not our kind of people at all."

Her mother's shoulders slumped as she said, "They get up to other antics too, or so I've heard. How did Ralph take it?"

"He was very gentlemanly. Tried to make out he was amused by it all."

"And was he?"

"Probably not. I think he was more disappointed than anything."

Her mother shook her head. "Oh, Ruby."

"Mum," seeing her mother lean on the shelf as if for support Lilith felt guiltier than ever. "I'm sorry, I shouldn't really have said anything. She just needs something to focus on. A job perhaps."

Though she'd tried to make out the answer was simple, in truth her sister had shown very little interest in finding work. She'd even baulked at helping out in the hotel, something that in the end Lilith was grateful for since it was far easier to get things done without the accompanying moaning and groaning.

"She'll come right eventually," her mother said, though not with much conviction.

"I know. And I'm not trying to come down hard on her, truly I'm not."

"She has to find her own way; the way you're finding yours." Moving another pile of linens, her mother continued without turning round. "It's Christmas Eve in two days. Are we ready? Or is there anything else we need to do?"

Lilith found herself straightening her shoulders, "As far as I know we're all set. The vegetables have been ordered and are coming up from the market first thing that morning."

"And the poultry?"

"The same."

"Good. We've plenty of bacon and eggs in for breakfast on both Christmas Day and Boxing Day?"

She nodded. "I made sure of it."

"Have our guests said whether they will be vacating their rooms over the holiday? Or will they be staying on?"

"Only Mr Appleside has made plans. The other two seem quite happy to carry on as usual. Apparently they still expect to be busy, but I can't see them being any trouble. Can you?'

Only then did her mother stop what she was doing.

"What do you think of Mr Tully," she asked unexpectedly.

Lilith frowned. "He seemed fine the last time I saw him. Is anything wrong?"

"Not at all. He gets on very well with your father, you know."

"They're fellow Irishmen. What do you expect?"

"I just thought…"

"Thought what?" she asked crisply.

"Oh, nothing."

"Good. Then let's leave it at nothing."

If her mother had been about to say any more the moment had gone, for the front desk bell was ringing.

"Bother," Lilith grumbled good-naturedly.

"I'll go," her mother offered.

"No, you stay here and carry on with what you're doing. With a bit of luck, it'll be a booking for two rooms and not one, otherwise we'll be eating goose pie for weeks."

After the gloom of the deep and windowless linen cupboard, the sunlight streaming in through the etched glass panels in the front door caused Lilith to squint as she hurried down the stairs to the foyer.

"Good morning," she said brightly.

And stopped dead.

Gazing around as if to take in every aspect of the place, the woman in the stylish cream jacket and pleated skirt had her back to the desk. And while the matching hat obscured both her profile and hair, Lilith knew the latter would be blonde and sleek, and cut short just like a boy's.

She couldn't speak. Couldn't breathe. Just stood there, clutching the bannister as the woman turned.

"Hello Lilith," Grace said, her face wreathed in smiles.

Clinging to each other far longer than might be appropriate, were there anyone to see, it was as if all things had ceased and time hung in the air, suspended.

Lilith wanted to stay crushed in Grace's arms forever, their bodies pressed tightly together and breathing so completely as one. Not daring to open her eyes for fear she was dreaming, she had no idea whether to laugh or to cry.

"I can't believe it," she leaned back, gurgling and choking. "I can't believe you're here."

"I am," Grace laughed gently.

It was on the tip of her tongue to ask, *how...when...* and retreat into the mundane to make something so unbelievable, so incredible, real.

Instead she whispered, "I've been so lonely."

"I know. That's why I had to come."

The urge to touch, to kiss, was more than she could bear, and leaning in and closing her eyes once more, she brushed her cheek against Grace's before letting her lips trail down to the corner of her lover's mouth.

"Heaven's," she laughed, grabbing her friend's hands in her own, "what are we doing standing here in the foyer. Come on, come with me. Leave your cases, they'll be fine."

Dragging her up the stairs and along the corridor, she called out, "Mum, you will never guess who's here!" before slipping her arm around Grace's waist and pulling her forward when her mother poked her head around the linen cupboard door.

"Look who it is! It's Grace," she burst out as if her mother wouldn't remember.

She knew she was beaming, knew her feelings were written all over her face. But right at that moment she didn't give a hoot.

"Goodness gracious," her mother was as taken aback as she'd been. "How wonderful. But where have you sprung from?"

"We docked this morning."

"This morning? You never said anything, Lil."

"I didn't know!"

"You mean it was a surprise?"

"Yes!"

"What's going on," Jim came stomping up the stairs behind them. "Could hear the racket in the cellar…Bloody hell!" he grinned.

Sitting on the bed in one of the better guest rooms, one that overlooked the street rather than the alley, Lilith clutched Grace's hand, still afraid that if she let her go she'd disappear in a puff of smoke.

"Tell me I'm not dreaming."

"You're not," Grace leaned in and kissed her for the umpteenth time.

"But why didn't you say anything about coming here in your letters?"

"It was a spur of the moment decision. I thought I could handle the separation, you know, be grown up about it because I do understand why you had to come here. I even tried force myself to imagine what it would be like before you'd gone. But really, nothing could have prepared me, and so when I woke up one morning feeling as miserable as sin I thought, what am I doing?

And since you couldn't come home, I decided to come to you. Besides," she said, "other than France I've never been abroad, so it was the perfect opportunity for a bit of travelling."

"A bit of travelling?" Lilith repeated in amazement. "You can't get any further than the opposite side of the globe!"

"Exactly."

"But your job? The movement?"

"All doing very well without me I imagine. The school was very good about my having extended leave, but they would like me back in time for the start of the Easter term."

"In four months." Lilith's tone was flat. "You'll need to go back in mid-February then."

"Don't think about it." Grace admonished before continuing, "And as for everything else, I thought while I was here it would be a good opportunity to see how things are run. You know, from women's right to equal pay and all that. Ask the hard questions. But enough of all that. Tell me all about what you've been up to recently."

"Let me see. Well, we're busy getting ready for our first Christmas - oh Grace, you couldn't have come at a better time."

"Really?"

"I was dreading it. Not that I could tell anyone. And Ruby…" she stumbled.

"What about her?"

"Not sure what I might have said in the last letter you received. That would have been when? End of

October? Had we made the arrangements when I wrote?"

"Yes. Your aunt was sorting something out. A family she knew?"

"Right. Well, obviously that's all behind us now, and the people who put her up adopted the baby themselves. Though it wasn't completely above board."

"Oh?"

"Yes. It was decided it would be better for everyone if the registration was in their name, rather than Ruby's. Of course, that means there was no formal adoption or paperwork, so the baby will never know it's real parents."

"Might be for the best."

"I know," even so, she wasn't convinced.

"So what's wrong with Ruby?"

"She's changed, and not for the better."

"How do you mean?"

"She's not her old happy-go-lucky self anymore. You'll see for yourself this evening."

"Perhaps it's still too soon?"

"That's what everyone else keeps saying. But let's not talk about her. My goodness, we've got such a lot of catching up to do, and I've no idea where to start. I know, let me help you unpack," and jumping up and pulling Grace to her feet she nodded towards where her father had stood her suitcases.

Only then did she realise unpacking was the last thing she wanted to do, and releasing Grace's hand in order to slip her arms around her neck she whispered, "Hold me."

46

CHRISTMAS PROVED MORE SUCCESSFUL THAN Dilys had expected, despite it being celebrated in temperatures more usually found in August back home. But once the decorations were tidied away she knew things couldn't be put off any longer. Lilith had Grace to lean on, at least for the time being, and Ruby had Lilith. Her only concern was Jim. And she needed him strong enough for everyone.

She'd waited until all three girls were out for the evening. Pictures, they'd said, though not what they were going to see and interestingly enough, Ralph and his friend Freddie had tagged along, so there was still hope a little romance might brew there after all.

"Time we talked Jim," she said, settling down on the brown and gold sofa.

He lowered his paper. Not that he followed much of what went on in New Zealand, but he'd started keeping up with the rugby much as he'd done with the football in England. 'It's the national sport, doll,' he'd told her not long after they'd taken the place over. "Got to be seen to show a bit of support, 'specially in the public bar. It's like a religion in there.'

Now he looked at her. "Oh yes? What do you want to talk about? Something on your mind, doll?"

"There is."

"Go on then. Spit it out."

"Why don't you go and get us a drink first."

He didn't move. Rather he looked puzzled. "That's not like you."

"Don't you worry about that, just go and get me a port and brandy. Get something for yourself too."

She could see he was uncertain, so she chivvied him, "Go on then."

He was back in a minute or so, a glass in each hand.

"Here you go, girl," he said, handing one to her before turning back to the table. "Now what is it you wanted to say."

"Come and sit over here," she patted the place next to her.

"Blimey! Sounds serious," he tried for a chuckle.

"It is," and when he sat down, legs apart so that his left knee touched hers, she took his hand. "There's something I have to tell you."

His palm was warm and his fingers reassuring, and she drew strength from believing that whatever she told him, nothing would break the bond between them. Hadn't they already loved each other through thick and thin? And dear God, there had been enough thin to last a lifetime. Now there was this.

"It's about my back. Well, my aches and pains, really."

He squeezed her hand. "Go on."

"I'm sick, Jim. Sicker than I let on, and you need to know New Zealand isn't going to cure what I have. Doesn't matter how good the climate is."

There was uncertainty in his gentle eyes. And something else, something she should have expected; a glimmer of denial.

"Thing is," she continued, willing him to take in how serious she was being, and willing him not to make light of what she was saying, for it would only make it harder for both of them, "I'm getting worse by the day. And I'm tired. You have no idea. Sometimes I can hardly get out of bed. I've got no energy, and no will to do things."

"I'll talk to Ruby," he cut in. "Get her to pull her weight. Give you the break you need."

But she shook her head. "Won't make any difference, Jim."

"Then you need to get yourself to the hospital. Have some tests and get them to sort you out," he said, firmly.

"Too late for that."

"You don't know that."

"I do."

He didn't move.

"You've got to face what's happening. I need you to be strong for the girls," she told him. "And for Alfie and Alice and the little one when it comes along."

Her eyes flicked to the mantelpiece, and the photo that had been enclosed in their Christmas card. Taken in Alice's mother's back garden a few months back, seeing how happy they both looked had brought tears to her eyes. Not that she begrudged them anything. It was the knowledge she'd never see or be held by her son again. Not in this world anyway.

Jim was breathing heavily.

"I knew you weren't right," he said, staring down at the fingers clutching his. "Known it a long time."

"You never said."

"Been waiting for you to tell me."

"Oh."

"It was the doctor."

"What doctor?"

"The one back home. When we got our medicals to come here."

She frowned. "What did he tell you?"

"Nothing. He just asked a few questions, that was all."

"Like what?"

"Like how you were at home. You saw him before I did and I knew he'd already given you a pass so it had to be something he was suspicious of, but you didn't want him to know. Tell you the truth girl, I was surprised you got your certificate so easily, what with your back and your belly and all that."

She nodded. "He wanted me to go to the hospital and see a specialist."

"So why didn't you," his voice rose.

"It was already too late."

"You didn't know that," he said sharply. "You should have gone. What stopped you?"

"Dunno really. Maybe I wanted one last chance to make a difference to our lives."

"You saying you didn't go, just so we could all come here?"

His cheeks had reddened and his eyes, those lovely gentle eyes, were staring at her in utter disbelief.

"We've had it good, you and me," she said, pulling his hand into her lap and placing her palm on top. "Might not have always seemed that way, but we have."

He opened his mouth to speak, but she got in first. "No Jim, don't say things you might regret later."

She saw it then. Saw it in his eyes. This thing had the power to defeat him too.

But it seemed he wasn't done yet.

"Now don't you go talking like that, girl, as if it's all come to an end. Because it hasn't. We're going to make an appointment in the morning to see someone at the hospital here and get this sorted."

"Look at me Jim. You reckon they can sort this?"

She saw his eyes drop from the dark rings around her eyes and sunken cheeks to her sparrow-like arms, and from there to her wasted thighs and bony knees.

"Need a bit of fattening up, that's all," he said gruffly.

"Can't eat. Got no appetite."

"I'm not going to let you go, girl."

He squeezed her fingers so hard, it hurt.

"We need to make plans," she said gently.

"No!" he'd stood. "No," he repeated, a little calmer this time, "no plans. We'll carry on as normal."

"But the girls…"

"Don't have to know anything yet. I'll talk to Ruby and get her to pull her weight a bit more. That'll help you. Otherwise why upset them? Bloody hell girl, you'll probably outlive us all."

"Wouldn't that be a turn up for the books," she smiled.

47

RUBY GLANCED OVER AT FREDDIE. Nowhere near as good-looking as Ralph, he did have one or two redeeming features. He was tall, like Bert had been, and his chest was broad. But that was where any similarity ended, for he certainly didn't have Bert's flirtatious charm or patter, nor would Bert have been as content to languish in Ralph's shadow. Funny that, since when comparing Ralph and Freddie it was the latter who had the money and influence. She'd asked around, discreetly of course, and it seemed his father might be in line for a knighthood. Services to industry and all that, which she supposed was a sign the family were doing rather well for themselves. Freddie was something in the city, she wasn't sure what, but it had to do with insuring cargos and the like, though he'd told them his ultimate aim was to get into politics and the sooner the better. Even now he was leaning forward, elbows on his knees, completely absorbed in the conversation he was having with Lil and Grace. They suited each other, those three. Not part of the real world.

Ralph was asking her if she'd like another drink.

"Love one," she smiled.

"You fancy a stroll later?' he suggested, topping up her glass from the bottle of wine on their table.

"What, at this time of night?"

"You'll be safe," he assured her, "you'll be with me."

There was a burst of raucous laughter from another table in the overcrowded Vulcan Lane pub, and she saw Freddie look over and nod a greeting to a fair-haired man. In return, an ink-stained finger was lifted to the brim of a hat. Journalists, she thought, since it was well known they liked to frequent the area of an evening. She'd overheard them talking too, though gossiping might be a better way of putting it.

Ralph was saying something.

"Sorry," she said quickly, "I missed that. What did you say?"

"I was wondering if you would like to come out to the pictures again before I return to Christchurch. Just the two of us this time."

"Oh, but that wouldn't be fair on the others," she protested.

"I'm sure they wouldn't mind."

"Ralph," she said, looking not at him but at her glass, "it won't work, you know. You and me."

"How can you be certain?"

"Because I am. We're two completely different people."

"I'm not so sure that matters. Anyway, what is it they say about opposites attracting?"

"Not in this case," she said firmly.

"Look, don't say no right away. Let's hold off and see how things pan out when I get back up from the South Island again. You never know," and now there was a mischievous grin on his face, "you might have changed your mind."

"I won't."

"You don't think there's any chance for us?"

"Not a one," and she smiled to soften the blow.

"Then I'll just have to pursue your sister," he came back.

Good luck with that, she wanted to say.

"You know, there are other girls in the world," she said instead.

"Not like the Doherty sisters," and he raised his glass.

It was just as well he had no idea of her yearning to reach out and smooth the hair at his temple. And more. She wanted to touch her hand to his cheek and draw his face towards hers. She wanted to breathe him in, consume him. And more again. She wanted that exquisite hesitation before their lips touched. And the sinking, drowning when they did.

Her heart ached, for she couldn't bear the thought of hurting him. But that was exactly what she would do. And badly.

Reaching for her glass, she drained the contents in one go.

"Anyone for another," she asked, a little too brightly.

Despite what her mother and father might hope, Ruby knew she and Ralph had no chance of a future together. He was too middle class for one thing - not that she held that against him. Heavens! Who was she to be snobbish, given where the Doherty's had come from? But his family would have the expectation his bride would come from similar circumstances to their own and more importantly, have a scrupulous background. And that was where things would unravel, for how could she put herself forward as something she was not. She was soiled goods. Tarnished. And when the McIntyre's uncovered the truth…?

She couldn't bear the thought. And even if it didn't come to that, how could she let him base his future happiness on a lie? He was too good, too decent.

Of course she could come right out and tell him how she'd borne a child to another man. Take a chance and do it now, before it was too late. But she hadn't the courage nor the strength to confront that particular demon. And not just for his sake. Imagine the look in his eyes as he edged away to put a little distance between them? She'd never cope, and wasn't she already struggling to surface from her dark moods?

No, she'd save everyone the hurt, and look elsewhere for a husband.

And maybe not too far, she thought, glancing across the table.

"Why not consider staying," Freddie was saying, "both of you. We do have a strong women's movement here too, you know. And not only were we the first country to give women the vote but ever since nineteen-nineteen women have been able to put themselves up as parliamentary candidates too," he finished proudly.

"Politics rather than unionism," Grace smiled at Lilith.

"You could do worse."

"Unfortunately, I'm due back at school for the start of the summer term."

"And I need to go back and get my teaching certificate," Lilith added.

"There's nothing stopping you getting it here, is there?" Freddie said to Lilith before turning to Grace once more, "And I'm sure you would easily find a position over here. If it was what you wanted of course."

"You are out to persuade us," Grace said.

"For my own ends. Yes, it's true. We have the same problems here as you have in England, and it would pay me to align with a number of those issues if I'm to get into government."

"But there are already strong female voices here."

"There are. But they're mainly affiliated with the Labour Party."

Grace was nodding. "Are you sure you're not simply paying lip service to such causes for your own ends?"

"Not at all. I really do believe an equal society is the way forward." And then he laughed. "As does my mother."

"It's something I'll think about. But I have to tell you, England is my home."

"I understand. And you, Lilith? Can I not persuade you to remain in New Zealand a little longer?"

"I'm sorry," she said, "I also have to return at some stage, though I will be here a little while longer. You might have noticed, my mother isn't at all well, and I have promised to stay and help out until she improves."

Freddie nodded. "Then I will have to make the most of you while you are here."

"You will," she smiled.

48

SITTING ON THE WHITE PAINTED verandah in a comfortable wicker armchair, Dilys thought Joe and Bessie's garden the height of loveliness. Here and there on the clipped lawn were sprinklings of creamy gardenia petals, while in the surrounding flower beds, statuesque lilies vied with showy chrysanthemums and blousy dahlias for attention, all under the under the watchful eye of huge glossy-leaved rhododendrons and mature elms and sycamores.

"It's just so perfect," she said to Bessie. "Like a park. All you need's a duck pond and a bandstand in the corner."

She gave a wheezing, laboured chuckle.

Her sister-in-law placed her cup and saucer down on the hammered brass tea table. "It is lovely. But as much as I'd like to take the credit, it's not down to us. No, it was the previous owners I believe. They put in a lot of effort into getting to look like a garden they'd had in Kent, or so I'm told."

"Doesn't matter. Everything's in bloom and the scent is quite magical."

"That'll be Joe's roses."

"Funny how they grow here too."

"It's all to do with the climate."

"Yes," she mused, "Jim used to go on and on about that. Telling me it was permanently warm and sunny here."

"Well, I wouldn't go that far. It does get chilly in winter."

"Ah, but nothing like as cold as in England."

"No."

"I'm glad we came here, Bessie. Glad we got the chance for an adventure really," Dilys said, tugging at the rug over her knees. Regardless there wasn't a cloud in the sky, she just couldn't seem to get warm these days. "I do hope Alfie and Alice come over too, especially once the kiddie's born. They should see the place for themselves."

"They should," Bessie agreed.

"Not sure Lil will stay, though,' she gazed into the distance for a moment. "Very close to Grace, she is. 'Course, they got plenty in common. I worried about that at first you know. Thought it might get her into trouble, all that championing women's rights, not to mention trying to improve the lot of women teachers. Yes, you can say one thing about Lil, she doesn't do things by half. Ruby now, well she's a different kettle of fish," and she rolled her eyes. "The only rights she's interested in are her own, though I have to say she's come good lately and taken over a lot of what I used to do. That's Jim for you. Said he was going to have a word with her, and he certainly did. Shame she wasn't interested in that Ralph Macintyre. He was a good catch, and I thought they might have suited each other. He's back in the South Island now."

"I didn't know that," Bessie said.

"Mmm. She says there was nothing between them, but I dunno. Jim had hopes of course. Well so did I if the truth be known. But you can't live your kid's lives for them, can you? All you can do is be there to pick up the pieces if it all turns to custard. I really wanted to see her settled down. Settled down and married with kiddies of her own. It's what she needs."

"And you will."

Dilys wasn't smiling anymore. "Don't do that Bessie."

"What?"

"Make out there's plenty of time left. I'm sick of people doing that. It's what Jim does."

"I'm sorry, you're right."

"I know it's hard to watch something like this. It's not easy from where I'm sitting either. We just need to be realistic, that's all. Otherwise there'll be regrets later."

"How's he holding up?"

Dilys looked into the distance again. "Only he could tell you really. He's not his old self but he's keeping it together for the girls, and that's not easy at times. I caught him crying the other day. Crying, can you believe it? My Jim." She shook her head. "Then he gives me that smile of his, as if nothing's wrong."

She said nothing for a while. Then, "You will look after him, won't you. Make sure he doesn't go to pieces and neglect the business or anything like that. He needs to be busy if he's going to take his mind off things. I know my Jim."

"We'll do that."

"And the girls. They'll need a bit of support too."

"Of course." Bessie cleared her throat loudly. "Are you cold? Do you want another shawl?"

"Wouldn't say no. If it's no bother that is."

"Don't be silly. Of course it isn't. I'll just pop inside and get one."

Somewhere a bee was humming, and closing her eyes she allowed herself to drift. Her granny used to say you could talk to bees. Tell them all sorts of stuff. But that was back at home. Doubt they'd hear you in Auckland, thanks to the cicadas with their infernal clicking, on and on until the sun went down. Jim said it would stop altogether when the weather turned cooler. The birds were nice though, chirping away.

She never dreamt New Zealand would be like this. But then what had she to go on when he first brought up the idea. All she knew was a crummy pub and a fifteen by twenty backyard stacked with crates and barrels. She wasn't daft though, not everyone who emigrated ended up with what Joe and Bessie had. Plenty were surviving on a lot less, even so, it wasn't like at home where families lived three or four floors high and never saw a ray of sunshine. No, this was paradise compared to all that. So, all-in-all he'd had been right. She'd tell him later when the taxi dropped her back at the Tivoli.

God, she was tired. It was all this fresh air. She just wasn't used to it.

It wouldn't be long now, she knew that. Accepted it too. She'd done her bit. Taken care of a husband and brought up her kids the best she could. Oh, there had been times she'd despaired but that happened to everyone. On the whole though, they'd had far more good times than bad and that's what mattered in the end. And even though she wasn't going to be around as long as she'd have liked, she'd given it her best. Her sister-in-law was a good 'un. Joe too. They'd keep an eye on things for her. Make sure the girls toed the line, and Jim came through alright.

"Here you are then. Ease forward so I can wrap this around your shoulders."

Opening her eyes, she couldn't help laughing. Bessie was holding out a large crocheted square.

"Lord," she said, "that's something my old mum would wear."

"Beggars can't be choosers," her sister-in-law laughed back.

"Wish we'd had more time together, Bessie," she said quietly, settling back and tucking the ends of the shawl about her.

Her sister-in-law nodded. "Me too."

"I think we'd have been really good friends."

A butterfly was flitting over the wide open blooms. Soon it was joined by another, equally as glorious, and she watched as they circled and danced closer and closer to the verandah, until for one tantalising moment they were almost in reach. Then with a flutter of wings, they rose up over the roof and were gone.

The End

THE BORDELLO GIRL

Hilary Murray

1

AT EXACTLY ELEVEN O'CLOCK THIS morning my great-aunt woke, stared wide-eyed as if witnessing something completely unexpected and then, with a long and contented sigh, departed this world.

Sitting at her bedside I thought I was ready. Thought I had every emotion in check, after all she was well into her nineties. But I didn't. It was as if my throat had closed over and I couldn't breathe. And suddenly I was weeping. Heavens! What would she have said to that! After reaching for the box of tissues and blowing my nose, I glanced around the private ward as if expecting to see - what? A ghostly figure floating towards the ceiling? Of course there was nothing of the sort. Just the usual cream painted walls and floral pink curtains half drawn over tropical shutters.

After that everything became very much a process. The duty nurse - lilac scrubs and salted hair scraped back into a large tortoiseshell clip - led me from the room to start the formalities. There no one else. No family. No children or grandchildren living close by.

Only me, and that was by chance after a failed marriage had led me to pack up my worldly goods and shift to Australia's Far North, a decision that turned out to be more of a challenge than I'd thought. I'd always had a vague idea of the existence of a distant relative in the area but I'd no plans to get in touch back then. It was an additional complication I simply didn't need. So it was a surprise even to me when I did. Perhaps I was feeling adrift and in need of a little grounding, a sense of who I was and the roots I had sprung from.

"Please don't call me great-aunt," she said firmly on our first meeting. "It makes me feel as though I've already got one foot in the grave. Why don't you call me Thea and I will call you Laurie. There, now we're friends."

My great-aunt was a lively, well-read, robust woman and, it turned out, one of life's rarities; someone completely at peace with the hand fate had dealt her.

"A good life," she said sipping on a glass of Madeira after one of our regular lunches. "It's all you can wish for. A good and happy life."

And yet from the little I knew it had not always been that way. Of her two sons, the eldest had been killed in the final months of the Second World War while Bill had long ago made his life in the United States. As far as I knew he'd not returned to Australia for God knows how many years, and at this point I was wondering if he would even bother coming back for the funeral.

I'd let myself into Thea's house, taking a moment in the hallway to let the silence wash over me. It was strange to think there was no one to welcome me, or call out, telling me to join her in the kitchen.

She had known this moment would come of course, and had asked me to take care of everything. We were in her cosy front room and she had just settled a pot of Earl Grey tea and two delicate china cups and saucers onto the low table between us.

"You can give my clothes to the Sallies," she'd said, as if we were discussing nothing more contentious than the weather. "Of course, they might consider them a little outdated but they might be pleased with some of the glassware."

I'd glanced at the old-fashioned, lead-lighted cupboard.

"Are you sure? Didn't you tell me some of it's from Ireland?"

"One or two pieces are. Why don't you have those?"

"I will. But I'd rather you had the use of them a while longer."

She'd smiled. "We all have to go sometime. And when I do, there is something else I need to ask of you."

"Oh? What's that?"

Thea was pouring tea.

"I have things that are precious to me. Items I can't bear to throw away. You must do that."

"Of course."

I was imagining redundant furnishings or unwanted books. The usual bric-a-brac found in an elderly person's loft or spare bedroom. But there was something in her tone that made me hesitate.

"What sort of things?"

Thea was already opening the carved wooden trinket box she kept on the side table.

"This," she said, waving a small brass key, "will open the bottom drawer of my writing desk. There's a box inside. Of course it's all ancient history. But I think I'd like someone to know the truth."

That threw me.

"Then why don't we do it together?" I suggested. "Now if you like?"

"No. It can wait."

I flashed my eyes as if we were co-conspirators. "Will I find the deeds to a fabulous fortune?"

"Would I be living here if that were the case?" she countered dryly.

I could see her point. The house was definitely on the small side and the garden even more so when compared to the vast property she and my great-uncle had owned in the highlands. I'd seen it first-hand one morning, when following her directions, I'd driven her up and parked on the verge near the gate. She'd gotten out of the car and bunching her hands into her jacket pockets, she'd gazed across the front paddock towards the house in the distance.

"I loved him with all of my heart," she said when I joined her.

She'd taken my hand then and I felt the fragility of her bones.

"It never dies, you know. It never goes away."

There is nothing worse than having to trawl through the belongings of someone who has recently died. Even more so when that person is close, and standing in the middle of Thea's front room I was already siding with those who would much rather leave things exactly as they were, as if the person would one day be coming back.

But I did not have that luxury.

I'd called Bill from the hospice and broken the news of his mother's death. It was late evening in California and I'd heard a women's voice in the background asking who was calling. This was not the first time we'd spoken as I had been keeping him up to date from the moment Thea had gone into care. But now it was different and there was a tremor in his voice as he told me he would get the first available flight in the morning.

With so much to be getting on with, it was all a bit overwhelming. I decided to take the easy option. To make myself a coffee and start with the bottom drawer of Thea's writing desk.

It was time to satisfy my curiosity.

The key was where Thea had left it in the trinket box, and kneeling on the carpet I soon had the drawer open and the box she'd mentioned, nothing fancy, just plain cardboard and similar in size to a large shoebox, on the floor in front of me.

I had no idea what I expected to find, and perhaps that was why I hesitated, running my fingertips over the mottled lid as if to delay the moment. In fact, the contents were disappointingly ordinary. Two bunches of letters tied up with ribbon, a large official-looking envelope, a cream and gold wedding invitation, an old passport - hers it turned out and bearing the name Crawford. Her maiden name I guessed. And there were other things. An old and crumbling pressed rose, a toy car and a small, leather covered photograph album. Turning the stiff pages, I studied the gray-toned images of a young man in uniform. Tom, her eldest child - he'd been so afraid the war would be over before he was old enough to join up. I found the telegram sent by the War Office and his birth and death certificates in the large envelope, along with the copy of the purchase contract for the property in the highlands and the birth and death certificates for my great-uncle. Strangely there was no marriage certificate, nor Thea's own birth certificate, and I would need one or the other in order to complete the information required by the registrar.

Oh well, I thought, no doubt they'll turn up elsewhere.

Picking up the smaller bundle of letters, the one bound in blue ribbon, I turned it over in my hand. The return address was that of an Australian battalion and I didn't need to be told that these were her son's and perhaps crammed with places he'd seen and people he'd met? Or had he already seen action and were his thoughts sober? Even then he would try to reassure her. She was his mother after all.

The other letters were bound in white ribbon and I wondered uneasily if they were intensely private love notes from my great-uncle? But the writing on the topmost envelope had a feminine style to it, though not that of someone proficient in the art. Turning up a few right-hand corners at random I checked the postmarks. More than a dozen or so, they were all in chronological order.

Given there was nothing else in the box I wondered what Thea had been referring to when she spoke of my learning the truth?

It could only be the letters, and suddenly I found it hard to breathe. If I slipped the bow, separated the envelopes, if I read the pages inside, what would I find?

I was gnawing on my bottom lip, something I always did when confronted by uncertainty.

Surely the contents couldn't be too terrible, for if they were, I simply wouldn't read them. I'd grown very fond of my great-aunt and nothing was going to spoil my memories.

I bit down a little too forcefully and winced.

For heaven's sake! Why should I be expecting the worst?

Easing back against the sofa and stretching out my legs I tugged on the ribbon. The long tails were creased from having been tied for so long and before lifting the first envelope from the pile I ran each one between my fingers.

Then I carefully extracted the folded sheets of lightly scented writing paper.

Originally from Sussex, England Hilary Murray now lives in Auckland New Zealand with her husband, grown up children and amazingly wonderful grandchildren.

If you have enjoyed this book and would like to keep up with her news and details of up and coming novels why not follow her on:

www.hilarymurray.co.nz

www.facebook.com/hilarymurrayauthor